A FINAL DEAL

BILLIONAIRES' BRIDES OF CONVENIENCE
BOOK 8

NADIA LEE

FOUR ISLES PRESS

A Final Deal

For my husband

1
————

Blake

Dressed sharply in a black suit, I stride through the bright halls of Digital Angel, a venture capital firm my cousin Dane and I started some years ago. Paintings that Dane's art curator picked out—many of them priceless—grace the vestibule and hallways of our Los Angeles location. The curator didn't touch our personal spaces. I'm more into postmodern pieces that many find incomprehensible. I like seeing what's underneath the seemingly random splatters and bizarre combinations of colors and shapes.

Usually I'm in the Boston office, but there's no way I'm spending more time than I need to on the East Coast. If I stay there too long, I'll get arrested for matricide. Although I gotta wonder if killing one's most annoying stepmother—who's barely old enough to vote —can really be considered a crime. Surely it would be viewed as a noble service, for the betterment of humankind...or at least an act of self-defense because the inane woman drives me crazy with her ostensible need to "mother" me.

My assistant, Cecilia Perkins, jumps to her feet as I walk in. A dirty blonde with sharp gray eyes in her early forties, she's still single, pretty and excellent at her job. She's married to her work—which I approve of— and dressed conservatively in an office-appropriate outfit of a pink blouse and navy blue skirt that reaches her knees—which I approve of even more. I can't stand women who come to work dressed like streetwalkers.

"Good morning," she says, giving me a cup of coffee. It's hot, strong and black, just the way I like it, and in my favorite mug, which says *Your misfortune is my opportunity*.

"Morning." I take a sip.

She follows me into my office. It overlooks down-town L.A., bustling with too much traffic and too many people. Some claim each city has its own charm, but to me, all big cities are the same—a concrete can of human sardines that just happens to be good for business.

Cecilia hands me a copy of my agenda for the week, highlighting all the main events. They're also in my calendar app, but this is how we go over any changes and plan our week.

I glance at the paper, noticing a newly added ten-minute appointment for nine thirty today. "What's this?"

"It's a courtesy, set up over the weekend as a favor to Samuelson."

I cock an eyebrow. Samuelson is a hedge fund manager in New York, and it wouldn't be a bad idea to have him owe me one. "All right. I can spare ten minutes for a pitch." I'm not interested in people who aren't prepared to impress me in the allotted time. If they can't intrigue me in ten, they won't be able to convince me in thirty. That's how business goes.

I give her a couple more instructions for the rest of the day, then finish my coffee in peace while checking a few emails that made it past Cecilia. After the strays have been sorted I sit back, drumming my fingers on my desk. My thoughts slide to my half-brother Lucas. After swearing up and down that he wouldn't get married, he's willing to go through the farce so all of us—the five people unfortunate enough to have Julian Reed as a father—can inherit Grandfather's portraits.

Which now puts me in the less-than-ideal situation of having to find a wife in under two months. Naturally, I've been procrastinating; who wouldn't, when faced with such a distasteful prospect? I'm not buying into the fantasy that I'll suddenly find the love of my life or any such bullshit. Stuff like that doesn't happen on a timeline.

Who cares? The marriage is only for a year.

The thought is hardly comforting.

Not to mention, there are logistical issues involved. My brother Ryder married his assistant, but I'm not marrying mine. Cecilia is far too valuable to lose to a farce of a marriage. And I'm certainly not propositioning a stripper like my half-brother Elliot did. It was easy for him, since he doesn't respect either of his parents, but I don't want to cause embarrassment for my cousins on the Pryce side. I actually like them, and the oldest, Dane, is also my best friend.

"Your nine thirty is here," comes Cecilia's voice from the intercom.

The door to my office opens, and a slim brunette wrapped in silk and dripping diamonds walks in. The hair on the back of my neck stands, and the moment she makes eye contact, I merely stare. I must be dreaming—having a nightmare, to be precise.

But she's definitely here, in real life, and I'm not hallucinating.

The woman is Faith Mortimer, age twenty-four, formerly a waitress at a diner in Vegas and now a wealthy widow. No college education, unless she's changed that in the last two years...but I doubt that since she doesn't need an education to be a rich man's wife, just a pretty face and a tight, hot body.

I know all this because she's my ex-girlfriend. That word is really too anemic to describe what she was to me, though. She could've been so much more. I wanted her to be.

She's as beautiful as ever, the same delicate face with high cheekbones and a small, straight nose. Her nude stilettos highlight the perfection of her legs, and the purple wrap dress shows off her pert tits and a very feminine flare of hips.

But it's her eyes that are truly sensational. Dark as bitter chocolate, they appear exceptionally large and expressive, framed by impossibly long lashes. Of course, the expressive part is a trick since they only show what she wants you to see, not what's really underneath.

And yet as her gaze clashes with mine, I feel ensnared in their extraordinary depth. My skin prickles with heat—from arousal or anger I cannot tell.

Sure you can't, part of me mocks. *You're getting hard.*

"Get out," I say, my voice frigid with disgust. I don't make a habit of lying to myself, but when the subject is Faith, it happens. "Or I'll have you thrown out."

She merely straightens her shoulders, then takes a seat directly opposite mine. "I'm entitled to my ten minutes."

"To pitch a venture. I don't know what you did to Samuelson to convince him you have anything worthwhile, but I know you haven't done anything meaningful in the last two years. And there's nothing you can offer that will tempt me." I deliberately let my eyes run over her body.

Red tinges her cheeks, but she doesn't back down. "I don't need to have done anything in the last two years to pitch something worth your while. And you haven't heard my proposal, so you can't make a judgment."

I steeple my hands and contemplate making good on my threat to have security drag her out. But instead, I regard her over the tips of my fingers. Why is she here? She has to know I despise her, even if I might still find her body attractive enough. I've deliberately—and unsuccessfully—done my best not to think of her over the past two years. When I excise someone, it's forever...even if my brain goes off on the wrong track for Faith.

I excuse that lapse with the fact that none of the cancerous people in my life has been my first. Not the first girl I fucked. I lost my virginity in high school. What Faith is is far, far worse: the first person—the only person—I gave my heart to...because I was that naïve, that foolish.

"I'm here to offer to marry you," she says, her voice firm.

I snort, then let out a belly laugh. Her gaze doesn't waver. The dispassionate response is what finally helps me calm myself enough to respond, "Usually it's the man who proposes, and I'm not crazy enough to want to marry someone like you. I'm fine with my marital status at the moment."

"Are you?" One carefully plucked eyebrow quirks. "You need a wife to ensure that not only you but your siblings inherit those multimillion-dollar paintings of your grandfather's."

Fucking Wife Number Three. My jaw flexes before

I can catch myself. She outed the entire sordid deal between our father and us to the tabloids. If her latest husband, Stanton, hadn't publicly humiliated and divorced her, I would've tossed her out of my plane. Without a parachute.

"Is this for real? You're wasting my time based on a tabloid article?" I give Faith a thin smile. "Have you also taken up chasing UFOs?"

She smiles—too smart for my bullshit. "Tabloid or not..." She crosses her legs. "Sure, you guys denied it. Are those denials believable? If you're two, maybe. The problem is, rich people always lie about things that make them look bad. But your siblings falling like dominos proves you're all full of it."

I give her a small smile. The kind that says *maybe you're right but who gives a shit anyway?* "Hypothetically speaking, if I needed a wife, I'd be looking for somebody younger, prettier and less headstrong than you."

She stiffens. "I'm twenty-four!"

Ah. The first crack in her composure. "My father married a woman who's barely twenty. Why shouldn't I aim for better?"

Her face reddens. "You always were shallow," she mutters.

Me? Shallow? Pot, meet kettle. "Faith, if I needed to marry in the next hour, you wouldn't do. You overvalue yourself. To *rich people* like me, a woman like you isn't even an afterthought. There are plenty eager to do what I want." I lean back in my seat. "Besides, when you come back to a man you walked out on over money, you really should show more humility."

"Humility?"

"Crawling on your hands and knees is usually a good start."

Humiliation and anger erupt in the dark depths of her eyes like bombs. "Should I suck you off while I'm at it?"

Her mention of a blow job heats my blood. She's damn good at it, and I haven't been with a woman in a while. I flip a hand back and forth. "Might improve your odds."

"You're disgusting."

"Did you really expect a different reception?" I push my chair back a little, creating some space between the desk and my crotch. "Well?"

She sways forward a little, and blood pounds in my cock with something that feels like about twenty-five percent derision and the rest anticipation.

Abruptly, she stands, her expression tight. "I should've expected this kind of swinish behavior from you. You were like that back in Vegas, too."

Outrage blazes through me. I was never, *ever* like that with her. I fucking adored her, treated her like a queen.

If she'd waited one more month, I would've married her.

Before I can tell her to shove her indignation up her ass, she's gone.

My hands curl into fists, then I inhale and exhale a

couple of times. Who gives a shit that I didn't get the last word? She's gone, and I made my point. Whatever she thought to accomplish by meeting me...she failed.

I let myself feel grim satisfaction, then throw myself into work.

2

Faith

I'M TREMBLING AS I LEAVE, NOT KNOWING WHERE to look. Blake's assistant gazes at me, her face curiously blank. Maybe it isn't anything unusual to have people walk out of her boss's office looking shaken and humiliated. Maybe the Blake I just met is the real Blake.

Why that thought guts me... I can't process my emotions. It can't be just because I didn't get what I wanted.

Maybe I was disappointed because he didn't seem interested in my offer or demand answers even when we came face-to-face.

Why did you expect that?

The time for all that was two years ago, not now.

The weight of the assistant's eyes grows more

stifling. I'll be damned if I let her see how much meeting Blake has shaken me.

Forcing a "nothing's wrong" smile, I walk into the waiting elevator. When the doors close and the car starts to descend, a sob pushes through my throat. I stop the elevator and put a palm over my mouth to contain the sound, then dig into my purse for something to wipe my eyes. My hand closes around a wrinkled tissue, and I dab it over my face.

What's wrong with me? Tears solve nothing, and I can't afford to be weak.

The back of my head hits the wall, and I let out a shuddering breath. The security camera blinks, and I sniff, then slowly raise a middle finger and flip the thing off. The chances of Blake watching the feed are probably zero, but it still makes me feel good to express what I think about him, the trappings of his wealth, and his treatment of me.

The last two years have been good to him. He's gotten even better looking, the veneer of his success shinier, and I hate it that I noticed the way his suit fits around his broad shoulders and arms, the way his skin stretches over the boldly carved bones of his face. If he wanted, he could be a successful leading man like his brother.

After restarting the elevator, I check myself with the compact I always carry in my purse. Makeup damage looks minimal, and people probably won't notice unless they really stare. I just need to maintain an "I'm fine" façade until I'm out of the building. I don't want anybody to notice my humiliating breakdown. It's already bad enough Blake more or less told me to suck him off if I wanted him to take me seriously. *Bastard.*

Two street blocks later, I find my ten-year-old Camry in a parking garage. I didn't want anybody in Blake's building to see me in that car, but I might as well not have bothered.

What wouldn't I give to allow myself a bit more time to cope? But I'm painfully aware the lot charges by the minute, and unemployed girls like me can't afford to waste money on something as frivolous as a coping moment. Jobs don't fall from the sky, and for a high school graduate, a decent-paying one is damn hard to come by. People wrinkle their noses when they see that my résumé lacks a BA and my most recent *paying* employment is waiting tables at a diner, then immediately assume I must be lazy or stupid...or both. They seem to forget education is free only up through high school.

I pay and exit the garage. *I should pawn the diamonds today.* I only hung onto them for my meeting with Blake. Going to him from a position of extreme vulnerability was out of the question. People like him don't respect anything but power and money. Samuelson would've never set up the meeting if he'd known how desperate I am.

My bank account shows I have enough for another thirty-four days. I don't know what I'm going to do after that. My late husband left me with nothing. Not because Jack lost everything before dying, but because the Villars would rather be poor than let me have a sum that would allow me to have a quiet, dignified life and provide for my mom. It never fails to amaze me how greedy rich people can be. Jack's family's fortune is valued at at least a billion. I would've been grateful with just a crumb or two.

I go home—a small studio apartment in a cheap part of town—and change into a shirt and jeans, no jewelry, and repair my makeup so there's no sign of my earlier tears. Unlike strangers, Mom *will* stare—rudeness be damned—if she thinks there's something wrong.

After picking up a small pot of daisies, I drive an hour to the hospice. Flowers are costly and perhaps even frivolous, but I can't visit her without something to cheer her up. She's in this place full-time. For the last two years, her doctors have been saying her tumor is inoperable and she only has three or four months to live. Somehow she's hung on through chemo and radiation therapies, although the specialists she saw recently seem convinced she won't make it this time. They even urged me to stop seeking curative treatment, because the new tumor isn't responding.

I don't believe them. It's true that if I pulled the plug my financial burden would go down to almost nothing, with Medicare assuming the vast majority of the cost. But that's such horseshit. Why would I stop trying to save my own mother because of what they think? They were wrong before, and they can be wrong again. They *will* be wrong again.

Blooming Flowers is a private facility that provides palliative care, among other services. It has a full-time medical staff that monitors the patients twenty-four seven. Putting my mother in a hospice wasn't my first choice, but this is what she wanted. "You're so young and pretty, Faith. You should be having fun, dating, finding a man who'll treat you like a queen. I don't want to be a burden."

But there's more. I can never forget the scare I had at the beginning, when I insisted on having her at home with me so I could care for her myself. She had a seizure, and the doctors determined it was due to my inability to recognize and judge her daily condition properly. After all, what do I know about medicine? It was then I made the decision to leave her care to the pros.

Nelly Friday, one of the nurses at Blooming Flowers, greets me with a warm smile. "Hi, Faith. Here to see Alice?"

"Yes. How is she today?"

"Hasn't complained about pain that much," she says, knowing what I'm really asking. Mom lies to me about her condition all the time. "She's a strong woman."

"That's for sure."

I go down to her room, a sizable semi-private with a shared bath, two beds and a writing table. The view from the deck shows flowers blooming below when the season's right. Mom shares it with another woman named Judy. They seem to get along pretty well, but then my mom's too laid-back not to.

"Hi, Faith," Judy says with a wan smile. Her blue gaze is hazy with pain.

I pretend not to notice. The one time I remarked on it she seemed really uncomfortable, and quickly I realized she wanted to be treated as though she wasn't dying. "Hey, Judy. How are you?"

"Doing great. How can I not be when you bring more flowers?"

I smile. "Glad to hear it." I've never seen her get any gifts. I'm not even sure if she gets any visitors. She told me once that her children live in New York.

Mom waves from a big comfy armchair, a book lying in her lap. "Faith."

"Mom!" I go up and hug her carefully, feeling the heartbreakingly fragile frame in my arms. It's like hugging a sack full of breadsticks. She's declined so fast, looking at least twenty years older than her age. Cancer is a bitch.

I try to be brave and tell myself she can beat it this time, too. But when she looks so frail, I can't help but think maybe the damned tumor's going to win after all. Every time I come by she seems pounds lighter.

I place the pot of flowers by the stand near the window and pull a chair close so we can chat. I search her expression for any sign of pain or discomfort, but her brown eyes are warm and bright, and her smile is exceptionally wide and open. Either she's become a better actress or she's actually doing okay. "How are you feeling today?"

"Wonderful. Especially when I get to see your happy face."

I let myself relax a little. *Thank you, makeup.*

"You look extra pretty today. Date?" Mom asks.

I laugh. "No. I just wanted to look nice for my favorite person."

She pats my hand. "You need another 'favorite' person...ideally a nice young man who'll love and spoil you the way you deserve." She sighs. "You're too young to remain a widow."

"Sometimes things happen."

"Poor Jack."

Yes. *Poor* Jack. "I know."

"Thank the lord he left you well off."

I merely smile. If I have my way, Mom will never find out the full truth about my late husband. As far as she knows, he was a nice man who swept her daughter off her feet and treated her like a princess in the glitzy part of Hong Kong.

One of the workers knocks on the open door. "Mail for you, Alice," he says, waving an envelope. I pat Mom's knee, then get up to take it. As I scan the outside, my smile crashes.

RETURN TO SENDER.

"Mom." I go to her. "You shouldn't have." I hand her the unopened letter. "He'll never read it. He isn't interested in us." If he were, he would've helped us out two years ago. All my emails went unanswered. I dialed his office, but his assistants hung up on me as though I were a sleazy telemarketer. The only reason I didn't call him on his mobile and cuss him out for his callousness is I had no idea what the number was. Not that I have a clue what I'd rail about if I ever got him on the phone. I can't decide if I'm angry or crushed that the early childhood memories of a loving grandfather are just lies, probably something my mind embellished after losing my father.

"He's your grandfather. It's my duty to reach out to him."

"He's my grand—" I stop when I realize my voice is too loud. No need to air our dirty laundry in front of Judy. "It's *his* duty," I hiss, "to reach out to *me*."

She studies my face. "Don't be so harsh on him."

"He's a racist."

"There are other reasons for him to disapprove of me."

"He called you a mongrel." Mom is half-Korean. "Who does that?"

She sighs. "When I'm gone, he'll be the only family you have left."

"Number one, you're not going anywhere. Number two, I'd rather be alone than play the loving granddaughter to a racist bigot."

Racist but rich, my mind whispers. I dismiss the reminder. He has the money I need, but he'll never give me a penny. He'd rather see Mom die.

Not wanting to think about Benedict Mortimer, I force a smile. "Mom, tell me about how you met Dad."

"I've told you that story at least a hundred times."

"So? It's worth listening to again."

She gives me a small grin, but she knows exactly what I'm doing. "Your father and I met at a Korean BBQ restaurant my dad owned. He was lost and needed help figuring out how to get back on the highway. I was helping out that night, and when I saw him, I thought I'd lost my mind. I was struck dumb by how handsome and smart he was."

"Even though he'd gotten lost?" I tease.

"I think it was a divine sign—or maybe fate—because otherwise we would've never met."

I squeeze her marvelously soft hand. It's adorable how Mom still believes in something so fanciful.

"I showed him how to get back on the highway. He thanked me, and two days later, he came back to have dinner at the restaurant. He was alone, and he had to wait for so long—we were always busy on weekends, but he waited."

"He knew how special you were."

"Love at first sight." She lets out a gentle breath, her gaze focusing on something beyond now. "We dated for two months, then he proposed."

"And you said yes."

"There was no other choice. He was it for me."

I adore this story. Dad married Mom despite his father's protests and turned his back on a multibillion-dollar fortune. He never regretted it—I've seen pictures of him smiling fondly at Mom—and he loved her unconditionally, pampered her like a queen. If it hadn't been for the plane crash, he'd still be with us, sharing in all our little happy moments.

My spirit, bruised from the meeting with Blake, slowly recovers as Mom tells me more stories about her and Dad. There's such healing and love in my mother's presence. I hold her fragile hand in mine and kiss the knuckles as she says, "I want that same kind of love for you, a man who will treat you like a queen, put you on a pedestal and worship at your feet."

I smile. I've suffered losses, I've experienced pain, but I'm not letting them turn me cynical, not letting them cut me off from seeking the unconditional love and rich life my parents had together. I lost sight of that when I went to Blake out of desperation today, and I suppress a shudder as shame unfurls in my belly. Thank God he turned me down. If he had responded the way I'd hoped, things could've turned out worse. After all, he isn't the kind of man a person can rely on.

I'll find some other way to make sure Mom is taken care of. I know there's a way. After all, every cloud has a silver lining.

After spending a couple of hours, I give Mom another hug and return to my apartment. A police cruiser outside makes me frown. The lights on the roof are flashing and a lot of people have gathered around.

"What's going on?" I call out to one of them. He's my next-door neighbor and a father of two.

"Your place got broken into," he says.

"*What?*"

"A few others, too."

I gasp. The diamonds!

I park my car and rush inside. A police officer blocks me. "Whoa. Back it up, ma'am."

"This is my apartment!" I gesture at the sad little space with the door wide open. There are cops inside with notepads.

"You live here? What's your name?"

"Faith Mortimer." I hand him my ID, and he checks it. "How bad is it?" I ask.

The place has nothing worth stealing other than the diamonds. I'm hoping the robbers didn't discover my hiding place in the bathroom. Since the main entrance door lock doesn't work anymore, I store my jewelry under a small potpourri sack in a miniature basket I keep in the bathroom.

"Not too terrible, although your sofa bed's been cut up," the cop says. "TV seems to be missing, too."

It's too bad about the sofa, but he's wrong about the TV. I don't have one. I want to get inside and check for my diamonds, but I can't with the cop in the way. "What are the chances that you'll catch whoever did it?"

"Honestly? Slim. You should talk with your insurance company to get your stuff replaced."

"I see." I smile tightly. I don't have renter's insurance. No money to pay for it, even though my lease stipulates I have some. "Thank you, officer."

3

Blake

I STARE AT THE SECURITY FOOTAGE FILE ATTACHED to an email I just received. The mouse cursor floats over it, but I don't double-click.

I should leave my confrontation with Faith on its previous high note. Did I not get the satisfaction of humiliating her...even if there was no one other than the two of us to witness it? Why should I go the extra mile of wanting to see the footage of her leaving my building? She probably fumed all the way to the garage, climbed into some fancy car—a Ferrari maybe—and drove off in a huff.

But I requested the footage from building security anyway, and they were more than happy to oblige.

This has to be a bad habit I picked up from Lucas. He's the type who just can't let go, and I've seen how his obsession with his ex has turned him into a quivering mess. My lip curls. How someone as smart as Lucas could unravel so fast over a woman as poisonous as that bitch, I'll never understand.

Cancer must be excised, done away with, never to be brought up or thought of again.

My grandmother Shirley Pryce often told me that, and it's a maxim that's served me well. The only cancerous entity I tolerate now is my mother, but only because it's damn difficult to excise the woman who gave birth to you and ostensibly "cares" about you.

Just watch the footage, the perverse voice in my head whispers. *It'd be a shame to trash it, and it'll sweeten the satisfaction you had.*

Can't argue with that logic. I double-click. The video plays in full color. Faith walks out, her knees a little wobbly, but she firms her expression and marches out like a trooper.

I let out a soft laugh. *Not bad.* I can't decide between admiration and contempt. The woman acts like a queen when she basically propositioned me and got shot down as she deserved.

She steps into the elevator, then I see...

Tears fall from her eyes, and she covers her mouth. Although the camera angle's too acute to show her full face, I can tell that much.

What the hell? I sit back, clasped hands cradling the base of my skull. I didn't say anything uncalled for. It infuriates me she's crying like she's actually hurt. Women like her become angry. Pout. Cajole.

They do not get *hurt*.

An unfamiliar ache passes through me, and I sneer at myself. *Don't turn into Lucas.* Faith was my first love, but that doesn't mean she isn't a cancer.

Suddenly she looks up at the camera directly, then bares her teeth and flips the bird.

I laugh. *That's better.*

My mobile buzzes. It's Elizabeth. "Hello, sis."

"Hi, Blake. Am I interrupting anything?"

"Nope."

"You sound awfully amused about something."

"I am." Then I remember how she can be interfering, and my mood darkens for a moment. Lucas is a basket case because of her. I wouldn't put it past her to try to mess with my life, even though the only person who knows about my history with Faith is Dane. On the other hand, Elizabeth has a way of figuring things out. And if she's calling to see if her scheme's worked... well... "I made a woman cry, and it was quite satisfying," I say.

"Jeez, Blake, why don't you go ahead and kick a puppy while you're at it," she says, no hesitation or consideration. Just the chiding tone she often uses with me when she disapproves of my heartless ways.

So. Elizabeth didn't send Faith. My mood improves, so I give her something to brighten hers. "She didn't cry that much. And it was nothing she didn't deserve."

I can almost hear her head shaking. "Such a lame defense."

"But the best you're going to get. Deal with it."

"Fine. But in return..."

"Yeees?"

"The foundation is short this year."

I chuckle. My sister is so transparent. She doesn't explain what the cause is, and I don't ask. I never do when it comes to her pet projects. If I'm not going to actively crusade on behalf of the less fortunate, I can at least fund the war. "How much?"

"How much can you spare? I know you love tax deductions, and it's almost the year end."

My lips twitch. *Sneaky.* But then she wouldn't be my sister if she quoted an exact figure. She knows she can get more this way. "Would a quarter million do?"

"Yes, that will do quite well. Thank you, Blake."

"You're welcome."

"Sometimes you give me hope."

"About?"

"You. There are times I think you're irreparably doomed, having spent all your time with someone like Dane—"

"Who gives generously to all your causes."

"—who's such a cynic he makes some of those old Romans look idealistic by comparison."

"You're wrong. He's totally pussy-whipped now."

"It's called falling in love. You should try it."

I did once and loathed the entire experience. Still do. I laugh instead. "You have a candidate in mind? I like mine pretty, with dark hair and enough tit to make a handful—" I stop abruptly. I'm describing Faith.

"Hair," Elizabeth says, sighing. "And tits. Anyway,

thanks for your generosity, Blake. You're going to make a lot of kids very happy this Christmas."

"I did it for you."

"I know, but thank you anyway."

"If you want to thank me..."

"Yes?"

"Back the hell off Lucas's case," I say. "You didn't see how bad it was, but he was a mess when I visited him in Charlottesville. He's finally getting his shit together, moving away from that toxic town and starting to rejoin the living. Whether he marries Faye or gets back together with Ava is none of our business."

"I just want him to be happy."

"The fact is, he was the exact *opposite* of happy after a second round with that bitch." If she hadn't been a woman, I would've punched her for what she's done to him. I might still. "So I'm asking you to stay out of it."

Elizabeth hesitates a bit, but finally says, "All right. I just wish he wasn't going to marry so...callously. Just for the paintings."

Lucas was adamantly opposed to getting married, but then caved recently, finally deciding to do whatever it took. I know it's partially to prove to himself he's gotten over the girl, but it's also due to familial loyalty.

You need to do the same, and you aren't even close to finding a candidate.

Only because I can't think of anyone to propose to.

A new email from Benjamin Clark pops up on my laptop screen. "I gotta go."

"All right. Talk to you later. You're coming to Ryder's Thanksgiving party, right?"

"Unless an asteroid hits, yes."

"Great." She hangs up, and I immediately open the email.

I shouldn't have asked the family's PI to look into Faith's finances, but I couldn't help myself. The only reason she would come to me like that is money. I'm curious how desperate she is to worm her way back into my life. Unless she's a complete moron—not the case— she has to know she isn't my favorite person.

Benjamin's report is brief and to the point, just the way I like it. I requested a high-level summary only; I don't care about the details. This isn't an audit, after all.

The report shows total amount coming in monthly —which is nil in the last four months—and total amount going out on a monthly basis, which is erratic but runs into four figures. She has a few thousand bucks in her account, about enough to last another month if her spending habits hold true. According to Benjamin, she has no other accounts or assets. What the hell? Her late husband should've left her with enough to live out the rest of her life in relative comfort, if not luxury. The Villars aren't doing that hot, but he must have had life insurance.

Maybe she's got a gambling or addiction problem...? Possible...even probable. Otherwise her rich grandfather would bail her out.

I lean back in my seat and smirk. If she has a money

problem, she should've done what I suggested—on her knees.

The insidious part of me whispers it won't be so bad if I marry her for a year. I only need a temporary wife who I can ditch easily, and I'll enjoy fucking her. A small sum should do it—she's probably desperate enough to do anything if she thinks she has a chance at getting the money she needs.

The idea has merit, and I like the image entirely too much. But the art of negotiation is to appear as though you don't give a fuck and are willing to walk away at any minute.

"Blake, you have a call. Simone Villar," Cecilia says over the intercom.

Faith's former sister-in-law. *Well, well, well.* "Put her through." I hit the speaker and steeple my fingers.

"Hello, Blake. Hope I'm not interrupting anything." Simone's voice is always so damn oily, speaking to her makes me feel like I've just drunk a pitcher of engine grease.

"Not at all," I purr. "What can I do for you?"

"It's about the venture in China."

"You know my stance on that. I'm going to personally inspect the manufacturing facilities since I'm not certain they're up to standard."

"The accident last month was a fluke."

"Fifteen people died," I point out mildly, suppressing contempt for the casual tone she adopts. This whole venture is about perfect timing. Right now is too early.

"Their families were compensated."

So many palms greased. I tap my lower lip. "Simone, I don't want to have any...negative publicity attached to my investments."

"It's not like it's through Digital Angel."

"Precisely. The Montresor Fund is more personal, so I can't afford any negative PR."

"Blake... Be reasonable. Just a little bit more time, and we'll all have a handsome profit."

I cock an eyebrow at her cajoling tone. She isn't the brightest, but she has to know I'm aware of her family's finances. If this venture fails—and it will if the Villars lose my funding—it'll ruin them. "I want all the problems corrected before the year's over. No more incidents like this. Is that clear?"

"Of course. I'll personally take care of everything."

"You do that. After all, you have the contacts there."

She titters. "Flatterer. I know you do too."

"Yes, but I have other matters taking up my time and energy."

"Oh. The gossip."

"Yes. The gossip. The woman I've been seeing was pissed." May as well start laying the groundwork for the upcoming nuptials so they're not a total surprise.

"I didn't know you were dating."

"I value discretion and privacy. If we're finished..."

"Yes. I'm done. I won't take up any more of your time."

"Have a good day, Simone."

I hang up, then drive over to La Mer, where I have dinner with my cousin Dane and his live-in girlfriend, Sophia. Sophia is a complicated entity on the Pryce side—the daughter of Wife Number Two. My mother —having been Wife Number One—despises "that crass usurper," and therefore hates Sophia as well, although she wouldn't dare express her feelings openly in fear of Dane's reaction. He's always been courteous and indulgent with her, but he won't tolerate anyone disrespecting Sophia.

La Mer is a seafood restaurant owned by another cousin, Mark Pryce. The man knows his food and wine. The exterior landscaping and design make the place look like an underwater palace. The interior is equally impressive: aquarium tanks everywhere with all kinds of sea creatures swimming inside. They're probably relieved they aren't on the menu.

I like the deep blue and the fish. There's something hypnotically relaxing about the place, and it helps me focus. The soft classical music from the sound system... Well, I don't care about it that much. It's just music.

The maître d', Larry Jones, smiles when he spots me. The man's never without his stiffly starched suit and a warm smile for the patrons. "Welcome to La Mer, Mr. Pryce-Reed."

"Is Dane here?"

"Yes, sir. This way."

A pert brunette in a black dress takes me to a private booth in the back, Dane's preferred seating location. She gives me a small, secret smile and puts a little extra sway into her hips as she walks. Normally she'd do, but right now I'm not in the mood. When I don't show any interest, she stops with the coquettish attempt.

Dane's already got a glass of chilled white wine. He's older than me, with dark hair and the classic Pryce profile the men in our family are known for. We started Digital Angel together as a show of defiance to our fathers—that we didn't need their damned money or connections to be successful.

The light from the tanks around us turns his suit almost navy in hue, although I know he mostly wears dark charcoal or black. His cold blue eyes warm about five degrees when he sees me. "Blake."

"Dane." I take an empty seat opposite him and tell the woman I'll have whatever he's having since he has good taste in wine. "Where's Sophia?"

"Stuck in traffic. She texted me about half an hour ago."

"Don't you live close by?"

"She was visiting Vanessa."

"You mean she went to see the baby."

"Yes." His mouth tightens. I give him an inquiring look but he doesn't elaborate.

A waiter delivers my wine and a menu. I take both with murmured thanks and turn to Dane. "Something's bothering you."

"People getting married bothers me."

I snort. "Then get married. Unless you don't think Sophia is the one."

The look he gives me is frigid enough to pack fish. I'm about fifty percent immune to it, though, after having seen it so many times. "Okay, fine. She's the one. So what's the hold up?"

"It's complicated. Ah..." A radiant smile suddenly brightens his face, and his eyes warm so quickly I'm afraid they're going to melt out of their sockets.

I turn my head and see Sophia walking toward us with a crooked grin. She's a petite gorgeous blonde, her body tight from dedicating most of her life to competitive figure skating. The dress she has on is the exact shade of Dane's eyes, and I'm certain it's no accident she chose that color. Diamonds adorn her ears and throat—most likely random gifts Dane picked up because he's whipped like that—and the sparkling stones remind me of Faith. She was wearing diamonds when she came by...

Don't think about her.

Sophia takes a seat next to Dane and gives him a quick kiss. Before she can pull away, he stops her with a hand on the back of her head and gives her the kind of kiss that makes me want to call my assistant to book them a suite.

When he finally lets her go, she blushes. "We have a guest," she says softly.

"He's seen people kissing before. It's not like Blake's a virgin."

"I'm right here," I remind him dryly.

He hasn't given me a single glance since she walked in. "And did I say anything untrue?"

I snort. "It's considered rude to talk like that."

The shrug he gives is barely noticeable. He doesn't care about what anybody thinks or says. The only exception is Sophia. Even a slight frown, and he'll have the head of whoever upset her.

In other words, the man is in love.

Ironic because that was me two years ago—and Dane told me how it turned his stomach to see me mooning over a woman. Now I'm the one whose stomach is turning. But it's envy, not disgust. I could've had this happiness...if I'd just chosen better.

"How are you doing, Blake?" Sophia asks.

"I'm fine." I notice a ring with a heart-shaped diamond on her finger. "Are congratulations in order?"

"Hmm?"

I gesture at the ring with my wine glass.

Dane frowns, and she flushes. "Not quite yet," she says.

He reaches over and takes the hand. "It's to show we're in a committed relationship...that she's mine." There's a tightness in his voice.

I don't understand what's holding them back. She has to love him too. He's rich, good-looking and crazy about her. What more does a woman need?

Our waiter breaks the tension by coming over to take our order. I get the six-course dinner with lobster and crab, and Dane and Sophia do the same. Dane instructs the waiter to have Mark select a bottle of rosé to go with the meal. Even though Mark can't cook, he has an amazing instinct for wine.

Sophia clears her throat, her fingers fidgeting with the stemware sweating from the ice water. "How are you really doing, Blake? I read about the whole... marriage thing. I can't believe they made all that up just to embarrass you guys."

"You know how Julian is. It's all true."

"Good God." She shakes her head. "I'm so sorry."

"Shit happens."

"So when are Lucas and Elizabeth getting married?" Dane asks.

"Beats me."

"You aren't going to do it, are you?" Sophia peers at me. "It's not like you need the money."

"Thomas Reed's works are in high demand," Dane remarks. "They auction for millions."

"Yes, but that's not why we want them. They're special portraits he did of us when we turned eighteen. He never meant for them to go to Dad, but the damned will was ambiguous, and..." I shrug. I should've fought like hell when it happened, even if everyone would've called me a greedy bastard. Then we could've avoided this bullshit.

"Hard to give up something sentimental," Dane says.

"Yeah. But I have a candidate."

"Do you?"

"Faith Mortimer stopped by earlier today."

Dane almost spews his water. "What the hell?"

"I know."

"Who's Faith Mortimer?" Sophia asks.

"A complete bit—" Dane pauses and regroups. "A gold digger from his past. I hope she came crawling and you kicked her out on her ass."

"Didn't want to scuff my dress shoes. But no, she didn't stay long."

Sophia puts a hand over Dane's wrist. "If you feel this way about her, why did she come to see you?"

"She wants to marry me."

Dane laughs, a short bark, while Sophia gapes.

"She believes the gossip is true," I add.

"At least she has good instincts," Dane says. "Too bad she screwed up. One more month, you would've married her."

"You would have? And why a month?" Sophia asks.

She's entirely too innocent about how things are for men like us. "I thought I was in love. I even bought the ring." I still have it. A marquise diamond with sapphires. When I saw it, I knew it was perfect for Faith. "And the month was to plan a one-of-a-kind proposal." People think how Mark convinced his wife to give him a chance was "grand." What I would've done for Faith would've made Mark's efforts look bush league.

"So what happened?" Sophia asks.

"She decided to run off with the first guy who flashed her some money." Dane alerted me before I made an idiot of myself, then prevented me from pursuing her like a pathetic loser. At the time I felt like killing my cousin, but now I'm grateful.

"Someone with more money than you?" Sophia tilts her head.

"She didn't know how much Blake was worth. She thought he was a tech firm manager," Dane says. "Good thing too. Marrying a woman who only wants your money is hell. Expensive, too, when you want to get rid of her."

Sophia is watching me. "You said you have a candidate. It's this woman?"

I nod.

"That's a terrible idea," Dane says.

"Not really. I know precisely what she wants —money."

"Why doesn't she run to Benedict?" Dane gives Sophia a quick aside. "Her grandfather."

"Don't know. Maybe she has a habit or something. Not that it matters. It's only for a year, and she's still hot enough."

"Probably diseased at this point. Get her tested." Sophia frowns at Dane's callous words, but he doesn't notice, his gaze intent on me. "And be careful."

"Why?"

"The first one you fall in love with is the hardest to get over. In fact, you won't until you fall in love with someone else. Don't let your guard down and don't let her try to worm her way into your life permanently. Most importantly, don't be overly generous. The only way to deal with a woman like her is a stick rather than a carrot."

Sophia gasps.

"I'm not advocating actually beating her," Dane explains quickly. "But there's no reason to give her things beyond what you have to in order to maintain appearances. Besides, she's going to pawn anything extra you give her to pay for whatever habit she has."

I nod. He's right. And if I want to pull this off—and ensure I have the upper hand—I need to make sure she knows she's not a critical piece in getting me what I want.

Three days of radio silence. Let her stew. Let her worry. Then when I finally tell her I'm interested, she'll take whatever I give her.

And that'll be an excellent start to our year-long marriage—me on top, her on the bottom.

4

Faith

"God. That totally sucks," Mimi Zhang says, stretching her long, golden legs out in my studio apartment as we split an order of chicken lo mein she got from the Chinese restaurant where she waitresses. My best friend since forever, she moved to L.A. three years ago to try her hand at modeling and acting. Given her supremely photogenic features and tall, lithe shape, modeling is definitely a viable option, and I'm sure she'll be great at acting too. "You should've punched him in the face."

"I'd rather not be tossed in jail for assault. Can't afford bail."

"I would've paid it, especially if you'd broken his nose."

I grin. "I know you would, but..." She works too

hard for her money. Since she hasn't gotten her break yet, she makes ends meet with waitressing and whatever odd jobs she can find, and splits living costs with her live-in boyfriend. Los Angeles isn't a cheap city. "Besides, it's been three days, and I'm over it." Although I'm not quite over the fact that I must've been temporarily insane when I went to him.

"Oh, before I forget..." She pulls a sleek laptop from her purse and gives it to me. "Thanks for letting me borrow it."

"No problem." She was having trouble pulling up some audition sites on her phone. Unfortunately her computer died last month, and she doesn't have the money to replace it yet. "It's actually a good thing you had it with you. I'm sure the burglars would've taken it."

"Thieves are assholes. Always looking for an easy way. It pisses me off that the cops probably won't catch them. You should sue your landlord for that broken front door."

"He said he'll fix it ASAP, so I'm going to wait until next week before I lodge another complaint. At least they didn't discover the diamonds." My stomach still knots every time I think about the mess they made of my place...the sense of *violation*. A sheet covers the cuts on the sofa bed, but I can feel the gashes underneath. "The pawn shop owner ripped me off though. Only gave me a thousand bucks."

"*What?*" Mimi screeches. "They're worth at least ten times that."

"Maybe, but nobody was willing to give me more."

"Bastards. There's gotta be a BBB hotline to report this kind of stuff."

"I'm pretty sure pawn shops don't care about ratings from the Better Business Bureau."

"At least it'd be something."

I merely smile at her mumbling. Mimi has no idea how dire my situation is. I haven't told her because if she knew she'd try to chip in, and I don't want that. Money's tight for all of us. She's one unforeseen emergency away from Brokeville. "Well, it'll pay the bills for the PI I got to track Jordan down."

"Did he find him?"

"Not yet, but hopefully he will. Soon."

My need to locate Jordan Smith is greater than ever before, even though the PI I hired warned me it'll be like looking for the proverbial needle. If it weren't for that man, I would've been entitled to a sizable trust— about three million dollars' worth—from my late husband's estate. I don't know why Jordan lied under oath and signed that affidavit, stating we slept together while I was married to Jack. But I'm not getting a penny unless and until Jordan recants. The prenup between Jack and me stipulated I had to be faithful during our marriage in order to get at the trust he set up for me, and since I was an idiot back then, I signed it without stipulating something equitable in return.

My phone hoots like an owl—my notification sound for new emails. Praying for a miracle, I open an email from my PI, Leslie Kent.

Subject: Jordan Smith

Sorry, couldn't locate him anywhere. I checked my contacts in Hong Kong and China, plus the States in case he came home, but...nothing. It's going to be a waste of time and money to pursue this further. I advise cutting your losses.

Closing my eyes, I sigh. I knew the odds were bad, but I was praying I'd catch a break.

"Bad news?" Mimi says sympathetically.

"Can't find Jordan."

She sighs. "You think your in-laws hired him to lie... and then vanish?"

"The thought crossed my mind, but I don't get why they'd go to the trouble. They have over a billion dollars. I would've settled for a quarter of the trust if they felt that greedy about it." I shake my head.

"They didn't get rich by being generous," Mimi points out. "Rich people are the worst when it comes to stuff like this."

I know that from my dealings with moneyed types, starting with my grandfather, but this still burns like a branding iron against my belly. I let out a forceful breath. I can't let the situation get me down.

"Hey, girl, it's okay. We'll figure it out together. I'll help in any way you need," Mimi offers, wrapping an arm around me. She doesn't really understand how bad my situation is...although I'm sure she can guess from the way I'm living. "God, if I were single, I would've moved in with you so we could save on rent."

"Thanks, but Andy's a keeper." I finish the last bite of my lo mein. Probably should've saved some for my next meal, but I'm too hungry to care.

Very deliberately, I change the topic to what's going on in Mimi's life. I live vicariously through her—her sweet romance, her dreams. If I'm not careful I'm going to forget what it's like to have dreams of my own for a better future, especially when my situation feels so hopeless. I refuse to become a shell going through the motions of living, so Mimi's talk is reminding me of all the things that make our lives worthwhile—the light at the end of the tunnel.

As we laugh at some ridiculous stories about Mimi's crazy photographer, my phone rings. *Caller unknown.* My mouth instantly dries. The last time I had a call like this, it was to inform me that Mom had passed out and was rushed to the hospital.

Mimi looks at me, the mirth evaporating from her face. "Who's that?"

I shake my head, unable to get any words out, then clear my throat. "Hello?" I rasp, willing this to be anything but bad news about Mom.

"Do you honestly think you'll get your lover to lie for you?"

There's no mistaking Simone Villar's upper crust diction, which came from top private schools in Hong Kong and Singapore. My stomach tightens with another kind of tension. Simone is my sister-in-law. Or, more precisely, was. She won't acknowledge me as her older brother's widow. Since his death, she's zealously guarded her family's fortune, doing whatever she felt was necessary to cut me out.

I don't understand how money could change her like this. Despite the difficult relationship she had with Jack, she gave me a very warm welcome to the Villar family, even making sure I joined the family charity so I'd have something meaningful to occupy my time as Jack's wife. But since his death, she's turned into a total psycho, determined that I get nothing.

"You'll never find him," Simone says with supreme confidence. "People like that aren't available to just *anyone.*"

I inhale sharply. The gloating way she speaks confirms my suspicions about Jordan Smith being a setup. How else could there be photos taken from angles that made it look like he and I were more than just friendly acquaintances? How else can she be so sure? "Did you hire him?"

"I'm not saying anything. Merely pointing out that you're wasting what little money you have. Wouldn't you rather spend it on your dying mother? Assuming she really *is* dying. She's been dying ever since Jack dragged you home like a stray dog."

The vise around my head tightens. She can say shit about me all she wants, but not my mom. Never my mom. "How dare you? What's wrong with you?"

"What's wrong with *me?* I'm just trying to protect

my family from an interloper. I can't believe you even tried to have a *baby* with Jack. Ridiculous, of course."

"What...?" I didn't tell anybody about the baby, except Jack, and I doubt he told his sister. He considered Simone vapid and better off uninformed.

"It's not that hard to tell when you don't use any sanitary napkins or tampons, Faith. Didn't you study basic biology in school? I know American schools are bad at that sort of thing, but I thought my brother had better sense than to pick up an uneducated idiot. Honestly, the complications from a child...especially a son..." I can hear a shudder in her voice, and I can't draw in breath through the searing ball lodged in my throat. "It's best the baby didn't make it."

My stomach cramps as though it's reliving the pain of the miscarriage, and I can almost feel the bloody flow between my legs. I pull my knees together and gather them close to my chest.

"You're going to go to hell, you unutterable bitch," I bite out the only response I can manage.

She titters. "Do you believe in fairy tales as well? Wake up. Heaven and hell don't exist. They're tools to control the unwashed mob, so they can mutter to themselves about how the rich and the powerful are going to *hell* and feel better about their pathetic existence. As though poverty were something to be proud of. How does it feel to know you're going to die broke and alone, Faith? I hope you live a long life...so you can experience it to the fullest. Or if you play nice and return everything you took when you left Hong Kong, maybe I'll be generous and throw a bit of money your way to tide things over until you get yourself a new sugar daddy. Tick tock, tick tock. Rich men don't like girls who are too old. Best hurry before you hit the big two-five." She hangs up.

My hand fists over my heart. The evil of Jack's sister never ceases to stun me, but this is more. *A lot more.* What Simone's saying is outright depraved. I was such a fool to have trusted her, no matter how nice she seemed. People from her social circle aren't like me.

Suddenly the feel of Mimi's hand on my chin jerks me out of my self-recrimination. "Oh my gosh, Faith! Your lip!"

I stare at her blankly. "What?"

She presses a Kleenex to my lower lip. Only then do I register the throbbing pain and coppery taste in my mouth. Mimi takes the Kleenex away and hands me a take-out napkin. I press it against my lip; it comes away with a large red spot.

"What was that call about?" she asks.

"Simone, wanting to crow about her victory."

"For real? What a bitch."

"It doesn't matter." My eyes are hot, but tears do not come.

"I could spend the night here if you want."

"No, you need to go home before it's too late. Didn't you say you have an early audition?" I squeeze her hand. "No missing your big break because of me. I'll be fine."

"But..." Her gaze drops to my mouth.

"It's just a little blood, Mimi. Please."

"Well...if you're sure."

"I'm sure." I need to be alone and think.

Mimi isn't convinced, but she gives me a tight hug, then tosses the empty Chinese cartons and leaves.

I clean up a little, then curl up on the couch and stare at a spot beyond the empty wall in my apartment. The throbbing from my lip is nothing compared to the ache in my heart.

If Jack hadn't died...

A hysterical giggle bubbles up in the back of my throat. Nothing would've changed except Mom's care would've been paid for, assuming he would've continued doing it. After all, he couldn't keep his vow to be faithful, and he made that in front of four hundred wedding guests.

I should know better than to trust anybody's promise, especially a rich person's. Their words have about as much value as used toilet paper.

Or the bloody towel against my mouth.

Knocks come from the door. I sigh and get up. Mimi can be forgetful. "What did you leave behind?" I say as I open the door...

...and stop dead at the sight of Blake.

5

Faith

I BLINK A FEW TIMES, CERTAIN I'M
hallucinating, but the pain throbbing in my lip isn't
enough to make me see things.

What's he doing here? The last thing I want is for
him to see my shabby studio apartment or me barefoot
in a thin white shirt and cropped pants. I'm not even
wearing a bra or makeup, for God's sake.

It's one thing to appear vulnerable because I chose
to, but something else to be caught with my shields
down. Especially when Blake is fully armored in an
expensive suit that radiates money and power in
expertly tailored lines.

Immediately my brain kicks in, and I try to shove
the door shut. If he wants to talk, he can make an
appointment like a normal human being.

But my strength is no match for his large, muscled body as he stiff-arms the door and casually strolls into the room. I inhale a whiff of something spicy and clean —the same scent that had me intoxicated with him when we first met—and steel my spine.

He stops in front of my coffee table, which is littered with bloody tissues. He frowns and spins around. "What happened?"

"Nothing," I mutter, holding the paper towel to my mouth. "What are you doing here?"

Ignoring me, he reaches for the paper. I jerk back, but too slowly. He pulls away the towel. I turn my head, but he catches my chin in one strong, implacable hand and tilts it up and toward him so he can study my mouth. It half-throbs and half-tingles.

"What happened?" he asks again, like he cares.

And I hate it that he can sound this way after our disastrous talk. I much prefer his rude and entitled attitude. "None of your business. It doesn't hurt and the bleeding's stopped, so you can turn off the fake concern."

His eyebrow twitches. "The bleeding *hasn't* stopped." His tone is mildly chiding, but it only gets my defenses up. The last time I took everything from him at face value, I ended up a heartbroken idiot at the end.

"It would have if you hadn't snatched away my towel."

"You need more."

He drops his hand from my chin. I feel the absence of the touch keenly, and my annoyance at myself doubles. Here's a man who told me to get on my knees three days ago. What the hell's wrong with me? Surely, I have more self-respect than this.

He goes into what passes for my kitchen and opens the small fridge. It has only one door, and the inside is pitifully empty except for a few eggs and butter. He mutters something that sounds suspiciously like "what the fuck" under his breath.

My face flushes with embarrassment, although I'm not sure precisely why. It isn't as though he can't figure out my awful money situation. My entire apartment is smaller than his fancy office, and it only has two pieces of furniture—my sofa bed and the coffee table. I'm their fourth owner.

He pops a few ice cubes from a tray and wraps them in a fresh paper towel. "Press this to your mouth. It'll help with swelling," he says, his tone a bit too brisk.

I stare at his offering like it's a rattlesnake. Actually a snake might be safer. When he quirks an eyebrow in silent challenge, I take it. I'll be damned if I'll give the impression that I'm uncertain and apprehensive in my own home.

The cold feels good. The throbbing in my lip subsides to a more manageable level, and I swallow a sigh of relief. I see him scan my place, undoubtedly cataloguing every flaw. The walls are empty, and the carpet's so thin the floor might as well be bare. At least it's clean, which is purely due to pride. I may live in a crappy place, but I won't let it become a pigsty.

I spread my feet shoulder width apart and

distribute my weight. Contrary to what negotiation experts say, I know having this encounter in my home confers me zero advantage. It's more of a liability because it reveals how little I have compared to him.

But maybe I can turn it to my advantage anyway. As long as I don't talk about Mom, he'll see I have very little to lose.

"Why didn't you go to Benedict?" Blake asks suddenly.

I blink. "Benedict?"

"Don't play dumb."

So he knows about my relationship with that man. "I'd rather die."

He raises an eyebrow. "Whatever he wants from you can't be as bad as...this."

I snort. Maybe someone like him doesn't think it's a big deal to cast aside his dying mother, but I do. I'll never give her up for Benedict's billions.

Blake's hand sweeps around my place. "This is a huge downgrade from your place in Vegas, not to mention the penthouse you shared with Jack in Hong Kong. You don't have to live like this to stick it to your grandfather."

"You don't know anything."

"I know you're suffering unnecessarily."

I roll my eyes. He'll never understand. "I'm not discussing him with you. I have no idea what you're doing here, but if you're here to tell me you're in the neighborhood, think again. It won't work."

"I came by to see you."

"And maybe get a friendly neighborhood blow job? Sorry, not gonna happen."

A hint of amusement gleams in his eyes; then he blinks and it's gone. "Hemorrhage isn't exactly a turn-on."

"Isn't it? Could have fooled me."

"Faith—"

"Whatever you want to talk about, I'm not interested. I'm tired, and I don't appreciate people barging into my home."

He leans against the wall, his limbs relaxed. His hooded eyes show nothing. "I've decided you'll do."

It takes me a moment to register what he just said. "What?"

"Your proposal. Surely you haven't forgotten?"

"Whatever happened to getting on my knees?" Because if that's the condition of this ridiculous... change of heart, I'm going to disabuse him of the notion.

He waves it away. "You happen to be the lowest cost provider."

I stop for a second, then laugh. Of all the things I imagined... "So, just like that? You don't even know what I'm going to want in return."

"Money, of course." His gaze sweeps around my place, then lingers on my body. "A hundred thousand in cash seems like a fair price."

"The portrait you're going to get is worth millions."

"So? *You* aren't worth millions. Like I said, I can always go to someone else."

I clench my hand. What wouldn't I give to bloody his nose. But that would solve nothing. My PI failed to come through with Jordan, and as insulting as it is, a hundred thousand will take care of the immediate problem: ensuring that Mom gets the best care until... My breath catches, and I can't continue the thought.

"Cash, upfront, you pay the tax," I counter.

"No on upfront. How do I know you won't take the money and run?"

"I'm a woman of my word."

"Your word." A small muscle in his cheek tics once. "When you disappeared, as I recall, it was *without* a word."

If he thinks it's a clever barb, he's wrong. "Only when the situation warrants it."

"Half upfront. Cash. I'll handle the tax since you obviously can't handle money." Blake gives me a cool stare. "And you'll move in with me immediately."

"No. I'm perfectly happy where I am." *Away from you.*

"You can't be serious." He gestures vaguely at my studio apartment. "This is a dump."

"It's *my* dump, and I like it."

"Lies are best if they're at least somewhat believable. Besides, regardless of how you feel about this place, appearances need to be maintained. I won't tolerate a separate living arrangement."

"Then it's going to cost you extra."

"Is that how you're going to play this?"

"Tolerating your presence day in, day out does require commensurate compensation."

He laughs. "A lot of women would pay me to spend time with them."

"Yes, well... I have better taste."

He considers. "An extra fifty thousand?"

I nod jerkily, surprised at how easy that was.

"Anything else you want extra payment for?"

I ignore his sardonic tone. "I'll live with you, but I want a separate bedroom. No sex."

"Is sex extra too?" he mocks openly.

"Five hundred dollars minimum per session," I respond, unable to be a mature adult.

He sputters. "I've never paid for sex."

"You're the one who wanted the lowest cost provider. Surely you weren't expecting full service."

"I'm not going to live like a monk, Faith. And you have needs."

"I don't expect you to," I say, ignoring his remark on my needs. That's what vibrators are for, but my toys will not be a topic of our conversation. Ever.

"I expect fidelity," he says darkly.

"I don't, but don't worry—I won't sleep around and cause you embarrassment. The only thing I ask is you have the courtesy to stay away from me on the days you take care of your...needs."

He stares at me, but I can't decide if he's shocked or angry or both. I forge ahead before I lose my courage. "I also don't want to meet your family...or friends."

"You will accompany me to social functions, Faith. That's non-negotiable."

"Once a month then, no more. And you can't make it up if you miss one."

"Any other stipulations?" he asks dryly.

"You can set any wedding date you want, but I prefer that it be in the next thirty days and my payment immediate upon the ceremony."

"How are we going to have a ceremony if you don't want to meet my family or friends?"

"There's this thing called a courthouse. The marriage is only for a year, so there's no need for anything extravagant." I quirk a corner of my mouth up. "I'm the lowest cost provider, remember?"

His expression shifts. If I didn't know better, I'd say he's almost sad. "You've changed."

"You haven't."

He pushes off the wall. "My lawyer will draft an agreement."

"Good. You know my address."

"I'll be in touch."

He lets himself out.

Breathing shakily, I plop down on the sofa. I got almost everything I wanted from the deal, including the money I need, but I can't help but feel I didn't come out victorious.

BLAKE

I LOOK BACK AT THE CRUMBLING BUILDING ONE last time. The intercom at the entrance is busted. It obviously hasn't worked in a while; the residents have made do by disabling the auto-lock on the door. Might as well put up a neon sign flashing "Criminals Welcome".

The carpet in the common area was worn, torn and stained with God only knows what, and the halls and stairs smelled like old animal urine. Wouldn't surprise me a bit if it also had puke and human waste.

I was so certain Benjamin Clark was mistaken— there was no way Faith could be living in a dump like this. I only went inside to confirm he was wrong. But I should've known better. Benjamin isn't prone to mistakes.

The sight of Faith with her face scrubbed clean of makeup and hair down jolted me, reminding me briefly of the simpler and sweeter time we had in Vegas, but the shabbiness of her home was shocking. And that nearly empty fridge—appalling. I tell myself my outrage is from my intense distaste for seeing people go hungry in a country as wealthy as ours, but I know that isn't entirely true. It's the idea of *her* going hungry that bothers the hell out of me.

And because I hate that I care at all, I told her I'd only pay her one hundred thousand dollars. The fact that she took it, knowing how much the portrait's worth, disturbs me.

I can't help but question my sanity at leaving Faith in that dump. Anger at her late husband knots my gut. I can't imagine a man leaving his wife in a situation dire enough to necessitate her living—hungry—in a slum reject like this...even if his family fortune *has* declined over the years.

On the other hand, the type of guy who cheats on his wife probably doesn't care enough to ensure she'll be okay after he's gone. And the vindictive part of me whispers she should've known better than to go with that son of a bitch because he dangled some money in front of her. What I don't understand is, why the hell he would want another woman when he had Faith? Then I stop, remembering how flagrantly my uncle Salazar cheated on his wife, who is still one of the most beautiful women I've ever seen.

Instead of leaving, I should go back and get Faith, drag her away from this hellhole. The problem is, she's made it clear she doesn't want to move in with me even to leave this behind. I could use force, but I don't have the appetite for that...especially after seeing the injury on her lip. I don't think she got it from fighting, but the obviously painful cut bothers me anyway, much more than it should.

Perhaps it's natural to react like this when you're dealing with the first woman you've ever loved, even if you don't care for her anymore. No wonder Dane warned me. After Sophia, he understands how insidious such feelings can be. And I almost feel sympathy for Lucas, since Ava is probably his first love.

Then I remember Lucas is staying at my penthouse, and my mood sours for a moment. I can't kick him out after asking him to move in, and I can't bring Faith over since she'll bolt at the sight of a family member. Guess it's time to look for another location. I text Cecilia to send me a list of suitable penthouses, preferably something close to Digital Angel.

I spot my still-intact Aston Martin. The neighborhood is so poor, I was certain the car would be stripped clean by now. Images of a cow in a river full of piranhas came to mind.

I climb into my car and pull away. I gave Faith more or less what she demanded because I want her out of this shithole.

And because I have no intention of honoring most of it—especially the part about paying extra for sex. I snort a laugh. She was always hot as hell in bed, and I doubt that's changed.

All I have to do is make her want it.

6

Faith

MOST OF MY NIGHT IS SPENT TOSSING AND turning. Despite Blake's promise to be in touch, I'm not taking anything for granted. To be honest, I don't know what possessed me to negotiate the way I did last night, and I'm pretty sure he's going to leave me high and dry. He has an insatiable sexual appetite, not to mention an apparent urge to humiliate me. I can't imagine him agreeing to my refusal to have sex with him...even with the proviso that he can screw anyone else he wants.

Despite my catty demand that it'll cost him at least five hundred bucks, there's no amount large enough for me to share my body with him. Some girls can fuck without having to like their partner. I'm not one of them. And I don't plan on liking Blake enough to sleep with him ever again.

At nine o'clock sharp the next morning, a special courier delivers a manila envelope. It contains a two-page document with a yellow sticky note.

Read, sign if you agree, then come to the courthouse at two for the ceremony. Dress nicely.

The end of the memo has an address.

So. Blake isn't changing his mind. Now that I have the papers in hand, I can't decide if I should be relieved or horrified that I'm actually going to do this.

The contract is short and refreshingly free of legalese, with all the points we discussed succinctly laid out. Of course it also includes a clause that sex is on the table so long as we're mutually agreeable.

I smirk. Then the next clause about fidelity makes me frown. Both parties are to be faithful? Whatever for? I meant what I said. I don't mind being faithful—he has to maintain the façade—but I don't expect, or even want, that of him. A small part of me burns at the idea of him with another woman, but it's better to go into the situation with eyes wide open.

With a black pen, I cross out the clause and write out what I told him last night, then initial and sign the agreement. For the first deposit of seventy-five thousand dollars, I go to a nearby bank and open an account. As soon as money shows up, I'm moving it to my regular account at another bank, then closing this one. I jot down the bank information on a sticky note and attach it to the signed contract to take with me.

Since it's theoretically a wedding, albeit a fake one, I wear a white blouse, matching pencil skirt and pink pumps. I don't have any fancy jewelry except for a pair of pearl earrings—something I absolutely refuse to part with since they're heirlooms from my dad. I put them on and carefully apply a vivid red to my lips to hide the cut, which is still tender. That done, I drive to the specified courthouse.

Blake is moving much faster than I expected, but that's actually a good thing. Less time to second-guess my decision—not that I really have any other options—plus he probably wants to get the whole thing over with as soon as possible to get his painting. Unless the tabloids misreported, he and his siblings won't be getting their portraits until they're married for a year.

I feel bad about not telling Mimi and Mom about the wedding, but my best friend is busy today—the audition plus a shift at her restaurant. As for Mom, she doesn't have to hear about this farce. I don't plan on having her meet Blake again. He didn't care about us back then, and I don't think that's changed in the last two years. There's a reason I don't want to meet his friends and family: I don't want him to meet mine.

Traffic's mercifully light, and it only takes me an hour to reach the courthouse. I'm a few minutes early, but when I walk inside, I spot Blake immediately. He's impossible to miss in his impeccable suit, tall and powerful as he stands in the lobby. The natural light coming in highlights his cheekbones, and his full lips are set in a firm line. Regardless of my feelings, I can't help but go still for a moment and admire the masculine beauty. There's something very wrong—unfair, even—about a man who is so perfectly created that his mere presence can leave you breathless. And it annoys me that I'm not immune to his magnificence.

Several women check him out rather blatantly as they walk past, but he treats them as though they're so many flies buzzing by. He glances at his Omega, then suddenly stops and swivels his head in my direction.

Our gazes collide; the fine lines around his mouth relax for a fraction of a second, and I inhale sharply at the impact of his dark eyes probing into mine. It's as though he can see right through everything, layer under layer, to my core, but I shake the fanciful notion off. He can't see anything at all. I've changed. I grew up, truly opened my eyes. For that I'll always be grateful to Jack and his family.

I walk up to Blake and hand him the envelope. "Here."

"Excellent."

"I made a small amendment."

"Did you?" He pulls the contract out and reads the clause I wrote over. His eyebrows dip into a V, but then he shrugs, pulls out an elegant black and gold pen, and initials it. He takes a picture of the page with our signatures, texts someone and places his phone back into his pocket. "Ready?"

"Yes."

He takes out a ring with a large marquise cut

diamond and slips it on my finger. "For the engagement."

I stare at it. The clear stone sparkles with exceptionally brilliant inner fire, and the sapphires embedded in the band are the color of the Arctic Ocean. It fits perfectly, and it's exactly the kind of ring I would've loved if this were a real engagement. I don't know when he had the chance to shop for one, much less find the right band size.

His assistant. And money makes a lot of things possible, my mind whispers. After all, it was Jack's assistant who picked out all his holiday and anniversary gifts.

Getting the marriage license takes no time at all, which is perfect since my nerves are getting worse with every ticking second. You'd think that a second wedding would be easier than the first, but it's not. At least back then I had no idea what I was getting into. I swore I'd never marry for anything but love, but that was when I thought I could count on the trust Jack set up. I rub my hands together. I should be grateful. It sucks that I'm marrying for money a second time, but it means Mom will stay alive. I'd marry Ted Bundy if it meant Mom would be taken care of.

The clerk informs us we'll have the civil ceremony in half an hour. The woman's tone says she can't believe we have our appointment so soon. Then I note why—I see a small notice stating that no appointment for a civil ceremony is allowed without a marriage license.

"Pulled some strings, did you?" I murmur.

"Time is money."

And probably everyone in the city who matters is his golf buddy. That's how things were in Hong Kong during my previous marriage. Jack had friends and acquaintances at every level, and they accepted me because it was expected, not because they actually liked me or wanted to be my friend.

I don't anticipate this marriage will be any different.

The ceremony is short. A witness is provided—for a small fee. The sharply dressed officiant smiles as though he's thrilled to bind us in matrimony, not knowing it's contractually stipulated to end in a year.

"Now I pronounce you husband and wife," he says, beaming when we finish our empty vows and exchange platinum wedding bands. Mine is rather elaborate, designed to cradle the engagement ring, while his is a simple gleaming circle. "You may kiss the bride."

Blake cradles my face, and I brace myself. I don't think he's going to devour me in front of other people, but he may do something to make a point after my refusal to sleep with him. The Blake I know is both persistent and determined.

He studies my mouth, and the cut from last night throbs—in anticipation of pain or something else, I don't know. He's always been an exceptional kisser, the first man to make me realize there could be more to the act than just a tangling of tongues and lips. The longer he stares at me, the more my belly flutters until it feels like it's full of starved ants desperate to feed. A slight frown creases his brow; he finally leans in and kisses me on the forehead.

It should be platonic and ridiculous, almost anticlimactic after his intense scrutiny of my face, but his lips feel like a brand on my skin, and the spot tingles. I swallow a gasp.

The officiant laughs. "No need to be shy, you're married now."

Blake smiles, the picture of an indulgent husband. "She cut her lip yesterday, and I'd hate to hurt her."

I'm a little surprised he remembers, and I guess he can read the thought on my face. The light in his eyes alters, taking on a serious note. "I remember everything about you."

Our witness sighs. "That's so nice. Enjoy it, sweetie. It doesn't always last."

Maybe she took his statement as some romantic proclamation, but I feel like it's more of a warning. It bothers me I can't pinpoint exactly what he's warning me about. Does he think I'll run off with the deposit? I signed the papers, and meant what I told him last night. I'm a woman of my word; I won't leave him until our year is up.

Blake takes my hand and leads me out. My phone buzzes, and I check the message. It's a notification from the bank about the deposit. Seventy-five thousand dollars. My mouth dries.

"Something wrong?" he asks.

"You're fast."

"Hmm?"

"The money." I swallow. "When did you arrange it?"

"As we picked up our marriage license. I told my assistant to make the deposit."

"I see."

He looks at me for a moment. "Did you think I'd drag my feet?"

"It crossed my mind."

"I don't back out of deals."

"Good to know. Neither do I."

He nods, his hand flexing around mine. "I'm sending movers to your place today."

"No need. I can fit what I need in a suitcase." I'm certain my beat-up sofa bed and coffee table will be unwanted in his fancy home. Ditto for my chipped plates and mugs. I'm going to box what I can for storage, so I don't have to buy everything from scratch when I move out. Seventy-five thousand is a lot of money, but I have to be really, really careful.

"Don't argue with me, Faith. People have been hired. Think of it as your contribution to the economy."

I sigh. "If you insist."

"You should also go shopping."

"For what?"

"Our honeymoon. All expenses paid, all luxury. Maybe some tropical resort...the Caribbean, the Seychelles...?"

I laugh. "Whatever for? It isn't even"—I lower my voice—"a real marriage."

"Regardless, we need to project the appearance."

"Sorry, I can't go. You'll have to make up some excuse if it's going to bother your father."

"You promised."

"I promised to make a good show of this marriage, not to actually do everything a married couple does." I can't leave Los Angeles. "Also, my passport's expired."

"I can get you a new one. And we don't have to go overseas for the honeymoon."

I look away. "I don't like flying." That part is true enough. Even though flying is statistically safer than driving, I still can't get over the fact that my dad died in a plane crash when I was six or that I'm in a tube of metal flying more than thirty-five thousand feet above ground at seven hundred plus miles per hour. But that's not something I want to get into at the moment. "Look, we can go later, just not now. Besides, I don't think your father's tracking whether everyone had their honeymoon, is he?"

Blake looks at me oddly. "What's really going on, Faith?"

"What I just told you." *Don't try to find out why.*

The arch of his eyebrows tells me he doesn't believe a word of it. "Fine. Pack whatever you don't want strangers to touch, and I'm sending you a car this evening. We're having dinner together."

"Where?"

"Where else? At our new home."

"I'm not meeting your family or friends."

"Don't worry." He smiles. "It'll be just the two of us, exactly the way you want."

～

BLAKE

FAITH IS LYING.

It doesn't take a genius to know. Maybe she really does dislike flying, but who turns down an all-expense-paid luxury trip to an exotic location?

I'm certain she doesn't have a job—Benjamin's financial report didn't indicate a steady stream of cash coming in. I assumed her money troubles might be due to gambling or addiction, but now I doubt that's the case. People with addictions don't tend to keep their homes up, and her place was spotless.

Since I haven't been living in a cave, I heard rumors about an affair before Jack died. Does Faith have a lover in L.A.?

I dismiss the possibility the moment it pops into my head. If so, she would never have agreed to be faithful, not when a breach would result in her getting nothing.

All I know for certain is: she wants money badly, and she's willing to do almost anything for it...except sleep with me or contact her wealthy grandfather.

Whatever she's up to... Is that the same reason she left me to marry Jack Villar? Back then she didn't know how much money I had or who I really was. I hid that, not for any perverse reason but because I enjoyed being with a woman who didn't look at me while calculating the amount of jewelry I could buy her, what expensive vacation I could pay for.

I even believed her when she told me she loved me.

What a joke.

Everyone has a price. Hers is one hundred thousand dollars in cold hard cash.

7

Faith

THE FIRST THING I DO WHEN I WALK INSIDE MY apartment is put on some music. It's free, it lifts my spirits, and I can use a pick-me-up to gird my loins for the move. Although Blake called it "our new home," I know it's really his. I'll just be a temporary guest.

As Adele's husky voice fills the air, singing about someone she used to know, I change into a shirt and jeans, pull out a suitcase and start dumping all my underwear and clothes into it. Although Jack's family fought to claw back everything from me, they didn't really want the clothes. Worn panties probably have no value to them, compared to the gorgeous Porsche he gave me on our wedding day. The only reason they failed to take my jewelry was the clause in the prenup that specified all jewelry as mine to keep, and Jack was exceptionally free with diamonds.

The rock on my finger winks, and I study the exquisitely cut stone, set perfectly in a sapphire encrusted platinum band. I love the elegant design, but I shouldn't get too attached to it. Blake will undoubtedly want it back when our time's up. Our agreement doesn't say I get to keep any of the trappings he's going to provide.

And I'm okay with giving everything back so long as I get to keep the cash, use it to help Mom beat that damned tumor one more time.

I carefully pack a couple of framed photos of me and my parents, burying them among the clothes to give them extra protection. They're old pictures, and I don't have digital copies anymore. Those, along with all the others, were lost when my computer died a few years ago.

My phone buzzes. It's Mimi.

"Hey," I say, as I hit the speaker button. Modern technology. Now I can keep packing and talk to her at the same time.

"Oh my God! I had to call!" The words are spilling out. "I wanted you to be the second person to hear this."

"What?"

"You remember the audition I did for that new sitcom?"

"Yeah." Mimi was inconsolable afterward, convinced she'd bombed.

"*I got it!*"

"*Oh my God!*" Hugging myself, I start bouncing around in a circle as though Mimi's right in the apartment with me. "That's *awe*some! Holy cow! I *knew* you killed it!"

"But the casting people never even smiled when I read for them! I was so worried."

"They didn't smile because they were too awestruck by your talent and beauty. Holy shit, we have to celebrate!"

"I know! Okay, okay." She breathes audibly. "Andy says he can get off work at five, and I thought you could join us for a couple of hours before I have to go work my shift. I need to see if I can get a reservation at some place decent."

My gaze lands on the suitcase. "Oh shit."

"What?"

"I'm sorry, I can't."

"Why not?" Suddenly joy drains from her voice. "Is it your mom?"

"No, she's okay. It's...um... Well." I huff. Mimi's bound to find out since there's no way I can keep my marriage a secret for a whole year. "I'm married, and I need to move in with my"—I stop, unable to spit out the word *husband*—"him."

"*What?*" She stops to take a breath. "Who, how, where, when?"

"Courthouse, today, nothing fancy."

"And you didn't invite me? What the hell, girl!" Mimi screeches. "Am I your best friend or what?"

"Of course you're my best fr—"

"I can't believe this! You didn't even tell me about the proposal!"

"Because there *was* no proposal," I say firmly, before Mimi works herself up for nothing.

She stops, and her voice almost returns to its normal decibel. "Okay. *What* are you talking about?"

"I married Blake."

I can almost hear Mimi blinking on the other side. "Blake? As in that guy from Vegas a couple years back?"

"Yes."

"I thought it was over between the two of you."

"Well...it was."

"Then what's up with the marriage?"

"You know that tabloid gossip about him and his brothers—Ryder Reed and all that?" I name the super-hot actor because there's no way Mimi's missed gossip about the Hollywood A-list star.

"Yeah, but I thought it was all bullshit. I mean, who could make Ryder Reed marry someone he doesn't want?"

"Well..."

The pause stretches, then Mimi finally says, "Um. It's true?"

"Something like that."

"Holy shit."

"You can't tell anyone."

"Fine, my lips are sealed. But why?"

I plop down on the sofa. "I need money. Blake has

it and is willing to give me some so long as I marry him for a year, but if the whole truth comes out..."

"Wow. Got it, but Faith, the situation sounds so...mercenary."

"That's because it is."

"How do you know he'll really pay you?"

"He paid me half upfront, and I already moved the money to an account at another bank."

"Smart." Mimi grows extra serious. "Does your mom know?"

"No."

"You gonna tell her?"

"She doesn't need to know. I made it clear to him we don't see each other's friends or family."

"I see. But shit. I wanted to celebrate with you, girl."

"I know. I want to, too, but..."

"Is he expecting a wedding night?"

"Nope. Sex is off the table. You know I can't sleep with a guy I don't like."

"What about Jack?"

"I liked him in the beginning." Or to be precise, I was *grateful* to him. Without him, things would've been a lot harder for my mom and me. Treating inoperable tumors isn't easy or cheap, and back then she wasn't old enough to be eligible for Medicare, and we weren't poor enough—quite—for assistance.

"Yeah, but you told me how much you hated Blake. Did that change?"

"It doesn't matter, as long as I get what I need out of this."

"Does he know what you need the money for?"

"Nope. I didn't tell him, and I don't plan to. It's not like he'd give a damn anyway. He didn't back then, and he isn't going to now." I'm sick of fake sympathy, fake *sorrys* and fake platitudes. It still makes my chest tight with humiliation to recall how I cried my eyes out on his shoulder, thinking he cared, when he was probably praying the waterworks would end so he could get the hell away from me.

"I'm sorry. I wish you could've had something better."

"I already do. I have an awesome friend—you." I sigh. "I'm sorry I'm in such a bind. I should be out celebrating with you."

"Hey, rain check. We can celebrate later. Making sure your mom's okay is more important."

"Thanks, Mimi."

"Don't mention it. I'm gonna visit her tomorrow, see how she's doing."

"She'll love that."

"So will I. Text me when you're free."

"Will do."

"And Faith?"

"Yeah?"

"Don't do anything you wouldn't want me to do. You aren't alone. I'm behind you one hundred percent, and I'll help with your mom. You know I don't mind."

My nose burns with unshed tears. "I know. You're the bestest girlfriend ever."

"So are you. Text me any time."

"Okay."

I hang up and pack the rest of my clothes, shoes, toiletries, then put all my kitchen stuff in a few boxes and label them. I stare at the sofa and table. Should I save them? Even cheap furniture isn't cheap. On the other hand, am I going to want a cut-up sofa bed when I have a few thousand bucks to spare? I run my teeth over my upper lip, thinking.

Ah, what the hell. They can go.

It feels weird that this is it. Maybe most people would be thrilled to leave a crappy apartment, but not me. It's mine—something I've paid for with my own money, a place where I can let my hair down and do whatever I want, including bawl my eyes out when I need a good cry.

Blake's home won't be like that. It'll be another gilded cage, just like Jack's penthouse was.

"Come on, girl," I tell myself, slapping my cheeks lightly. "It's only a year. Over before you know it. And this time, you know exactly what you're getting into."

Then there's a knock at the door, and a clean-cut uniformed chauffeur is saying hello, taking my suitcase, informing me that the moving crew is going to take care of everything else.

The car waiting out on the curb is a freaking white limo, gleaming with a fresh coat of wax. The driver opens the rear door with a flourish, and I stare at the pristine leather interior.

Any other woman would feel like a fairy-tale princess. I feel like one, too...one who's about to be dragged into a dark forest to be wed to an evil prince.

8

Faith

THE LIMO STOPS IN FRONT OF A SOARING HIGH-RISE not too far from Digital Angel. *Naturally. Blake arranges things for his own convenience.* The chauffeur opens the door for me and brings my suitcase from the trunk. "Thank you," I murmur.

"My pleasure, Mrs. Pryce-Reed." He beams.

I stare at him blankly, then realize with a start that the Mrs. Pryce-Reed he's referring to is me. I smile back, hoping to hide how awkward I'm feeling.

He gestures toward the revolving door, and I walk inside. The lobby is like a luxury hotel—all marble and gleaming brass and glass. A couple of asymmetrical leather seats are clearly there for aesthetics rather than comfort. I swallow a sigh. The décor reminds me of Jack's home. A million dollars' worth of interior decoration that looked expensive, but felt like it was to be seen and admired, not lived in.

If this is the lobby, I can only imagine what Blake's home must look like.

"Mrs. Pryce-Reed," a sharply dressed man at the concierge desk says in a warm voice. "Congratulations on your wedding. Do you need help with your luggage?"

Eyes wide, I shake my head. "I just want to go to Blake's uni—uh, home."

"Certainly, ma'am. Here's your security access code for the elevator and the gym." He hands me an envelope made of expensive, heavy paper stock. It contains an even stiffer card. "If you need anything, please don't hesitate to call."

He leads me to a waiting elevator behind a giant column. I walk inside and give him a small smile as the doors close. I pull out the card and punch the six-digit code into the security panel. The car starts upward.

I inhale and straighten my spine, push my shoulders back. I can't let anything intimidate me. This marriage has barely begun. If I start feeling depressed on the first day, how am I going to survive the next three hundred and sixty-four?

The elevator opens onto a small foyer. The double door's slightly ajar, and I walk inside, dragging my suitcase.

The interior is airy, with a light color scheme— beige, ivory and spring green—and an extra tall ceiling with modern crystal light fixtures. Vases full of fresh flowers sit on two stands in living room nooks.

One wall has a huge screen that shows orange jellyfish pulsing through a cobalt blue background, their movements surprisingly soothing. Blake showed me the same creatures on his phone once when we were on a date at an aquarium where we could snorkel with stingrays. He told me he loved aquariums—the blue, the calm and the languid movement of ocean life, and his favorite was sea nettles. He was disappointed the one we went to didn't have them.

I pick up the suitcase and take the three steps down, and Blake appears from a door. His hair is slightly damp, his mouth unsmiling but not tight with tension either. He's in a light, gray long-sleeve shirt with a pair of loose lounging pants hanging off his lean hips—a picture of a man relaxed and sure in his domain. His bare feet peek from beneath the hem of his pants, and they look surprisingly vulnerable in contrast.

I almost laugh. *He's anything but vulnerable.*

"You should've had the concierge deliver your suitcase," he says.

"It wasn't necessary."

He walks toward me. As he leans forward to take the bag from me, I get a whiff of soap and something spicy underneath. The side of his bare neck is so close, all I'd have to do is tilt my head forward a bit and I could press my lips to the pulse beating underneath the taut, bare skin. I try to let go of the bag before our hands can touch, but his fingers graze mine anyway. I flinch at the electric shock and pull away, swallowing hard. It's just static electricity, but my clit throbs as though it's gone straight to my core.

If Blake notices, he doesn't show any reaction. Instead he drags the suitcase to a room in the back. "Your bedroom," he says, opening the door.

It's enormous, with a sitting area that has an armchair where I can curl up and read and a low table. The bed is proportionately huge, with a lace canopy, just like the one I said I wanted once while we were dating.

I remember everything about you.

I shake my head. This isn't like my lip injury. Surely Blake didn't remember something so small and inconsequential. I mean, I mentioned it months and months ago.

Don't read too much into a coincidence.

"The closet's over there. If it's too small, I can get it expanded."

I check it, then stop in shock. The whole space is so big it's obscene, and it makes the furnishings and décor of Jack's home look sort of...anemic by comparison. Mirrors hang from all sides, so I can check myself over thoroughly. Shelves and a vanity are made of dark wood with recessed lights, as though the entire closet is some kind of display set up at a high-end department store, and a leather chaise occupies one corner. There's a separate storage unit in the center, sort of an island with drawers for accessories and belts.

"It'll do," I say, leaving my suitcase there.

The en-suite bath is as opulent as the rest of the house with a double vanity, a sunken Jacuzzi tub and a separate shower with triple heads. Two fluffy white towels sit on a warmer.

"I thought I told you we weren't sleeping together," I say.

"We're not. My room's through there."

I look over to the other end of the bedroom. A connecting door, ajar at the moment, shows another room that looks identical to mine, except it has a California king sleigh bed made with chrome and other metals that give it a modern feel. The frame gleams as though it's ready to be photographed for a catalogue.

Connecting bedrooms? "Kind of an odd arran..." Then it hits me.

The smile that curls his lips is an odd mixture of self-deprecation and amusement. "The previous owner didn't get along with her husband."

"And this was their solution? Like two connected suites could disguise the discord; they couldn't even share a bathroom."

"Why not?"

"You shouldn't have bought it," I say as I note how new everything inside is.

"I didn't. It's a rental. My home is currently unavailable."

I start to ask him why, but stop. Ours isn't that kind of relationship anymore. Does it matter where we live as long as the clock keeps ticking?

"Do you want to freshen up?" he asks.

"I'm fine."

"Hungry?"

"Yeah, actually." It's a little after six already.

The dining room is large—of course—with a gleaming table made of some really dark wood, maybe teak. Six contemporary high-back chairs surround the table, situated right below a large chandelier light fixture.

I follow him to the open kitchen. It's state-of-the-art, with every amenity I can think of and then some. I'm not certain why a two-bedroom residence needs three ovens, but what do I know? He turns on a burner over the grill, opens one of four doors on the stainless steel fridge and takes out two huge slabs of beef, some shredded romaine lettuce—already prepared in a beautiful multifaceted serving bowl—and a hunk of Parmesan.

He gestures at the pantry to his left. "You can choose the croutons. I think Lenore bought a few different types."

The walk-in pantry too is just as outsized as the rest of the penthouse. There's enough food to feed a family of ten for a month. I take a small package of plain croutons and run my hand over a box of dark chocolate longingly as I leave. I could really use some of—

"Bring that, too."

I start, then flush at having been caught.

Blake is frowning. "I told you, this is your home too. That means everything inside is yours."

"Okay," I answer because it's the right response

when people tell you something like that. But I don't take it at face value. Jack's family said the same thing to me, only to change their tune later. The weird thing is, I have no clue what I did to make them turn against me so abruptly.

When I don't take the chocolate, Blake reaches over and grabs it. His chest brushes against my torso, and I swallow at the feel of the hard muscles. If I didn't know what's under his clothes, maybe I wouldn't be such a bundle of awareness, but I do. I do so well that even after two years the same need pulses through me.

Just use a vibrator later.

Blake returns to the kitchen and tosses the steaks on the grill. The meat sizzles, and my mouth waters at the smell of browning beef. He moves confidently, as though he knows exactly what he's doing. My hormones like that entirely too much. I've always found men who are confident and capable supremely attractive. That's why I not only noticed Blake at the Vegas diner where I worked, but said yes when he asked me out. When we finally went to his hotel room after our third date, he used his more than capable hands and mouth to bring me to one of the most intense orgasms of my life, all without penetration.

Liquid heat pools between my legs, leaving the flesh tingling and swollen.

"I didn't know you could cook," I say, wanting to fill the moment with something.

"I can do a few things. Stuff I like."

"I thought we'd go out." I wish we had, so it'd be

less intimate. So I wouldn't be reminded of the qualities that had me mesmerized with him in the first place.

He flips the steaks. "We can, if that's what you want."

"And waste all this food?"

One broad shoulder rises in a careless shrug. "Doesn't matter." He expertly tosses the Caesar salad.

"It's late, and we probably won't get a table anyway."

"Again, doesn't matter. There's always a table for me."

Of course. He probably knows every maître d' in the city.

"Well?"

"We can eat in," I answer, suddenly feeling more off-balance than normal under his gaze. Now I wish I'd never brought up going out. The fact that he seems to want to cater to my wishes when he doesn't have to—he has the contract—disturbs my equilibrium, the paradigm under which I need to operate in this marriage. If I were the paranoid type, I'd think he was doing it just to throw me off.

When he's finished, he lets the meat sit for a moment, then cuts it with expert care and lays the portions out on plates with a dollop of Dijon mustard. Balancing both dishes and the salad bowl in his arms, he leads me out on a large balcony with a rectangular, glass-top table and an oversized sofa with ottomans. The city glitters at our feet. The wind is a bit cool but refreshing. My chest seems to open up, and I inhale deeply. There are throws on the arms of the seat. I note a bottle of champagne in an ice bucket, two sets of utensils and a pair of long-stemmed crimson roses. A decanted red also stands next to the bubbly, and multiple glasses glint by the silverware. Candles glow softly, and I count seven—my favorite number.

Another coincidence, I tell myself.

This whole setup feels ridiculously like something he might do for a real wedding night rather than this farce. I'm almost tempted to go back inside and forget dinner, but that would be akin to waving a white flag. It's obvious he's doing this to change my mind about the no sex rule.

With a determined smile on my face, I sit down next to him and cover my legs with a blanket.

"Champagne?" he asks.

"Thanks."

He uncorks it with a soft pop and serves with a flourish. If he'd done this in Vegas, I would've asked him if he worked as a bartender or waiter to pay his way through college. He would've told me whatever he felt like saying, probably laughing at my naïve question. And *that* hurts the most.

We clink our flutes. "To satisfaction," he says.

The skin along my spine prickles. "Are you satisfied? You don't have the portrait yet."

"No. But I have you. In my home."

My fingers flex around the delicate stem. "I'm holding you to all the terms of the contract."

A corner of his mouth curls. "I wouldn't expect any less."

I can't maintain eye contact anymore, not when my heart feels like there's a tornado inside. I look away, swallow the bubbly. It goes down smoothly, leaving notes of fresh berries and oak in my mouth. Only the finest vintages for Blake. If I hadn't been so infatuated with him back in Vegas, I would've noticed the signs—the way he splurged so often, the way he didn't seem to care about the cost of anything. I assumed his job at a high-tech company paid well, but if I'd been thinking more clearly, I would've known his lifestyle was too extravagant for a man living on salary in one of the most expensive areas of the country.

Not wanting to dwell on my naïveté, I take a bite of the steak and almost weep at how amazing it tastes. I haven't had beef in months. When you need to stretch your budget, you stick to rice and beans, and the occasional chicken for infrequent splurges.

Shamelessly, I gobble up the juiciest, most tender beef I've ever had.

"That good?" Blake murmurs.

I feel his gaze on me like a silken scarf, and my body seems to grow languid. *Probably the wine*, I think, then inwardly wince at how lame the lie is. I swallow and decide *what the hell*. We both know where this is going—nowhere. I have amazing food and wine, the view is breathtaking and I want to pretend I'm a carefree young woman enjoying her meal. "Yes. It is that good. You're a much better cook than I imagined."

"Always a pleasure to surprise someone. More champagne?"

"Please." I watch him pour, his motion elegant and easy as the muscles in his forearms flex. In the past I would've leaned forward and traced the sexy lines. Instead, I say, "By the way, is there a way you can drop me off at my place tomorrow?"

"Why? The movers are going to bring everything you need or place them in storage."

"I need to get my car. I forgot it in all the excitement." Mimi's news and the appearance of the uniformed chauffeur threw me off.

"It isn't at your old apartment. You have a car in the garage, space seventy-five. The fob's on your bedside table."

"Fob? My car doesn't have one."

"Of course it does."

I pull back and stare at him. "What did you do?"

"I had an Audi delivered. They didn't have silver, so they sent a blue one. Hopefully you don't object. It's fully loaded."

"But..." I fumble for words, shocked that he bought me a car and finding it difficult to believe he remembered my saying I wanted a silver car once in passing. "I don't want it. You aren't supposed to buy me things like this. The deal's strictly a cash transaction."

"I told you appearances must be maintained. No wife of mine is going to drive a junker like your old vehicle."

He's probably right, but that doesn't mean I'm

comfortable with the idea. It reminds me of the awkward time Jack gave me a Porsche. He didn't care that I couldn't drive stick shift. He only cared about how I'd look sitting in it.

"If it makes you feel better, it's automatic every-thing...except for auto-driving. I don't trust the tech-nology yet. The car's also registered under my name," Blake points out, his voice inflectionless. "Now, the correct response is 'Thank you,' not a wide-eyed look as though I just announced that we're going to lose every-thing in a market crash tomorrow."

"Right. Thank you."

He drains his champagne and reaches for the red, which has been breathing for a while. "It's amusing how you worry about the cash payment."

"I know it's not that much to you." Pocket change, really.

His brow creases for a fraction of a moment. "What are you going to do with it?"

I shrug. "Spend it on whatever strikes my fancy." *Whatever's necessary to help Mom beat the damned tumor one more time.*

"Such as?"

"None of your business."

Blake shrugs slightly and finishes his wine. "We should send Benedict a note at least."

"Remember our deal? We don't try to meet each other's family and friends."

"You aren't going to let him know?"

"He's like a stranger to me." I don't want to talk

about my family with Blake. Sharing personal struggles with people who don't really care is like having to scream for attention. It's humiliating and counterproductive. "Let's talk about something else," I say bluntly.

That earns me a hard stare. I just stare back.

Blake shifts his weight, pours himself more wine, then serves me the red. "We need to go to New York tomorrow."

"No." Tomorrow's Saturday, and I always visit Mom on Saturdays.

"Don't tell me you have things to do."

"Actually, I do—"

"Cancel. I wasn't making a request. You're the one who said I can only have you at public functions once a month. This is that time." He raises a finger before I can protest. "And you can't make it up to me later."

My mouth flattens. "I'm not meeting your family and friends."

"It's business, not social. I need to mingle a bit, and it won't hurt to have you there, so people know we're married."

"What's the cover story?" I ask sarcastically. "I'm sure you don't want to publicize our contract."

"Stick to the truth as much as possible. We met and dated, then separated when you fell in love with Jack, then we reconnected recently."

"That sounds almost romantic. A fated connection."

Blake's dark eyes glitter. "Is that what you want?"

"No. I just... When are we coming back?"

"Sunday morning. Then you'll be free for the rest of the month, and I won't ask you to come to Thanksgiving dinner at my brother's."

I frown. I didn't think about the holidays. "What's going to be my excuse?"

"Easy. You're too sick to attend after seeing how small my bank account is."

~

BLAKE

A DARK SHADE OF RED SLOWLY SUFFUSES HER cheeks, and she glares at me. The evening breeze brushes her unbound hair, and I tuck a loose strand behind one ear, uncaring of her anger.

The more time I spend with her, the more bothered I become. It's not just that I want to kiss her and palm her tits and run my thumbs over her nipples. My desire for her body is only a minor factor. The biggest issue is that I want her to come clean and tell me why she decided to marry me.

If she were a greedy bitch, she would've complained the Audi was too anemic for her new position as my wife...even though a Lamborghini would've been wasted since she can't drive stick shift to save her life.

If I hadn't made arrangements to ensure her mother

would be taken care of, I would've assumed she ran off with Jack Villar to fund Alice's treatment, but that can't be it. She got a letter—and a check—from one of the minor charities The Pryce Family Foundation is involved in to pay the medical costs of people who aren't quite destitute enough to be helped by the government.

I wait for her to explode, jump to her feet and call me names and tell me I'm mistaken because she needed money for this specific reason. Instead, she snorts a laugh. "You're right. That would definitely make me sick to my stomach."

She isn't biting. A smidgeon of admiration unfurls. But then I've always known she's no dummy. I wouldn't have fallen for her if she bored me.

Not that I'm in love with her now. That feeling died two years ago. But when I look at her, something stirs, as though the ember hasn't been fully extinguished.

A phantom pain.

I study her mouth. Generously shaped, it was so soft and responsive, like a talented dancer who was waiting for the right partner to tango with. I wish she hadn't hurt that lower lip. Then I would've kissed her the way I wanted at the courthouse, reminded her of the fun times we had in bed.

I want to know if it'll still be good. My mind could've embellished the past, making the memory better than the reality really was. Isn't that why Lucas ran after his ex like an idiot, only to be crushed when she rejected him?

"You have mustard here," I lie, just so I can cradle her chin and run my thumb along the corner of her mouth. Her skin is so damn warm, so supple, and the texture alone is enough to heat my blood. The long lashes lower, hiding her gaze from mine, but the uneven breath over my thumb betrays her. I could tilt her head, suck on her upper lip, carefully dip my tongue into her mouth for a taste. There are so many ways to kiss and seduce.

She stands abruptly. "I think I'm going to bed early. Let me help you clean up."

"If you want...but we have a housekeeper coming by tomorrow morning."

She swallows. "Okay. Um...I'll just put my plate and glasses in the sink then." She grabs them and makes a hasty retreat.

I watch her go, my body throbbing. Five hundred bucks and I can have her beneath me, legs spread.

But I'll be damned if I give her a penny for sex.

9

Faith

I was hoping our flight would be late enough that I could squeeze in a quick visit with Mom, but it turned out not to be. I forgot about the time difference. New York is three hours ahead, and we have to leave early.

Mimi's text arrives. *What time are you going to see your mom? Thought we could go together.*

Sorry, can't, I respond. *Have to go to NYC.*

What for?

Some party Blake's dragging me to.

That sounds like fun...

I can sense her dubious tone even through the backlit screen. *Don't really want to, but can't say no. It's our deal.*

Ugh. That's a long flight. You gonna be okay?

Bear and grin, girl. Bear and grin. That's how I survived all those trips Jack dragged me to. He wanted us to be seen. Thankfully that desire waned after a year. I pray Blake gets tired of it faster.

Maybe you can fake some illness.

Too obvious. Besides, a man like him won't care. Jack certainly never did about my fear of flying. What mattered was that we attended all those events and parties and looked like we were ridiculously in love.

I'll tell Alice you'll come tomorrow. You'll be able to, right?

Yes. I don't care what Blake has planned. I'm visiting my mom tomorrow.

Well...kinda sucks, but try to make the best of it. NYC is fun no matter how you get there.

Probably. And you're right. I'll try to enjoy myself as much as I can. And every time Blake does something hurtful, I'll just give a prayer of thanks. Just imagine how much worse it would be if he were nice to me.

I load my phone with a bunch of romance novels and movies for the flight. I don't expect to be able to enjoy any of them. But in case the flying bothers me less this time, I want to have something I can use to pretend I'm just like all the millions of people who fly without incident.

I pack a light bag, making sure to take only one change of everything. It's a lame way to make my point; if he wants us to stay longer, he can just have the concierge buy more clothes. That's exactly what he did when we went to the Grand Canyon for two days, then extended it to three because neither of us wanted to leave the majesty of those God-carved rocks. But I don't want to just meekly do whatever he wants. I didn't marry him for money. I married him for Mom.

Blake is waiting for me in the living room, dressed casually in a navy blue shirt and khakis. He's sprawled on the couch, one loafered foot resting on the opposite knee. Master of his domain and all that's within.

His shirt collar's undone, showing the play of muscles and tendons in his throat as he turns his head and looks me over. His expression remains neutral, but the dark light in his gaze makes me hot in places, and I resist an urge to shift my weight. I'm in jeans and a glittery pink shirt that reads *Hollywood Babe*. It isn't exactly my style, but it was on sale.

He quirks an eyebrow at my small carry-on. "That's all?"

"Only one night, right?"

"True." He stands and puts a hand at the small of my back, taking my bag.

The warmth from his body sends a rush of awareness through me, the fine hair on my skin standing up. My nerves are hyper-tense, and a sliver of apprehension sinks into my heart. He gave in too easily last night, without making a single move to get me into bed. And now he's too polite, too courteous.

"Where's your suitcase?" I ask.

"Already in the car."

The same chauffeur from yesterday waits for us by the curb, this time with a black Rolls-Royce. Our one-hour ride to the airport is silent. Blake doesn't try to engage me in conversation, and I don't have anything to say. I look down at my phone, reading one of the books I downloaded earlier. If I get myself really immersed in the novel, maybe I won't care that we're about to be catapulted through the air.

The car takes us to a private hangar away from the main terminal. There's minimal security, and people jump to do Blake's bidding. Then I see why. We're flying in a sleek private jet.

Figures. Jack's family is wealthy too, but they never flew on a private jet. Blake gestures for me to board first, so I do. I take a plushy seat and run my hands along the soft, luxurious leather and gleaming faux wood trimming. Even as I admire the beautiful interior, my heart beats erratically. No matter how pretty, I'm inside a tube of metal that somehow flies. Science. Physics. Engineering. I know all that, yet none of it means anything. My mouth still goes dry, my stomach still churns.

The sole cabin attendant offers me a drink, and I accept a mimosa.

Blake sits down next to me. "Any of this change your mind about a honeymoon?"

I shudder. "No. But it does make me wonder why you flew commercial to Vegas." He emailed me his itinerary so I'd make sure to be free on the days he came.

"I didn't. I just coordinated my schedule with a commercial airline's."

"I probably sounded stupid, asking if you wanted me to pick you up from the airport."

"I thought it was nice. You were the first one who offered."

"Because I didn't know how rich you were."

"Is that what bothers you? That I didn't tell you?"

"Partly."

"Would it have made a difference?"

I know what he's asking, and I consider his question with care. He merely patted my back while I cried my heart out over Mom's diagnosis. Then he had to leave that night for Boston.

Ultimately, how much money Blake has is irrelevant. I would've gone with whichever man offered to pay for Mom's care. If that makes me a mercenary bitch, fine. I'm not ashamed of my choices. If I could do everything over again, I'd still make the same ones.

"No," I tell Blake.

His gaze probes me as though I'm a messy chessboard he wants to figure out. "Did you love him?"

"No. The plain fact is, I was grateful." After that confession, I look away, downing the rest of my mimosa.

The cabin attendant closes the door, and engines start to rev up. I close my eyes.

"I'm going to nap," I murmur. "I'm tired. And it's better I nap than stay awake for the flight."

The plane starts moving. I know when it's made it to the runway from the way it turns and stops. Then I hear it...the roar of the engine and that feeling of pressure as the jet speeds up, gaining the momentum it needs to get airborne.

My grip on the armrests tightens, sweat soaking my palms and back. I squeeze my eyes shut and recite statistics. *Flying is safer than driving. Totally safe.* The reason crashes make the news is because they're so rare.

Except the stats didn't help my dad.

I clench my teeth and focus on breathing. The plane tilts, its nose going up. Air feels as tangible as a fist in my throat.

My whole body taut, I dig my nails into the padded armrests. Grinding noises come from below. Probably the landing gear coming up. Or maybe the sound is coming from the wing-flaps. Don't planes have to adjust them as they climb into the sky?

Or maybe they're a sign that something's wrong with the plane and we're going to crash, nose first, onto the ground below. I can imagine the explosion, the fireball erupting around us as the fuel ignites and the whole frame burns down. If we're lucky, we'll die instantly upon impact rather than suffering through smoke inhalation and having our bodies incinerated alive. Does skin bubble at such high heat?

Although I'm seated, I feel light-headed. I count, wondering if we aren't going to make it despite statistics. When I hit two hundred, I finally gather enough courage to open my eyes. The plane's made it to its cruising altitude. We haven't crashed. The plane isn't shaking.

I loosen my grip and suddenly realize—

I've been clenching Blake's forearm. There are small red crescents on the smooth skin. But he's reading something on his tablet as though nothing's happened.

Heat floods my face. God, what's wrong with me? I was so certain I'd grabbed the armrests. I drop my hand and slump in my seat. Emotions swirl inside, every single one of them elusive and confusing.

"Sorry," I mumble, closing my eyes.

"No problem," he says. "I didn't realize you hated flying this much."

"I can handle it."

"If you don't feel well, there's a bed in the back so you can lie down, and the bathroom's behind us, to your left. The cabin attendant's going to serve lunch, but you don't have to eat if you don't want to."

"Thanks. But don't worry. It's not airsickness. I won't ruin your jet."

"That's not what I meant." He hesitates, then finally adds, "If you want, we can turn back."

My eyes fly open. He's watching me, his face unsmiling. I think he's serious about turning back, but... "It's okay," I say. "I signed the deal."

The muscles in his jaw bunch, then he nods jerkily and turns his attention back to whatever's on his tablet.

I close my eyes again.

We don't speak for the rest of the flight.

10

Faith

By the time we reach our hotel, I'm ready to pass out. My skull is throbbing with a tension headache. Normally flying doesn't make me feel *this* awful, but we had frequent turbulence an hour into the flight and a rough landing. I almost reopened the cut on my lip when the plane jolted onto the runway.

The suite is nice, I suppose. It has a huge bed and a long, plushy couch, which is all I care about at the moment. The second I plop down, Blake says, "You're...quite pale."

"The landing really scared me."

"Want me to fire the pilot?"

"What? Why?"

"For the crappy landing."

My jaw drops. "Really?" I wave Blake away.

"Why am I even asking? Fire him if you want. It has nothing to do with me." I lean against the back of the couch.

His mouth curls into a lopsided smile that looks oddly self-deprecating. He picks up the room phone. "Bring two aspirins and a bottle of lemon-lime flavored Gatorade ASAP. Thanks."

My eyes half open, I observe Blake instruct the butler assigned to our suite to unpack and press all our clothes. I've never seen him in surroundings like this. Before, he was pretending to be an average Joe, and although I found him arrogant and bossy from time to time, that's nothing compared to him in his element. He speaks quietly and confidently, like he expects the world to realign itself to please him. He also doesn't treat others like servants, and he is unfailingly polite if a bit aloof. It's a contrast to Jack, who treated everyone who wasn't as rich as his family as though they were fundamentally beneath him. I still don't understand why he was so nice to me when we first met. He said he liked me, but surely there were plenty of rich heiresses he could've liked instead. That way he would've had a better marriage with a wife he could have considered his equal.

The front desk is quick to send the stuff up. Blake hands everything to me. "Here. Take these and drink all of it."

"The whole bottle?"

"You didn't have anything on the plane, so you're probably dehydrated. Once you feel a little better, have the butler bring you something to eat. Some food will get you back on track."

"Okay. Thanks." I swallow the pills and start sipping the sports drink. It's tart and sweet.

"I'm going out for a short meeting. The spa and salon inside the hotel are expecting you, and they'll make sure you're ready on time. If you decide you don't like the dress and shoes you packed, you can have the concierge bring whatever you want." His tone is matter-of-fact. Clearly, living like this...spending what could amount to tens of thousands of dollars in an afternoon is nothing out of the ordinary. Jack would've made a grand gesture out of it; to Blake it's just business as usual.

"Thank you," I say. "But you didn't have to bother."

"It wasn't a bother." He runs a finger along my chin, leaving tingling skin in its wake. "You're my wife, and you'll be catered to accordingly."

Then he's gone.

I finish the drink and ask the butler to bring me a grilled cheese sandwich and some yogurt. Sure enough, the food does make me feel much better. Once I'm finished, the butler reminds me of my appointments, and I leave, suddenly feeling unwelcome and awkward in the suite.

The spa and salon on the fourth floor are connected and beautifully appointed. Both have soothing music playing and apparently spend half their annual budget on candles. The staff doesn't begin with hair, nails and makeup—the first priority is a massage. "Your husband thought it'd be good to help you relax. Apparently your flight was a little stressful...?"

I nod and let them do whatever they were paid to do. But I can't help but wonder why Blake is bothering with all this. He insulted me when I went to his office. He called my place a dump...which was totally rude, albeit true. He said I was the lowest cost provider.

So why is he being so nice?

I counted on him being a jerk. Jerks are easier to deal with. They generally only have one facet, one motive. Nice guys, on the other hand, are more complicated. If Blake hadn't told me I should've come crawling on my knees or called me the lowest cost provider, I might actually assume that he still cares about me...but as it is, believing that would be criminally stupid.

The salon people make sure I'm finished on time, styling my hair in an intricate updo, applying smoky makeup to my eyes and highlighting my cheekbones and lips with an expertise that inspires awe. I end up looking like Mimi before a photo shoot. My stylist looks over my dress, which drapes fluidly over my body. It's a flame-red Versace that Jack bought. I've only worn it once.

"Do you have any jewelry?" the stylist asks.

"Just these pearls." I gesture at the stud earrings I've brought along, my cheeks hot pink. I should've realized the Versace wouldn't work since I don't have any accessories to go with it. It's not the kind of outfit you can pull off à la carte, so to speak.

He taps his inverted triangle of a chin. "Hmm. You really need a necklace with that dress."

He has a point. It's cut low in front, and the back is mostly bare, held in place with crisscrossing strings of faux diamonds. I place a hand around my neck and fidget, suddenly too embarrassed to stand still. "Sorry, I didn't bring anything else." *I don't have anything else.*

The stylist is squinting at me. "You really need some diamonds with that outfit. Chandelier earrings...a bib necklace...something elegant, but not *too* heavy..."

"Then she shall have them."

The stylist spins around. "Mr. Pryce-Reed."

I look at him in the mirror. Blake is absolutely stunning in a classic black tux. The beautifully tailored jacket and pants fit him perfectly, hinting at the lean, powerful body underneath. He's freshly shaven, his jaw free of scruff. If we were back in time two years ago and he showed up dressed like this...well, there's no telling what I would have done.

I drop my eyes to the pearls. They almost look sad, lying there on a bed of black velvet. Or maybe I'm just projecting my feelings onto the poor things.

I sense Blake's gaze on me, starting with the stilettos and going all the way to the top of my head, leaving hot tingling sensations all over my skin. I almost shiver as my breathing grows shallow.

"Beautiful," Blake murmurs. "You've done well, Mr. Inzarra."

"My pleasure."

"I didn't realize my wife wasn't finished with packing. I hurried her along this morning," he says with a small grin.

Stunned, I turn to watch him. It isn't like him to explain himself. He certainly didn't have to lie to spare my pride.

"Have the concierge bring whatever it is you have in mind," Blake instructs.

"Certainly." The stylist vanishes, leaving us in the huge dressing room together.

"You didn't have to do that," I say after a few moments of awkward silence.

"Do what?"

"Make excuses for me."

He shrugs. "It costs me nothing, and you're just the victim of an impatient husband." He flicks an artfully curled tendril that's brushing my collarbone. The hair tickles, and I look away, unsure how to feel about this... treatment from him.

A bit later, Mr. Inzarra returns, slightly out of breath. "Found just the right set." He opens two boxes. Brilliant diamonds sparkle on dark navy velvet. The pieces are fit for a princess.

"Perfect," Blake says. "Excellent taste."

The stylist looks pleased. "That's what you're paying me for."

Blake takes the necklace and clasps it around my neck. His fingers brush against my nape, the touch feathery and warm. I tell myself it's impersonal, but I can't suppress a shiver. Once finished, he presses a soft kiss above the clasp before I can move away. His lips burn against my skin, his breath fanning right above the spot, amplifying the effect. My heart flutters, and I feel like it's pumping liquid heat rather than blood.

I start to bite my lower lip, and he puts a finger over my mouth. "Don't want to reopen that cut."

I blink up at him, dazed. "No, I don't." I clear my throat. "I...can get the earrings myself."

He brushes the finger along the seam of my lips, the touch almost too light, his gaze intent. To anybody watching he might've looked like a concerned husband. I know better.

While I put on the earrings, he turns to Mr. Inzarra and hands him a few bills. The stylist lights up like a kid on Christmas.

As we leave the salon, Blake asks, "Are you feeling better?"

"Yes."

"We don't have to go."

"We're already here. There's no point in staying in."

"You always were stubborn."

"If you knew that, why did you ask?" I inhale deeply. "Look, you don't have to worry about me. I was fine before. I'm fine now. And I'll continue to be fine."

A small frown creases his face for a moment. "How can you say that, given the circumstances you're in?" he mutters. Then, without waiting for a response, he holds out a lovely white cashmere wrap.

We exit the hotel and get inside a black limo. Even though Blake said this isn't social, I know it won't be one hundred percent business either. There'll be people who are friendly with him, and I pray with everything I have that they aren't the same people who were friendly with Jack, who lived and did business mainly in Hong Kong. My nerves are frayed, my reserves depleted. I don't think I can pretend much tonight, and how I really feel about Jack isn't something I want to air to his friends.

11

Blake

FAITH IS STILL PALE UNDERNEATH THE EXPERT layer of makeup. If I had it my way, we'd just stay in the suite, but her jaw's tight, her mouth flat and gaze straight, like a mountaineer before an assault on Everest. If I insist on skipping the event now, she's likely to kill me.

Pieces of her don't add up, and that bothers me. Everyone adds up, even Dane.

Faith should have more money than she does, but she doesn't. She has some nice clothes, but apparently no jewelry, aside from those cheap pearls. She spent her first year of marriage jet-setting around the world—it was impossible to avoid all the news about her and her husband—but she acts like flying is pure torture, and my forearm still throbs from her death grip earlier. It won't surprise me if the spots develop bruises.

She agreed to marry me for a lousy hundred thousand bucks, plus fifty more for living together. That's such a pathetic sum of money that now that I think about it, the whole thing seems off. I've been looking for clues to what drives her—but she's tidy and her eyes are clear and her diction is normal. I've already decided she couldn't possibly be into gambling. The seventy-five thousand I gave her is a joke for a gambling addict.

If her mom were alive, I might think it was for medical care...but Alice probably died even before Faith married Jack. Specialists told her she had three months at the most. I still remember the heartbreaking way Faith sobbed when she received the news...and how helpless I felt, knowing there was little I could do even with all my money and connections.

Maybe she unraveled after her mother died. Some people do. Dane certainly did after our grandmother Shirley's funeral, and he went off-grid for a time to get his head screwed back on straight. So maybe Faith hasn't recovered, and her husband's death four months ago probably didn't help...although he wasn't alone in that mangled car—his mistress was with him.

The limo comes to a stop at a mansion on Long Island, and the driver opens the rear door. I start to climb out, then notice my wife. Faith is inhaling slowly, dragging her tongue along her lips. The girding of loins couldn't be more obvious.

"Faith—"

"Let's go," she says quietly.

Shaking my head, I get out first, then extend a hand to help her. She grasps it, her skin cool against mine. I notice how pale her hand is, how small, how breakable.

It isn't just her hand. It's all of her.

Flashes burst around us, and I force a smile despite the white spots in my vision. Ryder taught me the trick. Unless you want to look like a somnambulant idiot, you keep your eyes open and smile like being blinded by overzealous photographers is actually fun. Wrapping an arm around her, I pull Faith closer. She manages fine on her own, but I want to mark my territory, issue a subtle warning to everyone that they will give her the respect she deserves or they'll answer to me.

The place is just short of ostentatious. The party is the final charity event of the year hosted by Meredith Aylster, the wife of hotel magnate Daniel Aylster III. Instead of one of the numerous hotels and resorts he owns, they decided to host it at their second home.

Still, since Daniel isn't an idiot, the outside is crawling with photographers for publicity. I see him and his wife greeting guests. They make a handsome couple, both with dark good looks. His arm is around her as though he can't bear to have even an inch of space between them.

Faith and I make our way over to our hosts. Under my hand, the muscles in her back tense as we get closer. If I let her, she'd bolt.

Daniel raises both eyebrows briefly, but Meredith

smiles warmly. "Welcome," he says smoothly. "Glad you could make it, Blake. You too, Faith."

"Thank you," she says with a blank smile.

"Elizabeth told me you weren't coming." Meredith grins. "Guess I should tell her she's wrong and collect my winnings."

"You had a bet?" I say. "If I'd known, I would've been open to bribery."

Meredith giggles. "Yeah, like anybody can make you do anything for money." She turns to Faith. "I'm glad you're rejoining the living. I was heartbroken when I heard you were keeping to yourself after Jack's funeral."

"I needed some time to cope. It was very sudden."

"Indeed." Daniel gives me a speculative look.

"You don't have to worry about her, Meredith," I say. "She isn't alone or keeping to herself anymore." I pull her stiff body even closer. "We're married."

Daniel stares at me as though I've just shed my skin like a snake, and Meredith blinks a few times. He recovers first. "You are? Well, congratulations."

"Yup," I say. "We knew each other before, and when we reconnected again, I knew she was it for me."

"That's lovely! I'm so glad." Meredith beams.

"Thank you," Faith says.

"Love heals everything," I add.

"It sure does." Daniel nods although his expression says he doesn't believe such nonsense, not from me anyway.

"Well, we've monopolized enough of your time," I say.

"Enjoy yourselves. Oh, I almost forgot, but Elizabeth arrived not too long ago, if you want to say hi."

"Thanks. We'll find her." I lead Faith away.

Once we're out of hearing range, she stops abruptly. "I'm not comfortable with this."

"What's wrong?"

"I don't want to meet your friends. I told you that."

I frown. "They're your friends, too."

"No, they're not. They're *Jack's* friends." Her spine stays stiff, and her eyes are flat.

Did she have an unpleasant encounter with the Aylsters? Daniel can be an asshole. He didn't take control of his hotel empire by being a rainbow-shitting unicorn, but he knows how to smile and say the right things at the right time. After all, hospitality is his business. And his wife is an angel, sort of like Elizabeth. I can't imagine Faith having had any sort of trouble with th—

Someone taps my shoulder. "Hello, Blake."

Well, think of the devil. "Hello, Elizabeth." I hug her. She looks fantastic in a stylish pink dress with a side slit that emphasizes her small waist and long legs. Her golden hair cascades, framing her face. If she wanted, she could've had fame and fortune using that face, but she's dedicated her life to the family's charitable foundation, taking on the mantle left behind by Grandma Shirley.

"Who is this?" she asks, smiling at Faith.

"My wife, Faith. Faith, this is my sister, Elizabeth."

Elizabeth gasps. "Wife!? How come I wasn't invited to the ceremony?"

"Nobody was invited."

Faith's cheeks color, and although her mouth is smiling, her eyes are dismayed. "Hi. Nice to meet you."

"Same here. I'm genuinely sorry I missed the wedding. I didn't know, and this horrible brother of mine never told me."

"It's no big deal." Faith clears her throat. "I wanted a small ceremony."

"There's small and there's small." Elizabeth sighs. "I'm feeling left out now."

I roll my eyes. We didn't get to attend Ryder's or Elliot's wedding ceremonies. Why is she giving me and Faith shit about ours?

"My goodness, Elizabeth! *So* good to see you!"

Simone Villar comes over in a cloud of overpriced perfume and hugs my sister. Faith sways. Her reaction is so minute if I didn't have her so close by my side, I would've missed it. I'm about to ask if she wants to sit down, then notice her pallor as she eyes Simone.

Simone is pretty enough in black silk and a ridiculous amount of diamonds covering her throat and chest. Her ebony hair and bright red lips are a stark contrast to Elizabeth, who hugs her back. They exchange air kisses, then pull back, holding each other's hands.

"How are you doing, Simone?" Elizabeth asks.

"*Won*derfully. My family's organizing a fundraiser

to build more schools in Sudan at the moment, and I'm spearheading it."

"That's such a worthy goal." She beams.

"It is, but I'm afraid I'm terribly clumsy at raising money compared to you."

"Nonsense. You won't need any help, but if you do, you know my number."

"Thank you, Elizabeth."

"By the way, have you met my new sister-in-law?"

"No, not yet..." Simone's gaze lands on me, and she smiles. "Hello, Blake. How nice to run into you here."

"Indeed." I bet she didn't really want to talk to me face-to-face, not until she comes up with a fix for the disaster in China. "You're looking well."

"So are you, and this sister-in-law is your..." She trails off as she notices Faith. I'm not sure if she's aware of her lips twisting into an ugly sneer that doesn't jibe with the benevolent public image she's been trying to cultivate. "Faith."

"Hello, Simone," Faith says woodenly.

I put a protective arm around her. "Meet my wife."

Simone lets out a short, explosive breath. "Your...wife?"

"Yup. Eloped. Couldn't wait." I grin, laying it on thick.

She blinks. "Well. It must be...uh...true love."

"It is," Faith says coldly. "I'm too young to stay a widow."

"Of course. Of course. I'm so glad. Hope you two are happy." Simone's words are smooth, but her face twists as though she's bitten into something mushy and bitter.

"We are, and we plan to stay that way," Faith says, moving closer to me, the gesture subtly possessive.

A corner of Simone's mouth curls, then she puts a hand on my sleeve. "Blake, would you mind if we chatted privately for a moment? A business matter." Her gaze flicks to Faith so fast I almost miss it.

Is there a history between them? I can't think of any reason Simone would dislike Faith... "Not at all. Faith, do you mind?"

"Go ahead. I'll be fine." She gives me a perfunctory smile.

Elizabeth loops her arm around Faith's. "I'll keep her company."

"Good." I nod, relieved despite Faith's previous assertion that she didn't want to be around my family. My sister may look like a cream puff, but nobody messes with her.

I let Simone lead me away.

12

Faith

I watch Blake go with Simone. My stomach is in knots, and I wish I hadn't eaten anything back at the hotel.

Blake's sister, Elizabeth, clings like wet seaweed. I gently tug, but she doesn't let go. Either she's obtuse or wants to play a power game. My money's on the latter.

"I can't believe Blake got married," she says, almost gushing. "I was pretty sure he wouldn't."

I snort, but keep on smiling since we're in public. "You don't have to pretend. I know the score."

She pulls back, but the pleasant expression on her face doesn't falter. "That doesn't mean the inheritance is the only reason for his marriage." She peers at me. "He's protective of you. Interesting, isn't it?"

"I think he wants to make sure I don't mess

anything up in the next twelve months." I lower my voice. "You should look for a candidate too," I say, unwilling to let her think I'm ashamed of the choice I made to marry him temporarily. Despite her sweet woman routine, she probably isn't as angelic as she looks. I learned that the hard way with Jack's family, and I don't take anyone in their social circle at face value.

Elizabeth heaves a big sigh. "My problem isn't finding a candidate, but narrowing the field."

"Must be a nice problem to have." I look at her arm pointedly. "Do you mind?"

"Sorry. Am I holding too tightly?"

"You're holding. Period. Let go."

She does. "Are you always this hostile?"

"Only when people cling." I saw how she interacted with Simone, and how readily Blake went with my former sister-in-law. It bothers me, although I'm not sure why I'm letting it bug me since I've known from the beginning I'm on my own in this marriage. Just like I was in my previous one... I'm not part of the clique.

A tinge of bemusement colors Elizabeth's expression. "You know... If you open up a bit, you might make some friends."

Been there, done that. "Sure."

Meredith stops in front of us. "Hi. Hope I'm not interrupting."

"Of course not," Elizabeth says with a smile. "This is a lovely party. I'm thrilled you invited me."

"My pleasure. I wanted to invite Ryder, too, but Daniel wasn't too enthused."

Elizabeth chortles. "Just remind him that Ryder's happily married now. No longer interested in hitting on every beautiful woman in the room."

Meredith rolls her eyes. "I know, right?" She turns to me. "Are you enjoying the party?"

"It's very nice."

"I'm glad." She puts a hand on Elizabeth's arm. "I'm thinking about hosting a huge auction to raise a little money for..."

I slowly move away from the two until I'm free. I don't care to listen to their fundraising plans or spend any real time with them.

Maybe my demand that we don't meet each other's friends and family is a no-go. Although Blake'll never see mine—I can't imagine him slumming at the cheap restaurants and bars Mimi and I go to—I'm bound to run into people who know him unless I live like a hermit. And I'm not going to do that.

I pluck a flute of champagne and go out to a balcony. The November wind in New York isn't like L.A. It has a nasty bite, but the cold clears my head. I swallow some of the bubbly and take out my phone. There's a text from Mimi.

Your mom's doing awesome. We played Texas Hold'em, betting a penny a hand, and she won ten cents! This after telling me she wasn't good at poker! I didn't win a single hand. Pout.

I grin. Mimi's an excellent poker player, and I'm

sure she went easy on Mom. *Thank you. I'm sure it made her day.*

It was fun to see her laugh. Judy joined in for the last few hands. Alice asked me where you were, though, so I said she needed to ask you tomorrow since I wasn't sure what you were planning to tell her.

Thanks. I need to come up with a good story. I don't want to tell Mom about my marriage to Blake. She's going to know something's up, and the last thing I want is for her to fret about whatever's going on between me and Blake. *I owe you one.*

Don't even. Girlfriends gotta stick together.

I grin. *Love you.*

Love you too. And spill some wine on that son of a bitch for making you fly.

I laugh softly. *Will try.* I put away my phone. The flute's empty, and I'm too cold to stay out here any longer.

"So this is where you've been hiding. Like a cockroach."

Simone. I stiffen, then turn. "What do you want?"

"What *exactly* is it that you think you're doing?"

"Well, you know. Living in a dump lost its appeal, so I found myself a young, rich husband." The most comical expression of horror crosses the carefully made-up face. "What else did you think was going to happen when you decided to be greedy and lie about my 'affair' with Jordan Smith?"

"Don't blame me for Jordan. If you weren't such an

easy mark, you wouldn't have succumbed to his charms."

"We had coffee and lunch a few times." Because I was so lonely. I'll never make that mistake again.

"Naturally you say that. You have every reason to lie." She gives me a nasty grin. "Does your new husband know how easy you are?"

I laugh softly. "Why? Do you plan on telling him? Please."

"You don't think he'll believe me? I have a copy of Jordan's affidavit."

"Perfect. Go ahead. I'll sit back and watch."

"Shameless. Absolutely shameless." Hatred burns in her eyes, but it's tinged with fear. "Too bad you didn't die with your baby," she spits out.

I flinch, but there's no way I'm giving her the satisfaction of seeing me crumble. Besides, a repeated punch loses its impact. If she wanted to witness my devastation in person, she shouldn't have wasted the line over the phone that first time.

"Jack should've known better than to marry someone like you."

"I agree we should've never married," I say, because no matter what he said in the beginning, whatever he felt for me sure as hell wasn't love.

I turn away. I'm not in the mood to deal with Simone any longer, or listen to any more of her poison.

"Don't mess up what I have with Blake," she says.

The gall of the woman. Is she flaunting *her* affair? Despite her taking him away on some bullshit pretext about business, I don't believe business has anything to do with their relationship. I look at her over a shoulder. "If things go badly between the two of you, it'll be because you're lousy in bed."

"You bitch!" She grabs my wrist, her nails digging into me.

"Let go or I'm going to scream."

"You wouldn't dare."

"Try me. I'm crass, remember?" I open my mouth, ready to carry out my threat.

Simone lunges forward, shoving a palm against my lips. The cut on my lower lip burns, and I cry out.

"Ladies. Is everything all right?"

Simone jerks back, instantly letting go. "Benedict."

I press a finger between my eyebrows, tired and just *beyond* pissed off that now I'm suddenly face-to-face with my grandfather. Despite being in his seventies, he's still as tall and solid as a sequoia. And just like those colossal trees, he's going to outlive everyone, insulated from illness by his towering pile of money. The soft sheen of the black material and the neat way every fold and line lies on his body speaks volumes about the quality of his tux, and his silver hair is still as thick as it was in his youth. In his hand is a handsome cane, an affectation with an elaborate silver dragon twisted into some kind of figure eight, the top loop much bigger than the bottom.

If I'd known Benedict Mortimer would be at this event, I *would've* told Blake to turn the plane around.

He's looking at Simone. "Well?" His voice is stern.

"Sorry. I slipped and lost my balance for a moment," she lies, facing him with a contrite smile.

He gives the floor an exaggerated inspection. "Not frozen. Not even wet."

She swallows.

"She's clumsy," I say, not necessarily to help her but because I'm feeling catty and I want to get out of here before Benedict figures out who I am. We haven't seen each other since my father's death. "Clumsy people slip for no reason."

"Simone, could you give us some privacy?"

"Certainly." She scurries away like a mouse before a cat.

Disgusting. But then my grandfather has a lot more money than the Villars, and in Simone's shallow view, that makes him a force to be reckoned with. I start to leave, too, but he stops me.

"Faith."

So he does recognize me. I look up into his eyes. They appear gentle...and almost pleading, like my response here matters to him.

I shake myself mentally. A man like Benedict doesn't plead. He demands. He takes. He crushes anybody he deems beneath him.

"Sorry, I gotta go," I say firmly, my back stiff. "I'm freezing out here."

He immediately shrugs out of his jacket and moves forward with the garment spread, as though to drape it around me. "Here."

Stepping back out of reach, I stare at it like it's a

tarantula. "I don't want anything from you." I inhale deeply. "The letters Mom's been sending aren't on my behalf. If I had it my way, we wouldn't even be here, talking to each other."

His thick eyebrows pinch. "Do you know why she's been trying to get in touch with me?"

"I don't know, and I don't care. The only thing I feel is resentment that she's trying to get you to help out. I told her we don't need to beg you for anything. I can take care of her."

"By marrying a vulture like Jack Villar?"

My cheeks heat despite the cold. How dare he criticize my late husband? "He might not have been perfect, but he was a hell of a lot more generous than you."

"Because he paid for Alice?" he shoots back.

"Because he *cared* enough to pay. You...you couldn't even bother to return my calls. You thought if you held out, you could make me...what? Do whatever you want? Call you wonderful and awesome when I know you are just a horrible racist?"

He pales, then ugly red splotches his face almost immediately. "Is that what your mother called me? A racist?"

"She didn't have to tell me anything. I heard you calling her a mongrel."

"A far more polite term than what I wanted to use."

"I rest my case."

He looks away, expelling air audibly through his mouth. He turns back to me. "Faith," he begins again, his voice much calmer now. "I'm not here to argue about Alice or what I think about her. When I noticed you were here, I wanted to talk to you. You're my granddaughter, the only family I have left."

"Really? That's a shame. Because if that's the case, you have no family left." I take a half step toward the door. "I have nothing to say to you, Benedict."

"Faith, don't. You're going to regret this."

"No, I'm not. I didn't need you growing up, I don't need you now, and I'm not going to need you."

"You have your legacy to consider."

"Give it away. I don't want it."

"Faith, don't be rash. For once, put aside your pride and listen to me."

"To spare yours? No, thanks. I'm done." I start to walk away, and he uses his cane to block me.

"Careful with that thing, Benedict. People will get the wrong impression," comes Blake's cold voice. He slips his jacket off and drapes it around my shoulders.

My fingers are clumsy as I pull at the lapels and wrap the jacket more securely around me. The warmth from the fabric seeps into me, and I start to shiver uncontrollably, as though my body's just realized how bloody cold it is out here.

"This doesn't concern you, Blake," Benedict says.

"But it does. She's my wife, and she's freezing out here. Surely you noticed how unsuited her dress is for this kind of weather." Blake pulls me close against his body, and I let him, greedy for more warmth.

I bury my frozen nose against his chest and inhale

the spicy wood and soap and laundry detergent. None of it smells particularly alluring on its own, but on Blake, they smell like home and love and protection.

How stupid is that? It's got to be the freezing weather that's screwed up my head.

"You got married," Benedict says, stunned. "And I wasn't invited?"

"Don't take it personally," Blake says. "We eloped."

"I wasn't even told."

"Maybe that's because I didn't need your permission." My voice is thin. I loathe it that he acts like he's hurt when he didn't bother to come to my first wedding. I didn't care, but Jack was crushed by Benedict's absence.

"Excuse us. I need to take care of my wife," Blake says.

"This discussion isn't over."

"It is unless Faith wants to talk to you." Blake's voice is more frigid than the wind blowing over my face. "And if she doesn't, you *won't* bother her again."

A hand between my shoulders, he leads me back to the warmth of the main residence. I look at the glittering faces. So many of them...and given my encounters so far, probably none of them friendly.

As my body warms, an uncomfortable prickling sensation spreads through me. I raise a hand to place it over my face, and note with shock that it's shaking. I blink when my vision blurs for a second.

"I want to go home," I whisper, almost to myself. It's the same thing I've always thought every time I had to attend one of these high society functions. Jack, of course, always ignored how I felt since what mattered to him was being seen.

Blake holds my trembling hand. His hand is so much bigger, so much stronger, but unbelievably gentle wrapped around mine. "We can't fly to L.A. right now," he says. "But if you want, we can go back to our room."

I stare up at him, my mind completely blank at his response. I couldn't have heard him correctly.

A group somewhere erupts into uproarious laughter. The sound jerks me out of my shock.

"No." I lick my dry lips. "It's okay. I just need to sit down for a few minutes, then I'll be fine."

A fingertip under my chin, Blake lifts my face and studies my expression for a second. "I don't think so. We'll leave."

"But the party...your sister and friends..."

"They can go to hell for all I care. We're leaving *now*."

13

Faith

I'M SO MENTALLY DRAINED, I DON'T RESIST AS Blake helps me inside our limo. I also don't pay attention as he makes a quick call, my gaze focused on the headrest in front of me. The interior is blessedly warm, but I still hold onto his jacket. Absurdly enough, having that on makes me feel as though I'm not completely alone, and right now I want to cling to that. Tomorrow... Tomorrow I'll go back to being strong again.

When our car stops in front of our hotel, the doorman rushes over. Blake takes me to the suite, past the living room and bedroom to the bath. The huge tub is full of steaming water and covered with fresh rose petals as large as my palm. "How...?"

"I had the butler draw it. A hot bath will make you feel better. I don't want you catching cold."

"Is that where the rose petals come in?"

Blake gives me a small smile. "He knows we're newlyweds. Obviously, he's trying to help."

I just stand there with the jacket around me and stare at the water. It's such a thoughtful, nice gesture, and I don't know what to make of it.

I don't want to make anything of it.

"I'm going to need the jacket back before you jump in," he says, extending a hand.

I don't want to give it to him, but what claim do I have? Slowly, I let it glide down my arms, then hand it over. "Here."

The long lashes hiding his eyes, he takes it, then jerks his chin toward the tub. "Strip and get in. I'll give you five minutes."

"I can't undo the dress without help." The sparkling strips crisscrossing my back are securely hooked, and it's tricky to undo them on my own. Certainly, it's going to take more than five minutes.

"Turn around," he says, but doesn't wait for me to move.

Instead he shifts, draping the jacket over his forearm and unhooks the strings. Everywhere his dexterous fingers brush, goosebumps break out on my skin, and I shiver.

"Still cold?" he asks.

"No." I clear my throat. "I'm fine. Thank you."

He nods once, then leaves me to it. I kick off the shoes and sigh as my feet touch the heated floor. Such a small thing, but such a luxury. I let the dress pool at my feet, then take off my jewelry, not wanting to get any of it wet. My reflection shows small pupils and a pinched expression set in a pale face. No wonder Blake thought I could use a hot soak.

The over-the-top way the butler set the bath is ludicrous, but I'm happy to sink into the water anyway. The liquid heat is very different from what the vents in the limo were putting out. It warms me instantly, head to toe. Closing my eyes with a sigh, I tilt my head back, resting it on the raised, curved edge. Somehow, it's just the right height.

The left side of my face prickles, and I know without having to look that Blake is back. My fingers twitch, but I hold still. The water's surface is completely covered with petals, so unless he has Kryptonian vision, he won't see anything.

"Drink this," he says, sitting down on the step leading to the tub.

There's a glass of sparkling wine in his hand. He's in his dress shirt, the top three buttons undone, and black tux pants. The sleeves are rolled up to his elbows, and I run my eyes over the strong wrists and forearms, both lean and thick. The steam curls the long hair on the top of his head, and he almost looks sweet and vulnerable.

But that's an illusion. Underneath all the other stuff is a man—hard and unyielding.

When I don't move, he adds, "It's a Veuve Clicquot. Would be a shame to waste it."

"Okay." I take the cool glass and sip slowly. It tastes as though heaven has burst in my mouth. "It's good."

He shrugs, has a swallow of his. "It's not bad."

"Did you know?" I ask after another sip.

"What?"

"That Benedict would be there?"

"No. It's Meredith and Daniel's party. I wasn't privy to who they invited."

I digest that. "You should've been nicer to him. He's a useful man to have on your side."

"I have enough people on my side. You're my wife." Blake's quiet for a moment. "I didn't realize your relationship with him was this...strained."

"There's a reason I didn't turn to him for help, Blake." *Damn it.* I bite my tongue.

"What do you need help with?"

I force a careless smile. "Money, obviously. What else did I marry you for?"

Placing an elbow on his knee, he rests his chin in his hand and leans closer. "Money for what?" he says, enunciating each word deliberately.

"A shopping spree?"

"Faith..." It holds an edge.

"It's for me." I sink lower in the tub. "I need the money because I'm tired of crappy studios, empty fridges and lumpy sofa beds. Happy?"

"Not at all."

I blink. "What more do you want?" He doesn't know the truth. If he did, he wouldn't have asked.

"You should eat something."

I sigh. "I'm not in the mood." There's no way I can handle food after tonight.

"How about chocolate then? I recall you saying it's the most perfect food that has everything a woman needs to get through a bad day, a good day and an 'everything in-between' day." He magically produces a flat black box that says "Royce".

I stare at him. "You remember…"

"I told you I remember everything about you."

He did, but I didn't realize he meant literally every silly thing. I said that on a Valentine's Day when he faux-complained about my desire to have chocolate fondue for breakfast, lunch and dinner. We ended up having chocolate-themed meals all day long, even though we held off on the fondue until dinner.

"Here." He opens the box and uses a small silver spoon to lift a square of chocolate sprinkled with cocoa powder. I eye it dubiously—I've never seen chocolate served like this—but open my mouth and let him feed it to me.

The soft, buttery piece melts on my tongue, and I moan softly as the decadent flavor absolutely *takes over* my senses. "This is *amazing*."

He samples a piece. "Pretty good."

"*Pretty good?*"

"I'm not really into it the way you are."

Apparently not. I place a bent arm on the edge of the tub and rest my chin in the crook. "Don't be nice to me."

Incongruously, he offers another square and I take it. "Why not?"

"I don't want to like you." *I can't afford to fall in love with you again.*

"I'm not doing this to make you like me," he says softly.

I shift. "Then why?"

He runs a finger along my lower lip. It no longer throbs with pain...just longing. "I don't like seeing you doing your best to appear strong and firm when you're really stretched thin."

The sigh I let out is long and painful. "Am I that obvious?"

He shrugs. "I know what to look for."

It's true. He's always known what to look for. Back in Vegas, he knew before I could sort out my feelings for him that I liked him...really, really liked him—maybe even borderline loved him.

My heartbeat is erratic, my skin flushed and warm. Neither has anything to do with the hot water, the wine or the chocolate. Over the soft scent of roses, I can smell his cologne. His breath fans over my cheek, and his finger is still on my lip.

"Don't," I whisper.

He arches an eyebrow. "Me or you?"

I have no answer. He watches me in bemusement and presses a butterfly-soft kiss to my forehead, just like at our wedding.

The spot tingles, the sensation reaching all the way to my heart. I can't speak.

"Enjoy your bath," he murmurs, close enough that all I'd have to do is just lean a few degrees forward... And my head seems to tilt on its own, wanting to connect mouth to mouth...

But before we can, he's gone.

I'm disappointed, but relieved at the same time. If he'd stayed longer, who knows what I might've done? I look at the golden champagne still bubbling in my flute. As much as I want to blame it for my response to him, I know that's a cheap cop-out. I'm not some silly, inexperienced girl. I could've ended it by pulling away.

I pop another square of chocolate in my mouth and lean back in the tub, my brain whirring to process our interaction and how I'm going to proceed. After all, we still need to share the suite tonight, and we only have one bed.

If he doesn't bring up what just happened, I'm not going to talk about it either. But a small part of me whispers that maybe...just maybe...not talking about what I really think and feel is the root of all my issues.

14

Blake

I RELAX ON THE COUCH AND READ EMAILS AND proposals. Today may be Saturday, but I have some catching up to do after taking most of Friday off.

But my usual focus is shot to hell, and my mind keeps wandering. Faith's already dried her hair—heard the sound of the dryer more than an hour ago—and unless I'm mistaken, gone to bed.

I should too...or else get the damn work done...but instead I just stare at the ceiling. My phone rings, and I glance at the screen. It's Dane.

"You know what time it is?" I say.

"Ten. What's the problem?"

"I'm in New York."

I can imagine his slight scowl. "For what?"

"The Aylsters' party."

"That sounds boring."

"It was. Why aren't you in bed with your girlfriend?"

"She's indisposed."

"Headaches already?"

"Perish the thought," Dane says with a snort. "It's one a.m. there. Why are you still up?"

"Can't sleep."

"You can't be jet-lagged. It's only three time zones."

"It's my wife."

"Wife?"

"I got married on Friday."

"That was quick. So why is she keeping you up?"

"She's...doing things that bother me."

"Does she snore? Fail to floss and leave tampons everywhere?"

I make a face. "That's disgusting."

"If the answer is none of the above, just fuck her and go to sleep."

"Don't want to."

Dane pauses. "Who the hell are you? Where's Blake?"

I laugh dryly. "I'm right here, asshole. I'm not saying I don't want her, but I don't want to do it unless she begs for it."

"Who cares? You're paying her to be a wife."

"This isn't the Dark Ages anymore. Marital rape does exist."

"Fine. Seduce her then."

He has no idea how much I wanted to. She was so

vulnerable, sitting in the bathtub. Her eyes were dark and luminous as she regarded me, her breath going shallow as I ran my finger across her mouth. All I had to do was lean in and kiss her.

But I didn't. I wanted her body, to grip that great ass as I slid into her hot, slick depths, but I also wanted something far more.

And I'll be damned if I know what that is.

When I stay quiet, Dane says, "Don't tell me you don't know how. I'm not giving you a tutorial on that."

"She only wanted a hundred thousand, plus another fifty for living with me. And no sex unless I pay her an extra five hundred every time."

"Is her pussy worth that? No, don't answer. I don't need to know. But you agreed, didn't you?"

"Yes."

"A tactical error," Dane muses. "Should've offered at least twenty million."

I choke. "Would that be for an 'all you can fuck' sexfest?" My mind runs with math. Thirty-nine thousand seven hundred times for a whole year, which equals...one hundred and nine times per day. Jesus. I run a hand over my mouth.

"Sex is secondary, Gutter Brain. If she's that cheap, Julian can easily buy her, too. Hell, I could throw her half a mil and she'd dance naked in Times Square on New Year's Eve."

I tense. The image is so fucking obscene. And Dane might do it just to make a point. Older than me, he finds it something of a life mission to mentor me. He claimed it was something Grandma Shirley wanted him to do, that interfering old bat.

"But changing the deal at this point would look suspicious," Dane says thoughtfully. "Especially if you throw more money at her without demanding something in return."

"It would." And she's no dummy.

"Find her weak point. Everyone has one. Then apply whatever pressure you can to get her to do what you want."

The option is logical and exactly what I would've done normally. And yet... "Might be a little difficult."

"Why? Did Benjamin Clark quit on you?"

"No." I blow out a frustrated breath. "I hate the idea of coercing her."

He laughs darkly. "You paid her to marry you, Blake."

"Would you have paid Sophia to marry you if you had that option? Or exploit her weakness to have her do what you want?"

A warning frosts his voice. "Leave her out of it."

"You just made my point."

He stops for a moment. "But you don't love this woman."

"I don't." But that doesn't mean it doesn't bother me to see her suffer. I should just shrug it off, consider it penance for her betrayal, but somehow I can't.

"Then figure out what you're feeling so you can map out your action plan."

"Her pieces don't add up."

"Then find the missing ones. Simple."

"Easier said than done. I don't remember you being this logical and cool-headed with Sophia."

"She's different. There're only two types of people in the world—Sophia and everyone else."

"I'm hurt. What is this, hos before bros?"

He snorts.

"By the way, why did you call?" I ask. "I'm sure it wasn't to check up on me."

"I was going to ask you to host a party in the Maldives or Bora Bora or someplace so I'll have an excuse to skip Thanksgiving dinner. Geraldine's going to be attending, and I'd rather not have Sophia and her in the same room."

"Sorry. Can't do it."

"Why not? Drag your wife there too. Every woman loves a luxury trip to a tropical location."

"She hates flying."

"Did you show her your jet?"

"Yeah. Still hates it. Sorry, but you're on your own."

Dane makes a humming noise. "I guess I'll just attend the damned party. If Geraldine doesn't survive, it's on you."

"I'm sure Sophia'll rein you in."

He sighs. "Most likely. I don't know how she puts up with Geraldine. Half the time I want to strangle her for being catty."

"Thank you for not killing my mother. If you'd like, you can direct that rage toward my dad and thrash him while imagining it's Mom."

His cynical laughter rings in my ear. "You should just send him some anthrax. So much easier. Anyway, I gotta go."

"Sleepy already, old man?"

"No. Sophia needs a back rub."

"Pussy whipped."

"You're saying that only because you think you're safe. You aren't."

"Bring it, pussy boy. I can take you."

"Married...and now delusional." He hangs up.

I toss the phone on the table and sigh. Dane has a point. I need to know if Faith has any pressure point Julian can use. I need to find the missing pieces of the puzzle so I can understand everything that's going on.

But instinct tells me I may not like what I find.

15

Faith

THE FIRST THING I NOTICE AS I AWAKE IS THE BED
—the cloud-soft mattress and the silky sheet underneath. Then there's the blanket over me—a cotton
cocoon that's as outrageously warm as it must be cold
outside, from the way wind is howling at the windows.
After months of sleeping on a lumpy sofa, it's obscenely
luxurious. For a second I fear it's a dream. But if so, it's
a damn good dream, and I'm going to enjoy it until I
have to wake up.

But there's more. I'm enveloped in a sense of security. It's strange—but welcome—to feel this way after
the last two years. And perhaps that's what's making
me so languid, as though I'm not flesh and blood, but
gooey honey.

Then, as I become more fully aware, I note a strong

arm around my waist that's keeping me anchored. My senses register Blake spooning me, his bare chest against my back, his thighs against mine. Only a thin layer of nightshirt bunched around my waist separates us, but it might as well not be there. I can feel every hard line and muscle on his finely honed body. And his cock, which at the moment is very hard, very thick and pressed against my ass. My panties and his boxer briefs are insufficient since my memories supply everything I need to recall what he can do with that thing.

He shifts. His breath fans at my nape through the strands of hair. My heart tempo rises, but I control my breathing. Still, it doesn't do anything to stop the familiar lazy heat from coursing through me. Restless need pools between my legs, and I swallow.

Is this the result of having been lonely for so long?

As soon as the idea pops into my head, I shake it off. That can't be right. Jack tried on and off to fuck me or make it up to me when he felt particularly guilty—as though sex ever could make up for his infidelity—and his attempts always left me cold. But Blake... My nipples are hard. I'm already soaked. All he has to do is hold me, press his body against mine.

I don't get it. I wasn't kidding when I told Mimi I can't sleep with guys I don't like. That's why I don't do casual hookups—there's never enough time to find out if I like him or not.

Based on my interaction with Blake—what I know about him—I shouldn't like him. So what if his behavior since our marriage has thrown me off? I shouldn't read much into it. He was solicitous and attentive when we were dating too. Right now he's trying to make sure people believe that he married for love—or some such thing. His brothers Ryder and Elliot are doing their best to look that way, and it's obvious Blake doesn't want to ruin all their work.

It would be a mistake to forget the way he told me to come crawling in his office. Or said I should suck him off, albeit that was partially due to my angry retort.

He nuzzles at me, the stubble on his jaw scraping at my neck, while his soft mouth moves coaxingly. I press my lips together tightly to contain a moan welling in my throat. His hand moves, slipping under my nightshirt, but instead of pawing my girls, he runs a thumb under the curve where my breast meets my ribs, as though he's relearning the contours and shape of my body.

My hips shift before I catch myself, my ass nestling more firmly against him. My panties are worthless now —totally soaked through, and I would be shocked if his boxers aren't damp as well.

A soft groan tears from his chest, and his arm tightens around me. That clever, clever mouth loses its delicate moves. Now it samples me with teeth and tongue, and I realize I'm panting. He runs a finger along the hard tip of my breast, and I cry out. The ache in my pussy is painful now, and I slip my hand between my legs. This is always how it was between us—no shame, no barrier. Just pleasuring and making each other feel oh so good.

He nips my shoulder. "Jesus, you taste amazing." Cups the breast, pinches the nipple. "Feel amazing."

"Yes," I whisper, my hips moving mindlessly against him. I don't care if he's fully awake now or knows how turned on I am. Inhibition is the last thing on my mind.

He rolls me over in one smooth motion, putting me on my belly. I am trapped between his big, strong body and the mattress, and I love the solid feel of his weight. He's grown more muscular in the last two years.

He supports his weight on his elbows, his muscles growing taut. A string of curses pours out of him, but he's no longer touching me. Suddenly he pulls away and slides off the bed.

"What's wrong?" I ask, almost dazed with need. Heat prickles every inch of my skin.

He watches me, his cheeks flushed and his eyes dark and glassy. His cock tents his boxer briefs, which—sure enough—are damp in front. The vein in his forehead throbs. "I'm not going to have sex with you."

I blink, unsure if I heard him right. "What?"

"I won't pay to have you sleep with me," he says.

My mind works sluggishly, drugged with need. I'm still only half comprehending what he's saying. "Why not?"

"Because"—the muscles in his jaw bunch—"that would make you a whore, and I won't do that to you."

Then it finally hits me. The nasty barb I threw in my apartment about him having to pay five hundred bucks to sleep with me. Before I can come up with a response, he vanishes into the bathroom. I hear the shower running.

I roll over until I'm lying on my back. My whole body throbs, and I clench my teeth. He was so damn hard, and I don't know how he managed to pull away when I was clearly so ready and willing. All he had to do was put on a condom and go at it, then later pretend like he was too sleepy to know what he was really doing. Any other man would've.

And the fact that Blake didn't bothers me tremendously.

$$\sim$$

BLAKE

I TAKE LONGER THAN NORMAL IN THE SHOWER. There's the immediate issue of my dick. It's super easy to take care of —pathetically so—since all I have to do is give it a couple of good pumps while thinking about the way Faith ground her hips against me and the sleepy sexy way she looked, back arched and ass tilted back as though begging me to drive into her.

I almost regret that I didn't. Afterward, we could have pretended nothing happened—or, if she insisted, I could have given her the damned add-on money. But even thinking about paying her that way leaves a bad taste in my mouth. I don't mind spoiling her ridiculously. But treating her like a prostitute is another matter.

Jesus. I'm messed up in the head. Who gives a shit how I treat her? She might even appreciate some extra cash.

But I do. Entirely too much.

As I towel off, my gaze falls on my underwear. Going to need a new pair, obviously. My dick's already semi-hard again, like I didn't just come in the shower. *Fuck.*

Breathing evenly, I think about the emails regarding the latest venture I'm considering. In a few minutes, my body returns to an acceptable state. I wrap a towel around me and exit the bathroom. Faith is in the living room. I can see her sipping a cup of coffee through the open door.

"All yours," I say, gesturing at the bathroom.

She doesn't answer. Instead she studies me over the rim of her mug.

Shrugging, I go to the huge walk-in closet to pull out the clothes I've selected for the trip. I brought things that I can layer since the temperature difference between New York and Los Angeles is significant.

Faith follows me to the closet, leans against the doorframe. "Are you going to go to someone else?"

The sudden question makes me pause. "What?"

"I know what your appetite is like."

Then it dawns on me. And I'm absurdly pissed. "Until the divorce is final, I take my vow seriously despite your amendment to the prenup. I'm a man of my word."

"Not saying that you aren't."

"Yes, you are. Maybe you can go to any man to scratch your itch, but I'm selective about who I sleep with."

Her face turns bright red. "If you recall, I told you I'd be faithful in the prenup and the ceremony."

"So you did."

"I have a lot more to lose."

"Ah yes. The 'shopping spree.'" Sarcasm drips heavily, but I don't give a shit.

Anger twists her expression. I have a feeling that it's either that or shattering, and she won't shatter. "A girl's gotta have something to enjoy. Everyone does." She looks away, but her chin stays up. "That's why I didn't want to...restrict your activities."

Except I've seen how such things ruin relationships. My uncle Salazar has screwed half the young women in America because his prenup says he can, and his wife left him. From the way he mopes, I suspect he still loves her. Perhaps he's always loved her. Me? I don't think I love Faith—the feelings I have for her are very complex now, too contradictory, bouncing back and forth between wanting to see her hurt the way I did and wanting to protect her because I hate seeing her in pain. Until I know exactly what I want, I'm not crossing any Rubicons.

Finally, I say, "I won't have you humiliated like that."

"Because you're a man of your word?" She throws it back at me.

"No. Because it's you."

~

FAITH

SO BLAKE *DOESN'T* WANT TO HUMILIATE ME? ISN'T that one of the reasons he married me, so I'd be under his thumb?

I don't understand him, and I give up trying to solve the puzzle. Instead, I shower and get ready for the return trip. I hate the fact that we have to fly—again— but that's the only feasible option. Blake doesn't have the time to waste driving, and I don't want to be away from Mom for that long.

As our car moves toward the airport, I look outside. New York is very different from Los Angeles. It's more than the cold, it's the way people speak— fast, like they're getting charged by the second—and walk, like they have someplace important to be in the next minute. The city seethes with energy, and if I didn't have to go back so quickly, I'd love to explore it.

Our plane is the same jet—and I still hate it. The cabin attendant smiles at us, but I'm sure she knows what a baby I am onboard. I take the aisle seat; the last thing I want to do is look out the window. Blake sits next to me, casually placing his forearm on the armrest. He's in a white button-down shirt with the collar undone and black slacks. He layered the top with a gray V-neck cashmere sweater.

I planned poorly, so I'm in a green wrap dress that's too thin for the weather. If it weren't for Blake's instruction to the butler, I wouldn't even have the fitted cardigan to keep me warm.

Apparently remembering my preference, the cabin attendant serves me a mimosa and a finger of scotch for Blake. I drain mine gratefully, hoping the alcohol will help me relax.

Refusing to repeat what happened yesterday, I clasp my hands together and leave them in my lap. The thud of the door shutting makes me jump. It seems so loud, especially without the engines revving.

"Flying is very safe," Blake says.

"I know."

"Only one in four point seven million people die flying. You have a better chance of getting struck by lightning."

"What're the odds?" I ask to distract myself as the engines whir, and the plane starts to move.

"One in one point nine million."

"Lemme guess. Is this where you tell me driving is even more dangerous?"

"One in fourteen thousand."

His numbers are slightly different from what I've heard, but maybe the statistics he got were compiled from a more recent year. The ones I have are from almost ten years ago, the last time I looked them up as a way of coping with flying after my father's death. Still... since I need a distraction, I say, "You're making all this up, aren't you?"

"No. Google told me so."

"You believe everything Google tells you?"

"Depends."

The pilot positions the plane on the runway. I swallow hard.

"The odds are in your favor we're going to be okay," Blake says. "Heavily."

"Everyone thinks that, until they're not."

"When did you become so cynical?"

The jet accelerates along the runway. I grit my teeth, hating this moment with a passion. "When my dad died in a plane crash."

A stunned silence, then he says, "I'm sorry."

"Yeah, me, too." Cold sweat trickles down my spine. "It was during takeoff." I click my teeth, squeeze my eyes shut. I don't know why I'm saying this. But somehow I can't stop talking. "It was going up and up, then suddenly something went wrong and the plane fell. I was too young then, but I saw the footage later. The investigators said it was due to pilot error, of course." It's always pilot error. "And you know what's really crazy? Takeoff isn't the most dangerous time. Landing is. But takeoff is what I hate the most, since I can't *not* think about what happened to Dad."

"Faith."

"It's okay. You're right about the statistics. It's just hard to be rational about this, you know?" The plane's up in the air now, tilting toward the sun. One out of four point seven million. Those are damn good odds. Better than the ones I recited to myself on our way to New York.

But it doesn't do much to alleviate my phobia.

Blake reaches over and takes my clammy hand in his. I clench it. "How did you cope when you were jet-setting with Jack? Did you take some kind of medication? Do some therapy?"

"No. I just did it because he wanted to." It was the price I paid to make sure Mom would get the best care. And it worked. She's still alive.

"Did you hide how you felt about flying?" Blake's voice is taut.

"No."

He's quiet. Then after a moment, he says, "I promise I'll deliver you safely to L.A."

My eyes pop open. "How can you guarantee that?"

"Because I don't cheap out on safety. Because I have the best crew—pay to have the best—and because..." His mouth curls whimsically. "I believe in fate."

"Fate?"

"It didn't push us together again just to kill us in a crash."

I laugh. "I think you're confusing fate with irony.

Besides, fate didn't bring us together. Mutual need did —me for money and you for a wife."

"You're still beautiful and young enough to have gone to someone else for money."

I pause, surprised. I've met other men who had money and wouldn't have minded a trophy wife. But somehow, Blake was the only one I thought of...even though I knew he wouldn't welcome me with open arms. "Maybe," I say softly.

I wish I could lay my head on his shoulder, but I tilt it back instead. I don't know what's wrong with me, but I feel a little sad for some inexplicable reason.

16

Faith

I FEEL LIKE HELL, BUT NOT AS BAD AS YESTERDAY. The flight was smooth, and the landing so gentle I didn't even notice we'd hit the runway. When we arrive at the condo, I change into a long-sleeve cotton shirt and jeans. Blake offers another box of the mouth-watering chocolate I had yesterday. I take it, but don't eat any. I want to share it with Mom.

"It'll make you feel better," Blake says, noticing my restraint.

"I'll have some later." I place it in my purse. I grab the fob to my new car—the Audi—and start to leave, but Blake takes my wrist. "Where are you going?"

"Out," I say.

"Yes, I gathered that. Where?"

"I don't know. I just need to clear my head."

"You're pale." He scowls. "You felt awful when we landed in New York."

"I'm fine. Nothing some sun and a little time with friends won't cure. Besides, this time the landing was smooth."

"Are they coming to pick you up?"

"I'm driving."

"Faith, you're in no condition. Let me call you a car."

"No," I say quickly. I don't want a chauffeur who undoubtedly answers to Blake. "If I start feeling sick, I'll get a cab or something. I promise."

He searches my face, then finally lets go with a curt nod. Relieved, I leave. My new car is a beautiful blue Audi convertible with a luxurious leather interior. I sigh as I climb inside. Blake didn't have to bother, but I must admit it's lovely to drive something this gorgeous, even though I'll have to give it back after the year's up.

The first person I spot when I walk through the main entrance at Blooming Flowers is Nelly. I smile, but she doesn't. "Alice's been in a lot of pain since yesterday. Your friend visiting helped take her mind off it, but I think it's getting worse."

I inhale sharply. "Did she take some pain medication?"

"Yeah. But I'm not sure how much it's helping."

My gaze drops. "I should've been here," I whisper. *Rather than in New York, spending meaningless time with people who don't matter.*

"Don't beat yourself up for it," Nelly says.

"Everyone needs a little break. And trust me, Alice doesn't want you to spend the best years of your life on her. She isn't talking about it, but she isn't stupid, Faith. She knows what's happening."

"She beat it once. She can beat it again."

"Either way, it's not healthy for you to obsess about her all the time," Nelly says. "Anyway, go on in, but don't be shocked. That's all."

I nod, mentally readying myself. If Nelly feels the need to warn me, maybe Mom is really doing worse. Judy's not in the room when I peek around the corner, but I see Mom in bed, looking out the window. She's so small, her body so fragile. Maybe it's because of my conversation with Nelly, but I spot the signs of pain on Mom's face with ease—the small grimace, the three vertical lines between her eyebrows. A painful lump forms in my throat, and I can't swallow. What if... What if she *doesn't* make it this time? What if the tumor wins?

Come on. She looks bad from time to time. What matters is who wins the war, not the little battles along the way.

I paste on a bright grin and walk inside with a spring in my step. "Hi, Mom!"

She turns around, her mouth curving into a welcoming smile. "Faith. Mimi told me you'd be visiting today, but I wasn't sure when."

"Now, of course!" I giggle, then pull a chair and sit by her. "I brought you a treat."

"Oh good. What is it?" she says eagerly.

"A girl's best friend."

"Diamonds?"

I laugh. "Better. *Chocolate*." I pull out the box from my purse. "They're ah-may-zing! The best I've ever had."

"Ooooh." She smiles.

We take the small disposable fork inside and share the decadent squares. Mom moans. "My goodness, this is incredible."

"I know, right?"

"Where did you find it?"

"New York," I say without thinking.

"New York?"

Crap. "Ran into it during one of my travels."

Suddenly Mom's eyes narrow. "Is that a *ring* I spy?"

Damn it. I glance at my hand. Thankfully the wedding band doesn't show too obviously because it's intricately designed to cradle the engagement ring. "It sure is."

"Did you get engaged without letting me know?" Mom peers at me. "Mimi told me about your date yesterday."

"She did?"

"I won our poker match, so she was forced to tell me exactly what you were up to. And she said you were on a date."

Poor Mimi. She probably didn't feel right about lying, so she gave Mom a half-truth. I owe my friend a huge apology. "Why don't you have another piece?" I gesture at the chocolate. We've only had four total.

"No, it's all right. A bit too rich to eat all of them."

Not exactly true, but I know why she's really rejecting them—lack of appetite. "I'll leave them here for you so you can have some later."

She shakes her head. "You should take the box. Maybe share with Mimi. She'll love them."

This isn't good. "Okay."

"Now, tell me about this date of yours. If he gave you a ring like that, it must be serious."

"Don't read too much into it. I only put it on my ring finger because it didn't fit the other ones." Mom knows my right hand is slightly bigger than my left.

She makes a noncommittal noise. "Tell me about the man."

"He's...nice, I guess. Rich. Handsome." I shrug. "You know."

"Nice is good. So is rich and handsome. Is he the guy you went to New York with when you discovered this divine chocolate?"

"Yeah."

"Definitely serious. To get you into an airplane..."

"It's complicated."

"Is it?" Mom takes my hand between hers. She's so bony it pains me. "Do you see a future with him?"

I pause, giving myself a moment to think. Two years ago, I did. But now... "I don't know. Probably not."

"Hmm. What *do* you see in your future, if not this man?"

"Well... I want a house with a yard and a white picket fence. Maybe a two-car garage. And a dog."

"A dog?" Mom's eyebrows rise high. "What kind of dog?"

"A golden retriever. I always wanted one."

"You never told me."

"We couldn't afford one." We lived in small apartments and money was tight although she never denied me anything. Dogs aren't cheap.

"I'm sorry."

"Don't be. You did everything you could for me. Not having a dog was never a big deal."

She pats my hand. "What else?"

"Um... Two kids. A boy and a girl. Both with beautiful dark hair and dark eyes. Smart too."

"That's a lovely future, Faith. Have you told your man?"

I shake my head. She doesn't understand it's not about what I want, but what he wants.

"Why not?"

"He loves the city too much, and the convenience of a penthouse. And his home is such that I doubt we could have a dog in it. Everything inside is obscenely expensive. Can't have some big mutt's tail wagging around." I smile a sad smile. Two years ago, I thought I could have that with Blake. It's such a cliché vision of idyllic suburban middle-class bliss, but I wanted it because I didn't know any better. If I tell him now, he'll laugh at me. He'll find the idea of a picket fence and yard and a two-car garage ludicrous. He has multiple penthouses stuffed with elegant and expensive things. He wouldn't want a puppy chewing them up or getting in the way. As for children, he may not even want any. Or maybe he only wants a son.

"You should tell him, Faith," Mom says. "You never know."

"It's the man's job to propose."

She scoffs. "Nonsense. This is the twenty-first century, my dear. The modern era. No woman should wait for someone to give her what she wants. No! She should go after it with both hands!"

I grin at her impassioned speech. My mom, the original women's libber.

She continues, "It's lonelier now with people too busy to connect. That's why it's more important than ever for everyone to have at least one person they love unconditionally and who loves them back just as much."

"How do you know when you meet someone like that?"

Her smile grows wistful. "When a man puts you above his own needs, you know."

17

Faith

SOON AFTER OUR TALK, MOM DRIFTS OFF. I KISS her on the forehead and leave, asking Nelly to call if anything changes. She says sure, knowing what I'm really asking for. It bothers me how poorly Mom's doing. This damned disease is turning the strongest, most vibrant woman I know into a helpless invalid. I hate that, resent that it's going to take her away before I'm ready.

Like I'll ever be ready.

I sit behind the wheel. I don't really want to go back to Blake's, not yet. Nervous anxiety is bubbling inside me, and I know it's only going to get worse if I go home—Blake's home.

Wanting to delay that as much as possible, I text Mimi. *Hey, you free today?*

Yeah. Back in L.A.?

Yep. Just saw Mom. And I have chocolate to die for.

Ooooh gimme.

I chuckle. *Now?*

I'm at my place. So yes, bearer of chocolate! Stop by right now.

I drive to the apartment she shares with Andy. It's only about an hour from Blooming Flowers. Their place is in a nice part of the city, and the building, despite being old, is well-kept, with a new coat of paint and an intercom that works. It even has a security camera, which I don't think is just for show. I hit her numbers, and she buzzes me in.

The apartment is on the second floor, a nice corner unit. I walk inside with the chocolate and shut the door behind me. The entire place smells like lemon and apple.

"You aren't baking, are you?"

"Just whipping up some apple sauce," she says from the kitchen, turning off the stove, then gives me a quick hug. She's in a casual house shirt and cropped jeans, a wholesome, girl-next-door look that she wears with ease despite her model-gorgeous face. "Actually, just finished."

There are at least twenty apples in a box by her feet. "That's a lot of apples."

"Andy's mom sent them. The annual crate." His parents own an orchard in Washington. "If you want, you can take some."

"Seems like an unfair trade—apples for chocolate."

"Won't know until we check the goods, will we?" She crooks her fingers. "Let's see the merchandise."

I laugh and offer her the box.

"Ooooh, looks fancy." She opens the top. "And delicious."

"You need a fork or something to scoop it up."

She takes two out of a drawer, then grabs a chilled bottle of chardonnay and glasses. We go to the dining table to share the wine and chocolate. She groans at the first square. "Wow, this is almost worth a flight to New York."

"I'm sure they deliver," I say dryly.

"Probably. Damn. This is some good shit. Except for the needing a fork part. That I don't like."

"Why not?"

"What if I didn't have a fork?"

"Then toss the whole box into your mouth."

Mimi laughs. "Savage. So how's your mom?"

"Today's not her best day."

"Sorry to hear that. She seemed all right yesterday."

"I'm sure she'll be fine soon enough. She wanted to know all about my 'date.'"

"Sorry! She was very persistent. But you know she was going to wonder when you missed your visit." She shifts her weight, resting her chin in a hand. "Did you tell her?"

"Sort of. Not really."

"You didn't tell her it was Blake, did you?"

"No."

"Or that you're married?"

"No."

"Are you...um...ashamed?"

I blink. "Of what?"

"You know. The circumstances surrounding the whole marriage thing. I know why you're doing it, and I actually admire you...but maybe you feel bad about it?"

"I do feel bad. But as hard as it was, I'd do it again for Mom." I sigh and take a big swallow of the wine. "Mom thinks this 'date' I had is going somewhere. She wants me to picture a life with the guy and everything."

"Did you?"

"I told her some stuff. A house, kids. And you know, I did kind of keep seeing Blake in it."

"Oh."

"But it's so stupid. He didn't come for me two years ago. He knew I was going to marry Jack—and why—but...he never came for me." I sniff. "I wanted him to."

Mimi reaches over and squeezes my shoulder.

"I thought if he cared, he'd come clean about himself, then tell me he wanted me...that he'd make everything right.

"Mom said I'd know when I found the right man because he'd put me above his own needs...but Blake didn't."

"You think he'll...dump you when he gets what he wants?"

"I kind of did, but then he confused me." I tell Mimi what happened on the plane to New York, how he stood up to Benedict last night and then refused to sleep with me this morning.

She's quiet for a moment, processing my story. "Maybe you should let go of your preconceived ideas about him. People can change in two years, and he may be different now. *You* aren't the same you from Vegas, either."

I hesitate. What she's saying is possible, but...

"What would you have done with Blake if all the stuff two years ago never happened?"

"If I only went by what happened in the last few days...?" I let out a shaky breath. "I think I might fall for him."

"Uh-huh. Except you won't because you already know—or *think* you know—what kind of man he is. Stop stressing and live in the moment. If it's going to end in a year, why not just have fun rather than overanalyzing everything and making yourself miserable? That isn't helping anyone. And trust me, your mom's too sharp not to pick up on your tension. Maybe this is another chance, and it won't turn out like, you know...Jack."

The memory of his betrayal still stings. My feelings for him started out as gratitude, but in time they could've morphed into something more...if he'd been just a little more considerate...and faithful.

"You've been stressed out for at least two years because you can be very black and white about things, and you hold that bad feeling inside you when you've been wronged. But life isn't supposed to be fair."

I smile a little at Mimi's speech. She tries really hard when she thinks I'm not handling pressure well.

"Ever since your mom's diagnosis, you've been pretty tough on yourself."

I start. "What do you mean? I've never..."

"Yeah, you definitely have. You don't allow yourself any missteps. And that's a difficult way to live."

Mimi's revelation makes me pause, and I realize she has a point. I *have* been feeling guilty. I failed Mom because I wasn't lovable enough to convince Benedict to help out with her care. I used Jack for his money. Maybe it wasn't as crude as demanding money every time we had sex, but it was pretty close. And a tiny sliver of me wonders if he knew I never loved him and that was why he strayed. It couldn't have been easy to live with a wife who only felt gratitude for his wealth.

With the feeling of guilt came resentment for Benedict. Even if he couldn't bring himself to love his only grandchild, he should've still helped us because that's what family does. But obviously our blood ties mean nothing to him.

And those emotions have complicated my interaction with Blake. If he hadn't lied to me about who he was... If he hadn't looked the other way when he knew I needed his help... If he hadn't kept his distance when he knew I was about to marry another man...

But why would he care about a woman whose own grandfather doesn't hold her in any regard? Why would he want a woman who married someone for money?

"It's okay to make mistakes," Mimi says. "We're only twenty-four. If we don't screw up now, when *can* we screw up?"

She's right.

"Appreciate all the shades between black and white, and enjoy every moment now. When today's gone, it's gone forever. Why not get what joy you can? That includes sex."

I sputter.

"It's a great stress reliever, and orgasms are always nice as long as you remember they're just that and not anything more. And sex is a great lubricant in a relationship. Don't think of it as putting out, think of it as using him for sex."

I choke back a laugh. "Oh, like that's any better?"

"Better than a vibrator, I'm guessing." Mimi gives me a level look. "Besides, I hate the idea that you might second-guess yourself or overthink everything to death while married to Blake. It's not worth it. Just do what you'd do if you didn't have to worry about tomorrow. Or if that's too difficult, just ask yourself WWMBBFD?"

"What's that?"

"What would my brilliant best friend do?" She grins, fluttering her eyelashes.

I laugh. "That you are, Mimi. And you're a friend anyone would be lucky to have."

"That's God's truth. Now promise you're going to take my advice."

"Okay. I promise."

18

Faith

Since I promised Mimi, I take some time to consider what I should do for the rest of the day. Something I enjoy...

Impulsively, I stop by a grocery store en route back to Blake's penthouse. I haven't bought groceries in a while—butter and eggs don't count—so I get some chicken breasts, a small bag of sticky rice, some veggies, spices and herbs, and a tub of double chocolate ice cream plus a bottle of rosé that looks promising. The penthouse is dead quiet when I get back a little after five. The door to his room's ajar, but I don't see Blake inside. Maybe he's gone out to eat. I'm sure he has friends to meet, colleagues to discuss business with, even if it's Sunday. He probably doesn't stay rich by working a regular nine-to-five.

I change into a black shirt and cropped teal pants, twist my hair up in a messy bun, put on some music and start cooking. The kitchen's surprisingly well-stocked with everything I could possibly need, so it's super easy.

The act of washing the rice and veggies, dicing everything and sprinkling herbs and spices into a pot is soothing. I've always enjoyed cooking, even though I haven't done much in the last two years. Jack had a live-in chef, saying it was beneath his wife to be in the kitchen. After he died, I didn't have money to waste, so I lived on ramen noodles and mac and cheese out of the box, eggs and cheap meat on sale being my occasional splurge.

Singing and moving my body to a jaunty tune by Beyoncé, I make enough for two, just in case, and put everything in the preheated oven. Once that's done I pour myself a glass of the rosé. It's a bit sweet but otherwise okay. Not bad for a sub-ten-dollar bottle.

If I'd known Blake wouldn't be home, I might've asked Mimi to come over. She loves my chicken and rice. While they're cooking, I halve a ripe avocado I picked up from the store.

"You seem to be enjoying yourself."

I almost drop the knife.

"Careful." Blake comes over and uses the knife to get the pit out. "Here."

When I don't take the avocado, he places it on the cutting board. He's in a gray T-shirt and loose, black pants. His hair's damp, and I can smell soap and shampoo on him. I'm tempted to lean closer and bury my nose in the hollow of his neck. "I didn't realize you were home."

"I was on a call in the office."

"Oh." I cringe inwardly, wondering if he saw me dancing in the kitchen. The most charitable thing you can say about my moves is that I don't look *completely* spastic.

"What are you making?"

"Chicken and rice." I take a quick sip of the wine, suddenly feeling stupid. "But you don't have to eat it if you've got something else coming, or..."

He leans over and sniffs appreciatively. "I'd love some."

"Okay. I was just making some salad to go with it."

"Let me help."

"Um..."

He gives me a small grin. "I can handle washing vegetables. I'm not as helpless as Mark."

"Who's Mark?"

"A cousin. He owns some of the best restaurants in the country, but he can't cook for shit. Probably doesn't even know how to hold a knife."

I choke on a laugh. "Really? That bad?"

"Yup. Not even his executive chef could teach him."

"Okay. You can wash the veggies over there. Or chop. You decide."

"I'll wash."

We stand side by side and work in a companionable

silence. Not that it's relaxing. Our fingers brush every time he hands me something he washed and dried, and I feel the zing like a little shock to my system each time. Heat spreads through me like warm honey, and my body all too quickly remembers the unfulfilled need from this morning.

I steal a quick glance his way, but he seems totally unperturbed. How irritating. I take a gulp of the rosé.

What would my brilliant best friend do?

She'd rub herself all over Blake because she doesn't believe in holding grudges or overthinking anything. Maybe that's why she and Andy were able to get back together after six months of separation. She said they both needed a break, even if neither wanted to acknowledge it. When I asked her how she'd feel if Andy slept with other women during that time, she said she wouldn't feel anything different because they weren't together. She's a lot more practical than me in that regard.

I finish the glass and pour another. "Want some?" I ask impulsively.

"Sure."

"It's kind of cheap."

"Cheap is fine as long as it's good."

Raising a skeptical brow, I let him taste first. "Well?"

"It'll do."

I serve him a glass, and we clink.

"You're in a good mood," he says.

"I'm not flying," I say. "And I'm away from—" I wave my hand in the general direction of New York.

"Next time you won't have to come."

"But I said I would in the contract."

"Sometimes you have to bend a little, Faith."

I regard him over the rim of my glass. "Do you want me to?"

"Yes."

"Okay."

His eyes narrow suspiciously. "You're entirely too agreeable."

"What? You want to fight?"

He shakes his head. "Did your afternoon outing go well? Is that what this is about?"

"It was a mixed bag." If Mom had been better, I would've said it was a lovely afternoon all around. "But—"

The oven dings, interrupting me. I open it and pull out the covered skillet.

"What's that?" Blake asks.

"Herby chicken and rice. It's my mom's recipe."

"Chicken Alice," he murmurs.

I nod and let the skillet sit. It needs to wait about five minutes before serving.

"I'm sorry," he says.

"For what?"

"About your mom. I know she meant the world to you."

I stare at him. He looks so sincere, his gaze full of sympathy. His brother is a brilliant actor, but Blake? I find it hard to believe he's faking it, but if he knew how much my mom means to me, why did he leave me the way he did back then? I don't get it.

I don't want to rehash the past, but the words slip from my lips anyway. "Why did you lie about who you were back then?" To disguise how much his answer means, I start portioning out chicken and rice. The food smells amazing, and I know I've outdone myself.

Blake helps me carry the plates and salad bowl to the table and set it with utensils and napkins. I bring the wine. When we're seated and each take a bite of the juicy chicken, he finally says, "I didn't lie *per se*. I was helping a start-up manage some supply chain issues. I just didn't want to tell you the whole truth. This is good."

"Thanks. Why not?"

He moves his fork through the rice, then stops. "I liked the way you looked at me. You know, just as a guy you found interesting, not as a two-legged ATM."

I have another bite. "Ironic, isn't it then, that I ended up leaving you for money?"

"Ironic's one word." We eat in silence for a moment, then he asks, "Was it worth it?"

The answer is too complicated, but it's a yes or no question, and I don't want to explain myself. "Yes."

"Even putting up with his affairs? The publicity?"

I nod. "Even then." I would've done much worse for Mom.

"I don't understand you."

"What's there to understand?"

"From what you told me about your parents, I thought you'd want what they had."

"I did, but practical considerations won out." As I say it, I realize that is the sum total of how our relationship ended two years ago. Yes, it hurt like hell when I realized Blake lied, but contrary to what I told myself over and over again, I wasn't angry he didn't offer to help with Mom's care when he had more money than he knew what to do with. Even if he'd been truthful about who he was, I still would've gone with Jack, because Jack offered to pay for Mom.

What upset me ultimately was my failing...even though I've been lying to myself about that too. I wasn't smart enough to go to a kick-ass college or get a job that paid oodles of money. I wasn't good enough to convince Benedict to pay for Mom's medical needs. His minions didn't even let my calls through—that was how little he thought of me.

"Would it have made a difference if you hadn't had to worry about paying for your mother's hospital bills?" he asks.

"Maybe, but that's not how it happened." I finish my dinner and the rest of the wine.

Blake does the same, but his gaze never leaves me. It's like he wants to unravel me, but there's nothing to uncover, especially if he's trying to figure out the answer to his question—because it isn't what most people would conclude.

After dinner I load the dishwasher. "I don't know what I would've done because that doesn't change the fact that you lied about who you were. Maybe I carry some old baggage because of my relationship—or lack thereof—with Benedict, but I think it would've bothered me a lot more than it might other women, who probably would've been thrilled you're rich."

"You don't like money?" He places his dirty plate on the rack, his hand on my left side, effectively caging me.

"Money's nice, but I like other things more. Respect. Trust." I turn around and face him. We're so close, I can feel his body heat through the small gap. "If you ever wanted to take our relationship to the next level, you would've had to tell me the truth. What would you have done if I'd looked at you like a meal ticket at that point?"

His brows pinch.

I put the tip of my index finger on the furrowed spot between them. "I can see why keeping your identity secret held some appeal, but it didn't for me. And learning the truth from Jack didn't help."

"I would've proposed if you'd waited another month."

I flinch, my finger dropping from his forehead. His mouth immediately sets into a firm line. The inadvertent talk makes my heart ache. Maybe I should rage about it now, tell him how he screwed up by waiting, keeping things to himself. But maybe I'm too tired from the trip. Or it's the alcohol. I can't muster anything except a sad little smile. "Does it matter now?"

"It matters to me."

"Well, I didn't know. And I didn't wait, and you didn't propose."

"Did you hate me that much?"

"No... I think I blamed you for things that were ultimately my responsibility. But I don't hate you. You've been remarkably nice, considering, and I would've been in a real bind without this marriage."

I duck around him and go to my room. The talk was productive. I think we understand each other better now, and that's always good.

But my heart is sore, like I've been in a boxing match with an opponent who connected with one too many body shots.

19

Faith

I can't sleep. The temperature in the room's perfect, and the bed is utterly comfortable. The sheets are soft and clean, smelling of fresh detergent. But sleep eludes me, so much sand slipping through my fingers.

Annoyed, I pick up my phone and check the time. One seventeen. If I could, I'd blame jet lag, but that's not it.

I'm just restless. The talk I had with Blake keeps circling in my head. His question about whether it would've made a difference if I didn't have a money problem nags at me. Without a pressing need for a large sum immediately, I would've never gone with Jack. But even with the financial issue, if I'd known Blake was going to propose in a month... Maybe I would've waited, even without knowing he was a billionaire, because it's a crazy kind of commitment, given my situation, and I would've found it incredibly touching and heartfelt, the kind of foundation a forever could be built on.

I roll over and bury my face in the pillow. This is what Mimi meant by overthinking. I'm analyzing so much I can't even cut off my brain to go to sleep.

Not that knowing that helps. My thoughts bounce back and forth between past and present. I'll never be able to undo what happened. Blake and I are never going to get those two years back. But right now? I want him. Maybe it's because I'm just horny or maybe because I've been lonely. There's something singularly pathetic and soul crushing about being faithful to a husband who cheats on you publicly, even if you don't love him. Even when he approaches you with a frisky grin on his face, you pull away because you don't know if he's being a damned douche—a likely scenario—or if he's trying to rekindle something—unlikely...but possible. But nothing happens because it's impossible to have sex with a guy who leaves you colder than a fish in an icebox. Then he gets angry and accuses you of being frigid. Because you're not getting wet? Your fault, one hundred percent.

I sit up in the dark. Blake's probably asleep now. It'd be crazy for me to go jump into his bed and try to seduce him. Disgusted, I get up and go to the kitchen. A glass of ice water should do the trick. If I want to seduce him, maybe I shouldn't think about Jack—or any other unpleasant topics.

A small lamp in the living room's on, and I frown. Did Blake forget to turn it off? I take a bottle of water and walk over, then stop.

He's stretched out on the couch, tablet in hand, a finger of scotch on the table in front of him. All he's got on are the loose black pants from earlier and a pair of glasses. The effect is devastating, all the more because he doesn't mean it to be—a perfect combination of lickable body and amazing brain. His torso is totally bare, his shoulders broad, chest thick. His abs are ridged with clear definition even in repose, and his arms are lean and muscled and eminently nibbleable. The dusting of dark hair below the navel disappears underneath the waistband of his pants, and I pull my lips in, wishing I could do more than just look.

He glances up from his tablet.

I flush, embarrassed at being caught staring. "I wanted to get something to drink." I gesture at the kitchen. "Why are you still up?"

"Couldn't sleep, so I was reviewing a few proposals."

"I see." I clear my throat. "Well...think I'll go back to sleep now," I say, then stop. He knows I wasn't sleeping.

He sits up and places his tablet on the coffee table. "Before you go... About what you said during dinner—"

I raise a hand. "Don't."

"Faith—"

A Final Deal

"It's in the past, and I don't want to talk about it again, Blake."

His eyes get that stubborn look I'm all too familiar with. He had the same expression when he asked me out that first time and I declined. I had an early shift the next day and I didn't want to waste my time with a guy who was in Vegas for a couple of days on business.

I put the bottle of water next to his tablet. "I mean it. You got all your questions answered." My heart thuds. This is my chance. I place my palm against his chest, then push him against the back of the sofa. His skin's hot underneath mine, and I lick my lips. "The only thing I want out of your mouth is something filthy. Otherwise..."

He drops his gaze to my lips, his throat working. But the words out of his mouth are anything but filthy. "I meant what I said in New York."

This man is slaying me, little by little. "I know." I place my left knee by his right hip. "That's why I'm taking advantage of you late at night—to use you for sex." I swing my right knee over to where it's flush against his left hip.

One dark eyebrow quirks up. "Is that so?"

"Uh-huh. You're going to be my boy toy and you don't owe me anything for what I'm about to do to you." I place a hand on his cheek, tilt his face up.

I lower my head, let my lips hover over his, only a hairsbreadth away. Our breaths mingle, and he doesn't move. My heart hammers, accelerating painfully as the moment lengthens.

I angle my face, and our mouths fuse. He parts his lips, and I lick them all over, relearning the shape and the impossible softness. He doesn't try to take control or overwhelm me. The pace is easy, exploratory, our tongues stroking, caressing, each touch gentle and sweet. His hands slip under my nightshirt, hot skin against hot skin. The calluses on his palms leave my back tingling. Sweat mists over me as his fingertips trace every bump along my spine, then skim along the elastic waistband of my panties.

A soft moan tears from my chest. I'm starved for his touch—for him. Need runs in my veins like lava, and I don't want the shirt between us. I pull it up roughly, tossing it over a shoulder, not caring where it lands. Breaths shudder out of me, and my nipples bead until they almost hurt under Blake's hot gaze.

His voice is gravelly as he stands, his hands impatient as he palms my ass. "Wrap your legs around my waist."

I do, and his mouth is back on mine, the kiss deeper, more intense. Our tongues tangle mindlessly, and I clutch his shoulders, my nails digging into the hard muscles as he walks toward the bedroom. Every step bounces my breasts, nipples rubbing against his bare chest, and my spread legs leave my pussy rubbing against the thick erection trapped between our bodies. White-hot pleasure streaks through me, pooling between my thighs, where I'm already soaked. I moan into his mouth, wrapping a hand behind the back of his head and pulling him even closer.

One of his hands shifts, and he fingers my slick sex underneath the panties. My body winds tighter, and I squirm and finally pull back. "Don't."

"Why the hell not?" His thumb slips inside me, and I bite my lower lip.

"Because... I had this idea of driving us crazy by prolonging it."

He lays me carefully on his bed. The sheet smells like him, and it's another turn-on. "Damn, wasn't all day enough?"

I blink.

"I was hard in the plane, hard in the car, hard all day long, including dinner."

"That's a lot to bear without relief."

"I cheated a little. I beat off in the shower before we left New York."

I choke back a laugh at how unrepentant he sounds. "Did you? That's not just a little bit cheating. It's nuclear cheating."

"If I tell you I was thinking about you all the while, would that make it better?" He flicks his tongue over my nipple.

"If you tell me...exactly what was going through your mind...yes."

"Simple." His mouth trails between my breasts and down my belly as he drags my panties along my legs. "I was fantasizing about eating you out."

"No way. Not the other way around?" I could have sworn blow jobs were what guys masturbated to.

"I thought about that a little, too...but going down

on you is so much more fun." He flings my panties away, then kisses me on the back of each of my knees, slowly pushing my legs apart, then studies the exposed flesh. "You're incredibly pretty here...and responsive. I missed your hot taste, that little sound you make when you're turned on, the way you scream when you come." He runs a thumb from my clit to the opening of my pussy, the motion deliberate.

And sure enough I make a soft little sound. Just like he said.

"The way you smell changes, too. Muskier and earthier as you get more excited. Just from that I can tell when you're close." He breathes over me, and my whole body tightens.

"And your taste. Sweeter..." He licks me, holding his tongue flat and hard, from south to north. "Saltier."

The effect is devastating, stretching my nerve endings until they're taut with anticipation. My thighs spread wider. He reaches up and palms my breasts. My nipples stab against his hands as I arch my back, and he laughs darkly, the vibration pulsing through me in waves. I'm impossibly wet now, and the sheet under my ass feels slightly damp. I don't care so long as he doesn't stop.

"Fuck, just look at you," he grates out, then pushes two fingers into me. They glide in easily, and I tilt my pelvis for deeper penetration. He curls them, hitting the bump...just...perfectly...and I clench the sheets. "I want to taste you when you come." Pumping his fingers slightly, he sucks my clit into his mouth, and I'm a goner. A mind-destroying orgasm rips through me, and I'm wrecked, my voice hoarse as I scream. But he isn't finished. He pushes me higher, his hands relentless, his lips and tongue absolutely ruthless.

I want to get away, and I don't want to get away. I feel so good, but also quite vulnerable, like a hermit crab that's outgrown its shell.

But through it all, I hang on to Blake because part of me trusts that he'll anchor me, keep me safe.

I hear foil tear, and seconds later, Blake is kissing me. He smells like him, but he also smells like me—us. I taste myself on him, and it only turns me on more, like I'm barely getting started. My fingers dig into his silky hair, and he cradles my head, his elbows supporting his weight.

"I want you inside me right now," I whisper. "Thick, hard and deep...just like how I wanted it this morning."

"You're killing me."

"No, I'm telling you to fuck me." I press my feet flat on the mattress and rock against him. "*Right now.*"

I know the moment his control slips. His pupils are so dark and so large, I feel like I'm being drawn into a black hole. He drives into me, each plunge rough, and I love it. I revel in it.

We're lost in each other, the slick friction between our bodies giving and seeking pleasure. His lips find the sensitive spot at the base of my neck where it meets my shoulder, and I sink deeper into the sweet sensation.

Then his mouth is on my lips, and every time he

thrusts and rolls his hips, an electric heat sizzles through my veins.

Somehow his hands find mine; our fingers link.

Only then do I let go, sobbing his name against his mouth.

"Faith... Faith, my sweet girl..." He shudders, then groans loud and hard as he comes inside me.

He rolls off to avoid crushing me, then drags me toward him, spooning me like he did in New York. An incredible lassitude comes over me.

I should go back to my room. After all, I told him I was just using him for sex. But this feels way too nice to give up. I yawn. *Just five minutes*, I tell myself. Or whenever Blake falls asleep, whichever comes la...

20

Faith

SLEEP DISSIPATES, AND I WRINKLE MY NOSE AS I blink. Something feels off. This bed's not mine—no canopy—and the sheets are tangled and I'm totally naked and my pussy is throbbing gently.

It's a good throb, though.

My cheeks heat as I remember what happened last night. I must've fallen asleep in Blake's bed. *Argh.*

An arm pulls me back, closer to Blake's warm body, and it's impossible to stay stiff. His thighs are hard and hot against my hamstrings, and his thick erection pushes at my backside. He nuzzles me. "Morning," he murmurs softly.

"Morning." I shiver at the gentle scrape of his stubble across my skin. "You have to work today, don't you?"

"I'm the boss," he says. "So I can play hooky whenever I want."

I laugh, but the sound quickly turns to a throaty moan when he presses hot, open-mouthed kisses along my spine, one hand cupping my breast and the other gliding down below.

His fingers find my clit and stroke gently. I'm already wet, embarrassingly so. I arch my body, shifting and adjusting to open up, then I hear something out the door.

"Wait. Did you hear that?"

"Hear what?" He licks my skin.

I hear it again. "*That*. Blake...someone's *here*."

He finally pauses and listens. "Oh, it's just Lenore."

"Who?"

"The housekeeper. I told you about her."

Sleep and arousal vanish in an instant, although it takes a moment before my brain catches up.

Blake shrugs as though he can read my mind. "She's always here in the morning."

"Oh." I sit up, pulling the sheet with me.

He props himself up against pillows. "What's wrong?"

"I'm...not comfortable with other people around." Jack had servants too, lots of them. They were always scurrying around, making notes of what I was up to every second of the day. "It's hard to let go when there are others in your home."

"Give yourself a chance to get to know her. She's a nice woman. Besides, if she weren't around, the place would turn into a pigsty. I hate cleaning and doing all those chores."

Understandable. But that doesn't mean I'm comfortable. "Let's go out," I suggest impulsively. "If you really don't have to work, that is."

"Where do you want to go?"

"Anywhere. I'm open to suggestions."

He gives me a heated look. "If you just want us to be alone, I have the perfect thing."

"Then let's do it."

I hop out of bed, run to the connecting suite and into the attached bathroom. As hot water sluices down my body, I berate myself. I'm probably being unreasonable. Blake's housekeeper probably isn't a spy. I remember him mentioning her right after I moved in. I doubt he hired her to keep track of me the way Jack did. I couldn't even make a phone call without having it observed and reported. Normally I'd think he was trying to control me or isolate me from everyone, like a lot of abusive men do. But Jack just wanted to know who I called, and when it was either Mom or Mimi, he'd deflate some and encourage me to call Benedict.

It doesn't matter how you feel now. You two are blood, Faith. And one day, you're going to need him and he won't be there for you because you're a stranger.

Jack didn't know shit. Benedict was already a stranger, had already ignored my attempts to beg on my mom's behalf.

When I'm out of the shower, my hair dry and skin coated with drugstore lotion, Blake's waiting for me in my suite, sitting in one of the plushy chairs and tapping on his phone. He embodies casual elegance, his big, muscled body relaxed, his gray shirt and knee-length dark olive cargo shorts simple but expensive. His hair's still a bit damp. He looks up and puts away his phone.

"You can keep fooling with that," I say, going into the walk-in closet. "I'm going to need more time to get ready."

"I prefer to watch you."

I look at my selection of outfits and choose cropped denim pants and a bright orange, long-sleeve UC Irvine shirt.

Blake tilts his head. "Nice. Irvine, huh? Not UCLA?"

I flush. "It was an impulse buy. I happened to be on campus a few months ago." I should stop but I can't, needing to explain such a frivolous purchase when money was so tight. "Since lots of those life gurus say you have to visualize your future self, I wanted to have the shirt so I could imagine myself as a college student."

"If you want to go, you can," he says, his expression soft. "If it's important to you."

His comment surprises me. He could've easily dismissed me or asked why in the world I'd want to bother with an education when I can just get myself a rich husband. "It is. I feel like it's a way for me to better myself... You know, become independent." I put on some lip gloss, mascara and blush at the vanity. It's an ordinary activity, but having Blake watch makes it seem a lot more intimate.

He comes over and props his hip against the edge of the vanity, tucks an errant strand behind my ear. "If you want independence, you should've asked for more money."

I shake my head. This attitude... Yes, it's familiar and I know precisely how to deal with it. "That isn't the same."

He looks slightly puzzled. "Money always makes people independent."

"But not when it's *given* like that. If money was enough by itself, all those lottery winners would be living happily ever after in wealth and luxury. But most of them lose their windfalls pretty quickly." I open the jewelry box and take out the pearl earrings. "I want to earn my own way, using my own ability. The money I asked for when marrying you... That's just some emergency funds."

He presses a kiss on my temple, and I feel its warmth all the way to my toes. "You fascinate me."

"Why?"

"All the layers." His eyes are dark and shuttered, but I see questions in their depths. He doesn't know what to believe. But that's natural. I've been in his face about needing money.

"I'm not that complicated." I just don't want people to know me that well. People aren't that nice when they get to know me. They think I'm crazy for not wanting to brown-nose my grandfather, or they think I'm some weird heiress trying to rough it just for kicks. Some even assume I'm lying about everything. Mimi is the only one who knows me well. And Blake's a very close second.

He glances down at my jewelry box, then frowns. "Where are your diamonds?"

The set he bought me in New York glitters inside. "They're in there."

"No, the ones you wore to my office."

"Oh, they're in one of the moving boxes." It's easier than telling him I had to pawn them because he'll want to know why. I grab my purse. "Okay, I'm ready."

He takes my hand. And just like that, I let my worries go...for the moment.

21

Faith

BLAKE ISN'T STUPID. HE KNOWS I'M NOT TELLING him everything. It's in the way he glances at me from time to time as he drives his Aston Martin. Even behind his sunglasses, I can sense the speculation in his gaze.

Still, he doesn't press for answers I'm not willing to give, for which I'm grateful. It would've ruined an otherwise fine day—and the sweet peacefulness between us.

The drive is relaxing, and it's extra fun in the convertible, the wind in my hair, sun in my face. The caffeine from my Americano is starting to circulate in my system. The traffic isn't too bad since it's well past ten.

"Where are we going?" I ask after half an hour or so.

"You'll see."

"We aren't flying, right?"

"Nope."

"No parties or events?" I look down at my clothes. "I'm not dressed for anything."

"Don't worry."

He pulls into a marina and kills the engine. With a small grin, he opens my door and leads me to a sleek, single-mast sailboat that looks relatively new.

"You don't get seasick, do you?"

I can't help but tease. "What if I do?"

"I have some pills in the cabin."

"I don't need them. Boats don't bother me. But... impromptu sailing? Are we going to catch our lunch?"

"Nope. I had the boat stocked with something to munch on...although you're welcome to try to catch something. It does have a kitchen." He reaches over and takes my hand. "You wanted privacy, and there's nothing like a boat for that. Just the two of us."

I can just imagine...and I do. It's perfect. "I figured you'd have a huge yacht. You know, one of those super ostentatious ones where you can park your smaller yacht inside."

He laughs. "This one's a forty-four footer, not quite big enough to be considered a yacht. But if it makes you feel better, I have more than one boat. And if you want to experience a super ostentatious yacht, we can always borrow Ryder's."

I make a face. That probably means I'll have to see Ryder in person and thank him. Probably any other woman would kill for a chance to see the man up close —he *is* one of the world's biggest movie stars after all— but him being Blake's younger brother makes me less than willing. "No, thanks. I'm perfectly happy with this."

Blake and I climb on board. While he checks a few things, I explore. The ship's positively luxurious. Belowdecks has a fully functional kitchen, living room, office, full bath and two bedrooms. The walnut finish is elegant and ultramodern in feel. I test the mattresses, and they're just firm enough, the sheets fresh and soft.

"Like what you see?" he asks, popping into the stateroom. He smells like coconut, and his skin glistens with a fresh coat of sunscreen.

"Yes. It's amazing. I didn't know smaller boats could be this nice." Jack had a yacht, but it was way too large and always full of people I didn't know or care about. Hardly an intimate experience.

"If you're tired, you can get more rest."

"No way. I'm too wired." I follow him up topside. Blake hands me a bottle of sunscreen, I slather it all over myself, and we're off.

He's an excellent sailor, handling the rudder with ease, his body relaxed. We share a bottle of chilled Riesling, and I draw in the salty air. It's a bit chillier out on the Pacific, but the sun makes it warm enough. The cloudless sky is a brilliant azure, and I raise my arms, spreading my fingers. As we cut through the water, I feel all my worries leaving me, one by one.

"This is nice." I grin at Blake. "I can see why you like this."

"It's fun." He smiles, then presses a quick kiss on my lips.

"Do you sail often?"

"No. I don't come to L.A. that much, and I'm often too busy in Boston."

"But you've been in L.A. for a while now."

He cocks an eyebrow. "Been tracking me, have you?"

I squirm. "I had to figure out where you were."

"I'm usually in Boston, but right now, I'm here to get away from my father and his new wife. Murder is illegal, alas."

"You don't like them?"

"That's putting it mildly. I despise them both."

"Why? Because he married a trophy wife?"

"I couldn't care less about his domestic life. He can marry as many trophy wives as he wants." He squints into the horizon. "Come to think of it, he has."

I prop my chin in a hand. "Then what's the problem? Unless you don't want to say?"

He considers, then finally says, "She has this unnatural urge to mother me. And like I told you before, she's barely twenty, if that."

"Jeez. I'm sorry." I can see how awkward—and infuriating—that could be. "Did you tell your father?"

"Why? He wouldn't care. He's only interested in

controlling us. The whole inheritance bullshit is the latest in a long string of schemes."

"He sounds like an ass."

"He's the most indented portion of an ass, although he doesn't like to think so." Blake turns to me. "How about you and your grandfather? It sounded like Benedict wanted to talk to you in New York."

"He's like your father, except he wants to pretend I don't exist." What's up with rich old men? "He's ashamed of me and my mom."

"Why?"

"In case you didn't notice, my mom's not white." I stop, realizing my slip. "Was. It's still hard for me to talk about her as though she's gone."

Blake squeezes my hand. "He hated it that she wasn't a Texan beauty with blond hair and blue eyes or something, I guess. He called her a mongrel."

Blake curses under his breath. "That's no way to talk to a woman, much less in front of her daughter."

"Oh, it wasn't in front of me. He did it behind my back. I only know because I overheard Mom talk about it." I huff out a breath, trying to disguise the old ache in my heart. Knowing that your grandfather is a racist hurts; somehow it's a poor reflection on everyone in the family, even though it has nothing to do with the rest of us. "We've never hung out or anything like that. Benedict wouldn't accept my calls two years ago. Maybe he's decided I look more white than not, so I'm acceptable now. I have Mom's eyes, but I mostly took after Dad."

Blake pulls me into his arms, and I let him comfort

me. And I realize I've never talked about my family with anybody, not to this degree. Mimi knows because she's pieced things together, not because I told her anything outright.

Maybe I'm changing. Maybe I'm finding it easier to open up and talk about my old pain.

Or maybe it's just Blake, my mind whispers.

That might be right, too. I assumed he'd be difficult and overbearing, but instead he's been surprisingly considerate. And I feel myself opening up, the tightness in my heart easing, little by little, making me vulnerable to him again.

Unwilling to take the thought further down this dangerous path, I throw myself at him, wrapping my arms around him. I dig my fingers into his sun-warmed hair and bring his mouth down for a long kiss, our lips open, our tongues gliding against each other.

This is just physical. His palms slide over my skin through the shirt, leaving hot trails that prickle. I arch into him, the hot slickness gathering in my pussy, and that too is physical. His cock is hard and thick, pulsing against my belly through his shorts.

It's just biology. We're both healthy, young animals that are attracted to each other. It's that simple.

I pull my shades off. Blake's boat is the only one on the horizon. I unbuckle his pants, drag the zipper down. It hisses, parting. I push the clothes out of the way, and grip his cock, my hand wrapping around the hard, veined shaft. The head is plum-shaped and beautiful, its color dark. A bead of clear liquid seeps from the end, and I run my thumb over it, spreading it all over the cockhead. Then, very deliberately, I suck my thumb, my eyes on his.

Blake's breathing grows shallow, and more precum seeps out of him. His excitement fuels mine, and I know I'm going to have to get rid of my panties.

"You know, I was thinking about your dick for a while," I whisper, my hand back around him.

"Were you?"

I bite his lower lip gently, then tug. "Uh-huh. When you were eating me out, I thought you'd taste amazing too."

"I see."

"I'm not the only one who changes scent and taste when they get excited." I pump him once. He groans. "But sadly my memory is somewhat dim."

"A terrible shame."

"That it is." I lick my slick fingers. He's slightly salty. He jerks his pelvis forward, and I love him—no, his reaction.

I drop to my knees and let the tip of my tongue trace him, base to crest. He grips the metal bar behind him, thick tendons standing out in his arms and neck.

"Delicious," I say with a wanton smile, then pull him all the way into my mouth.

He groans loudly. I bob my head. He isn't the only one who remembers. I recall all the ways he loves to be touched—the gentle scraping of nails against his balls, my tongue teasing the small flap of skin where his cockhead meets the shaft.

His scent is getting headier, muskier. He pulls back a little, trying not to come too soon.

"Jesus, you haven't forgotten anything," he hisses between clenched teeth.

"Not much," I say throatily before I take him back in my mouth, increasing the suction.

"Put your hand inside your panties."

I do it.

"Touch yourself."

I do, letting my fingers glide through the slick folds.

"Are you wet?"

I nod.

"How wet? Show me."

I pull out the hand, lift it so he can see the glistening juices on it. He touches it, then tastes my fingers. *Damn* that's hot.

"You love sucking me off, don't you, dirty girl?"

I nod, taking him deep until he is almost touching the back of my throat. He's so long and thick.

His hands let go of the metal bar and cradle my hollowed cheeks. "Put your hand back into your panties and fuck yourself with your fingers just like I'm going to fuck your face."

I do and slip two digits into my dripping pussy. He pulls back, then glides forward slowly. He isn't rough, but he's firm, his strokes deep and sure. Having me fuck myself with fingers isn't enough though. His instructions roll over me:

Use three fingers. Your hands are so much smaller than mine. Feel how they stretch you.

Push your bra out of the way. Massage your tit. Is your nipple hard? Show me. Good, now pinch it as hard as you want. Tug on it. Roll it between your fingers. That's right, Faith. You always loved having your tits fondled.

Don't slow down. Grind the heel of your palm against your clit. Roll your fingers, curl them, touch your G-spot.

My breathing's impossibly shallow. My body's a mass of quivering, stimulated nerves. This is so indecent—me sucking him off on the deck while masturbating to his instructions as the sun's shining upon both of us, the cool ocean breeze brushing our heated skin.

Blake curses under his breath, and his driving grows more frantic. I love the way he slowly loses control, succumbs to the need searing between us.

His hands fist the hair at the base of my skull, his hips flexing. I suck more strongly, more desperately, all the while I pump myself to the same frenetic rhythm, pinching my nipple until it hurts because right now that's how I want it.

I thumb my swollen clit, and it pushes me over the edge. An orgasm consumes me, my scream's muffled against Blake's hard dick. As though the vibrations were enough, he spurts into my throat, his taste and scent saturating my senses. I swallow, still shuddering in orgasm, manage to hang on long enough for Blake to get full satisfaction, then collapse back on the deck. My limbs feel like soggy pasta, and I'm too relaxed to care if anybody sails by while I have my pants undone, my hand wet with my juices.

Some moments later—I don't know how long—Blake picks me up. "Let's go below."

I wiggle, feel his still-thick erection against me. I give him a dreamy smile and put an arm around his neck. "Yes. Let's."

22

_____

Faith

I thought Blake would screw my brains out below, but instead, he shows me the bathroom so I can freshen up. "I'm going to get lunch ready."

"You'd rather eat lunch?" My tone is slightly petulant, and he merely grins.

"You need to be fed." He kisses me. "I didn't bring you out here to starve you."

I sigh, then clean myself as best I can. I _really_ need a new pair of panties, but there's nothing I can do about it. I stick mine in the back pocket of my pants and dry myself. My eyes are bright and my cheeks are glowing —my "I just had a fabulous orgasm and I want more" look.

Still, Blake had that determined expression, so he's not going to budge on the food. By the time I'm finished, Blake has taken out two large lobsters—thankfully already dead—and a platter of huge shrimp cocktails and a bowl of fruit salad. He's at home in the small galley, placing a grill and starting the gas stove.

"You can go ahead," he says.

I squeeze a lemon wedge over the cocktail, dip two shrimps in the sauce and feed him one while munching on the other. The meat is succulent and tender, the coldness refreshing. I nod with approval. "Very good."

"Only the best." He gestures at the open bottle of Riesling. "Want some?"

"Of course." I pour two glasses and we toast.

"To a perfect day," he says.

His gaze is so intense, it feels like a physical caress on my sun-flushed cheeks. "Hear hear." I drain half the glass and reach for another shrimp.

"Don't fill yourself up. You haven't had my lobster yet."

I give him an impish smile. "How are you going to cook it?"

"Just watch." He throws a couple globs of butter on, then tosses the crustaceans onto the hot grill. Immediately the meat starts sizzling, the bottoms of the shells changing from blue-green to orange to red. Drizzling on some kind of liquor—at least I think it's alcohol—and sauce later, he uses a cooking fork and knife to expertly shuck the shells and cut the meat into bite-size pieces.

"If that's half as good as it smells, it's going to be awesome," I say, my stomach growling.

"It will be awesome. I've tried this recipe before, and it was a resounding success."

"On this boat?"

"Yup."

Suddenly I wish I hadn't asked. Whoever he cooked for on board must have been a woman. An ugly feeling twists inside me, and I realize it's jealousy. I take a quick sip of wine.

"In case you're wondering, the guests were my sister and Elliot."

I choke on the Riesling. Am I that transparent?

"And yes, I can tell what you're thinking."

"I wasn't thinking anything except I'm hungry."

He snorts. "It's fine. If I were in your place, I'd be wondering."

I raise an eyebrow.

"Look, I'm possessive. So are you." He serves the lobster on two plates, and we move to the table in the living slash dining area.

"Sounds like a euphemism for jealous."

"Whatever you want to call it. Point is, I'm the same way around you."

"Are you..." I take a bite of the lobster. It's juicy and tender, the sauce enhancing the sweet flavor of the meat without overwhelming it. "But you never came after me," I murmur without thinking.

Blake stills for a moment. "Did you want me to?"

Damn it. I wish I'd kept my mouth shut. Why did I bring that up after telling myself I'm letting go of our past? "It doesn't matter."

"Yes, it does. Otherwise you wouldn't have brought it up."

"But you didn't, so who cares?"

An edge sharpens his voice. "Faith."

I shrug. "Maybe if you'd come after me, I might've chosen differently. But we'll never know." Sighing, I close my eyes. I hate that I've ruined the easy rapport between us.

"I didn't go after you because Dane told me not to."

My eyes pop open. "Who's Dane?"

"My cousin and best friend. He's very cold and methodical about a lot of things, and he said going after you would be like begging to be abused. And I agreed."

"I see."

"And it made sense. You don't run after a woman who leaves you over money."

"You know why I needed money."

He gives me an unreadable look. "I do, but you didn't need *his* money."

Blake doesn't get it. I needed Jack's money because it was either that or nothing. I can't believe Blake hasn't figured out Benedict wasn't going to lift a finger for me two years ago.

I drain the rest of my wine, then get another glass. "Sorry. I shouldn't have brought it up. Water under the bridge."

He frowns. Suddenly I don't want either of us to think. Resting the empty wine glass on the table, I straddle and kiss him. If we're fucking, we can't be thinking.

I do my best to devour his mouth, but he holds my head, slowing me down. I make an impatient noise in the back of my throat. This isn't how it's supposed to go down, but he's stronger and more determined.

His tongue touches mine, stroking me slowly. I press harder, but he stays irritatingly resolved, his mouth not letting me take more than he's ready to give.

"Easy," he whispers, his breath tickling my lips. "We have all day."

I groan softly, and he relaxes his hands, letting go of my hair, and traces the slopes and lines along my spine. I don't know what kind of magic this is, but the calm within him settles my turbulent emotions until I slow down, too.

His kisses are leisurely but no less hot for that. He kisses as though he has all the time in the world, as though I'm the only thing that matters to him. Pleasure unfurls inside me, pulsing through my veins. I feel like I'm sinking into the sweetest oblivion, inch by painstaking inch.

And all the while, he's exploring me as though we've never done this before. His fingers ghost over the sides of my breasts, down the narrowing slope of my waist and the flare of my hips. He runs his palms over my legs, and I feel the warmth through my pants.

He kneads my ass as though he's worried about scaring me. But I'm not scared. I want this—and more. I want him to hurry up, be rough, and fuck me like a porn star.

But he takes his time. There's liquid fire coursing

through my veins, and my skin is so sensitized it almost hurts. "Blake..." I whisper.

"I know... We're still taking it slow."

His mouth seeks the pleasurable spot at my neck, and I let my head tilt so he can do what he will. He licks and nuzzles. Goosebumps pop up all over me, and wet heat pools between my legs. My pussy and clit ache, pulsing in unison. I want to be filled, I want him grinding over me.

But instead, he pushes my shirt and bra out of the way and kisses my breasts, then palms one, running his thumb over the tip, while pulling the other nipple into his mouth. He traps it between his tongue and the roof of his mouth and sucks until his cheeks hollow. My head falls back.

"Why are you torturing me?" I whisper.

He merely chuckles with the nipple in his mouth. I feel the amused vibration all the way to my clit. My toes curl.

When he switches nipples, I reach for him. My hand slips under the waistband of his boxer briefs and grips his hard dick. It twitches, and I give it a few good pumps, strong and tight, exactly the way he likes it. His body reacts, and he groans harshly.

He picks me up and carries me to the bed in the back, his mouth on mine. My fingers dig into his hair, and I devour him, knowing he's going to plunge into my aching pussy in any minute.

He rips my pants off. His eyes go utterly dark when

he notes the lack of underwear. "You've been commando all this time?"

"Yup."

"Jesus. Good thing I didn't know."

I can't help but smirk as I lie on the bed and spread my legs in shameless invitation. "I should've told you."

"Minx." He sheds his clothes like they're on fire and puts on a condom.

Then he's on me, his dick sliding along my folds. I whimper when his cockhead bumps against my clit.

He glides into me, and my breath catches. He moves slowly, his thick erection dragging along my slick, sensitive channel. His fingers link with mine, and he gazes deeply into my eyes. I swallow. I want to turn away, close my eyes, anything to break this connection, but I can't. I'm hopelessly drowning in the dark depths, every thrust dragging me just a little bit deeper.

The air around us seems to grow syrupy sweet. Pleasure swells like a monster wave, but it's not ready to break yet. Blake kisses me hard—finally!—pinning me on the bed with his strong hips. I feel his heart thunder over my breast, and my heart matches the rhythm beat for beat.

We move in unison. Bliss saturates my senses, and all I feel is Blake, reaching into me as though he can shatter all my walls and defenses.

The orgasm builds and breaks, builds and breaks. Each peak is sharper and sweeter than the one before. I taste his patience, his drive in our kiss.

When I finally let go, I fly so hard, so high, I'd feel

lost if it weren't for his hands holding mine. He joins me, then rolls to his back, pulling me on top while making sure we're still fused together.

It takes a long moment before I can breathe in air. And as my brain starts working again, I realize I've given him far more than a year of my time.

~

FAITH

I PULL THE SHEET ALL THE WAY TO MY NECK WHEN I hear somebody moving right outside the door. Jack had servants who waited on us all the time. I hope Blake doesn't have people who walk around the boat like they belong there. I'm really not happy with such...attention.

Or maybe they were on board all along, just hidden.

The thought makes me scowl...then I blink, realizing I'm no longer on the ship. *I'm in Blake's bed.* How?

The door opens, and Blake strolls in. "Hey."

"Hey," I say, my mouth dry.

He's already showered and dressed in a charcoal suit. A blood-red tie is knotted impeccably and stands out against the somber broadcloth.

"How did we end up back here?"

"I brought us home after you fell asleep. I think that sixth orgasm did you in."

I flush at the memory. Blake was insatiable, and I was an eager participant in all the dirty things he wanted to do. "What time is it?"

"A little after eleven."

I gasp. "In the morning?" I can't believe it's so late. I yawn. "I'm still so sleepy."

He grins. "Eleven p.m."

I blink. "Then why are you dressed like that?"

"I need to be in Boston for three days."

"Oh." I push hair out of my face. "Do I need to come as well?"

"No. It's just some business stuff. Lenore's going to be here in the morning to take care of everything."

The housekeeper. Tension creeps into my shoulders. "Okay," I say, feigning nonchalance.

He hesitates for a moment, then adds, "There's one more thing."

"Yes?"

"I told you about my brother Ryder's party on Thanksgiving."

"I remember."

"I'd like it if you could come. It's family only."

I bite my lower lip. "I meant what I said about families."

"But..."

"Sex changes nothing." The light in his eyes dims, and his face chills. I reach out. "I don't mean it like that. I just... I really don't want to meet them."

"Why not? They aren't ogres. You didn't mind Elizabeth."

Because we were in public, and she behaved. But I don't say that because families stick together. Generally. "Family can complicate things." I swallow. "Besides, I already have plans for Thanksgiving."

"Doing what?"

Spending it with Mom. "Spending it with friends."

"Then maybe I'll join you instead."

"You aren't invited." I smile to take the sting out of the words, rise to my knees and give him a quick kiss on the mouth. "Have a safe trip. I'm going to shower."

I scramble out of the bed and almost run to my bathroom before he can argue. It's one thing to have sex and realize I care for him a lot more than I ought to, it's quite another to take him to meet Mom again.

Really? WWMBBFD?

Mimi would agree with me.

23

Blake

THE BUSINESS IN BOSTON IS EVEN MORE BORING than I anticipated. And my home in the city is colder and emptier than I remember, even though the weatherman assures me that the temperature's the same it's always been.

Maybe the Californian sun's turned me soft, but I want to get out of here ASAP. I work nonstop until I'm done with all the meetings and follow-up issues. After three, I get inside an elevator heading to the café on the first floor to grab a very late lunch. I pull out my phone and text Faith.

I start typing "Miss you" then delete it. That's too sappy and not like me. *Miss me?* No, not that either. I try a few more messages, then finally settle on the first one—*Miss you.* I hit send.

A moment later she responds, *Miss you too.*

Everything okay? Lenore taking care of you?

Everything's fine. Don't worry.

Her texts are perfect, just what I want to hear, but my gut says something's wrong. Maybe it's how she refused my Thanksgiving party invite or how she told me I wasn't welcome to join her and her friends for the holiday before I left.

I start to call, needing to hear her voice, then stop myself. What the hell am I doing? That's pathetic. She said she was fine, so why call like some stalker?

You're not sure about her. That's why.

After sex, I assumed something had shifted between us...which just goes to show that what people say about *assuming* is one hundred percent correct. She's still skittish, especially when it comes to my family. Did she meet any of them before, as Jack's wife? They would have been polite to her, since I've never advertised our relationship to anybody. The only one who knows is Dane, because he happened to be in Vegas with me when I met her. But Dane is the furthest thing from a gossip.

I text Lenore instead. *How's everything?*

She responds: *So far so good, but I'm afraid I might've offended your wife. She packed a bag and left not too soon after breakfast.*

Where did she go?

She said she was staying with a friend, but didn't say who or leave me a number to get in touch.

I don't like it. Her home is at the damned penthouse. She doesn't get to pack a bag and leave as soon as I'm out of town, then pretend everything's peachy when I text.

If I were the jealous type, I'd suspect an affair. But no. Faith will keep her promise. I know that much.

I probably shouldn't, but I can't stop myself from taking out my phone and opening a tracking app. It keeps tabs on where the Audi's been for the last thirty days.

She regularly goes to an address I don't recognize. I enter it into the map, and it pulls up a place called Blooming Flowers—a palliative care center slash hospice.

What the hell?

This doesn't make any sense. Faith doesn't have anybody else dying in her family. Her father passed away when she was a young child, and her mother succumbed to an inoperable tumor during her marriage to Jack, if not sooner. Benedict is still remarkably robust, and even if he were dying, he's in Texas.

A friend, maybe?

No. She's there too frequently and stays for too long. Then I remember why she married me—money. She wouldn't say what it was for, being coy every time I asked. Is she footing the bill for the facility's care?

That seems too extreme. Who goes that far for a friend?

A lover, on the other hand...

My molars grind together. She went to Blooming

Flowers on Sunday too...and that evening she cooked and seduced me.

"What would you like, sir?"

I blink and stare at the expectant face of an aproned worker at the counter. I guess somehow my body did what it usually does and got in line. "Americano and a turkey sandwich," I croak out through a tight throat.

"Got a cold?" she asks sympathetically.

I tug at the collar of my shirt. It's not some damned virus. It's the stuffiness in the café. I can't breathe.

I toss her a couple of bills. "Put my food over there." I gesture at an empty table and stumble out into the cold, slushy Boston winter.

The air cuts like a scalpel, stinging my nose. I drag the chill into me, hoping it'll cool the ugly feeling boiling inside.

"Blake, just the person I was hoping to see."

I jerk my head. "Simone."

Damn bitch is only six feet from where I stand. She approaches fast, the door to a silver Maserati closing behind her. A mink coat is wrapped snugly around her, the hem swirling a few inches below her ass. The dress she wears is wool and as black as her heart. Her skinny heels are laughable for snowy Boston in November, and I find myself hoping she trips and breaks both ankles.

The muscle in my jaw ticks. She must've been stalking me. Cecilia told me she's been trying to get an appointment, and I instructed my assistant to evade all attempts to get in touch. "What are you doing here?"

"You're a difficult man to reach."

"For good reason." I start to go back inside the secured building that houses Digital Angel's Boston office. She can't follow me in. No clearance.

"Wait!" Her manicured fingers dig into my sleeve, her hold stronger than I expected.

"Let go."

"We need to talk about the China venture."

"I'm pulling out."

"Blake, let's not be hasty. I'm sure we can—"

"I'm pulling out."

Her eyes go flinty. "Your family's reputation will suffer. I'll make sure of it."

"I don't give a shit." I turn so we're facing each other, my gaze boring into her. "My family will still be worth billions, while yours is going to be in rags. After the IRS and FBI are through with you, you may even get to wear orange. I hear it's the new black."

She pales, and I enjoy the expression of terror ripping through her heartless visage.

I let out a derisive laugh. "Didn't think I knew about your sticky little fingers?" I wriggle mine. "I knew, which is why I never donated a penny to your 'cause.'"

"You set me up."

"Did I? You're the one who begged me for money, remember?" I start to turn away. I'm done.

"Is this because of that worthless whore?"

The question stops me. I slowly turn back to face her. "What did you just say?"

Simone smiles a genuine smile. *Fuck.* I've betrayed myself.

"Faith Mortimer. She might be your wife now, but she's a worthless whore."

"Insult her again, and your face'll never look the same."

"You wouldn't dare hit a woman."

"Try me."

"All she had to do was keep her legs closed, and she would've received millions in settlement after Jack died, but she couldn't. Within a year, she started fucking around, making a fool out of my brother. Have you thought about that?"

"*Jack* should've thought about it before cheating on her," I bite out.

"She started it. She even got pregnant with her lover's baby, the stupid cunt."

I take a menacing step forward. I warned her.

Simone scrambles for her Maserati. "If you don't believe me, look him up. Jordan Smith. That's his name!" she yells before shutting the door and speeding away.

My fists clenched, I almost start after her, but her car's already gone around a corner. How dare she show up, threaten me and slander Faith? Does she think it's going to save her?

At the same time...

Jordan Smith. She didn't toss the name out for shits and giggles. She knows I can easily check her story.

Is he the man in Blooming Flowers?

I have a massive urge to fly out now, but there's an absolutely critical meeting with one of the people whose businesses I'm backing. Tomorrow's meetings, on the other hand...

Fuck 'em.

I call my assistant. "Cecilia, cancel everything for tomorrow. I'm flying to L.A. first thing in the morning."

She doesn't miss a beat. "When do you want to reschedule?"

"We can do a teleconference while I'm flying."

"Got it. Anything else?"

"Have a car ready for me at the airport. No driver."

"Certainly. Have a productive trip."

I narrow my eyes. "I will."

24

Blake

MECHANICAL ISSUES WITH THE JET AND POOR
weather delay my flight. By the time I land, it's almost
three, and the traffic is so bad it might actually be faster
to walk.

Should've asked Cecilia to have a chauffeur pick me
up. Then I could've ditched the damned Aston Martin.
Can't leave it on the road even if the 405 is a parking lot.

By the time I reach Blooming Flowers, it's five
fifteen. A frumpy receptionist in her late forties with
frizzy red hair gives me a small, polite smile. Her plastic
name tag reads Candace McKenzie. "Welcome to
Blooming Flowers. Can I help you?"

"Yes, Candace. I'm looking for..." I stop, debating
what would be the best thing to say.

"Yes?"

"My wife, Faith... She comes by every day, and I wanted to check on things." I give her my warmest "I'm a good guy" smile. "We just got married, and I haven't had a chance."

"I see. Congratulations." Her eyes flick to my hand; the wedding band there seems to satisfy her. "I need to see an ID though."

"Of course." I hand it to her and scrawl my name on the visitors' log.

Candace checks me out thoroughly, cataloguing my clothes, the Omega on my wrist and the ridiculously expensive haircut I happen to indulge in every month. "Don't think we have a visitor named Faith Pryce-Reed."

"Faith Mortimer is her maiden name."

Her expression brightens. "Oh, *that* Faith. She didn't tell me she was married."

"Have you seen her recently? We got married last Friday."

"Goodness. Maybe that's why. I've been working late these past few days." She gestures at some vague spot behind me. "Room Four-Oh-Two." Her gaze softens with sympathy. "We're providing the best care possible, but"—she sighs—"it's not going to be easy this time. I'm sorry."

My gut tightens. So somebody's dying. Jesus. My body moves on autopilot, taking me to the fourth floor. Maybe I should just...leave. If it's her lover, what am I going to do? I can't possibly punch the guy—which I might under normal circumstances.

But at the same time, I've come too far to turn back. I need to see the man who's gotten Faith to go to this extreme...

Room Four-Oh-Two is average, nothing special compared to the luxurious private room Grandma Shirley had when she was dying. The floor is linoleum, the walls are painted an industrial beige and the curtains are cheap polyester. At least there are quite a few vases and baskets of flowers to liven up the space. Probably Faith's doing. There are two beds, and one's empty. The other one...

I stop abruptly, blink a few times. The woman is thinner now, her dark eyes like a pair of craters in a skeletal face that used to be plump and round. Gray now dominates her previously inky hair, and her skin's so thin, I can't help but wonder if it's going to tear when she moves.

"Alice?" I whisper, needing to make sure this husk of a woman really is Alice Mortimer, Faith's mother.

Her head turns toward me, and she squints. "Blake?"

"What..." I swallow. "I thought you were dead."

She coughs. "And I thought you were no longer in my daughter's life."

Faith hasn't told her. "We...got back together." I stay rooted to the spot. My head is totally scrambled, everything inside a total mess like a ransacked house.

"Come sit for a bit," she says, pointing at a plastic

chair next to her bed.

I do as she asks—more out of shock than a genuine wish to please—and stare at her. "Faith told me you weren't going to make it, and that was two years ago."

"Somehow I did. My doctors called it a miracle."

"I see."

A corner of her mouth twitches up. "Did you want me to die?"

I flinch. "No. I'm just"—I drag my hand through my hair—"surprised."

"Me too. You here to see somebody else?"

"No. Faith's been visiting you so..." I start diplomatically, although I'm not sure precisely what to say.

Alice nods.

Damn it. Why didn't Faith say something? "Are you getting everything you need?"

"People here are wonderful at keeping me comfortable. Faith doesn't want to hear this, but I'm not going to make it this time."

"You've made it so far."

"I have, but I know my body. I can feel it giving out a little more each day." She reaches out and places a shaky hand over mine.

I look down at the frail, pale hand mottled with spots. Her skin's so cool that I can't believe she's kept it under a sheet all this time. Shirley was cold too, when she started to go.

"You feel it too, don't you?" she asks.

I swallow. How the hell can you answer honestly?

"You don't have to lie. I've accepted it."

I put a hand over hers, trying to warm it.

"Tell me, Blake. How are you and Faith involved again? I thought you two were through."

"We were when she married Jack Villar."

She sighs. "It's my fault. She did it because of me."

"She didn't have to. I had a foundation arrange to pay for your care. All Faith had to do was accept the check."

"What check?"

"A check for a hundred thousand dollars, which would've taken care of the immediate problem. It should've arrived within a day of my leaving Vegas."

"We never got anything," Alice says.

"That can't be right. My sister took care of it personally." I asked her to over the phone, made it clear how critical it was that Alice was helped. Elizabeth seemed surprised since she's the one who contacts me for money, not vice versa, but she promised.

And one thing Elizabeth never does is break a promise.

"I'm afraid not," Alice says.

I can feel myself start to burn with anger. The only thing preventing me from clenching my fists is Alice's hand between mine. Elizabeth dropped the fucking ball on *this*? When she knew how important it was to me?

Alice continues, "If there was another way, Faith would've never married Jack. She never loved him."

I know that. I know his only appeal was money.

Which is why I approached the Villars to destroy

them. I wanted to take away the one thing Faith desired the most by marrying him. And funnily enough, they took the bait. But then they were desperate. And once I'm through with them, they'll be nothing.

"You're upset," she says quietly when I just sit there, trying to digest what she told me. If it weren't rude, I'd jump to my feet and dial Elizabeth to demand answers.

"Why wouldn't I be?" My tone is curt. "My fu— sister screwed up."

"I'm sure she had her reasons. Anyway, it's in the past. Best to let it go."

Easy for her to say. If Elizabeth had done as I asked, Faith's and my lives would've gone very differently.

"You still have feelings for Faith."

I nod once. I have them—complicated and messy and so visceral that I'm not capable of sorting them out.

"Then would you do me a favor?"

"What is it?"

"Can you be good to her?" Alice sighs. "She never asks for anything—too much pride you know. It's sad because she doesn't want anything grandiose either." A wistful smile fleets over her. "You know what she told me she wanted?"

"What?" I prompt after an extended pause.

"A house with a big yard and a two-car garage. A white picket fence and a golden retriever. Two kids— one boy, one girl. That's what she said she wants for herself. Her dream."

The vision is so ordinary and sweet my heart twists,

as my mind conjures her in a neat suburban house with the dog and two beautiful children who look just like her.

"You know who her grandfather is, don't you?" Alice asks.

"Yes. Benedict Mortimer." The man made his fortune in oil. And he didn't keep betting on oil either. He was smart enough to diversify, which is why he's been able to weather the huge dips in commodity prices over the years.

"If I hadn't caused the rift between her and Benedict, she'd be living like a princess, wanting for nothing."

"Living like a princess is overrated." I mean that.

Alice wheezes a laugh. "It would have kept her from marrying a man she didn't love. She puts on a brave face, but I know when she isn't happy."

I take a moment to digest that. "Do you think she's happy now?"

"I believe she wants to be happy, but..."

"But...?"

"She's afraid." Alice sighs again, deflating like a popped balloon. She seems to age twenty years right before my eyes, and the muscles around my shoulders and neck tighten.

"Do you want me to call a nurse?"

She waves a hand, the wrist bending like a weed. "No need. I'm just tired."

Her physical frailty leaves me speechless. All we did was talk. "Sorry."

She gives me a small smile. "I enjoyed the talk. Nice to have a little variety, much as I love Faith." Her eyelids droop.

"Get some rest, Alice," I say.

She doesn't respond, but she's breathing. I step out of the room, find a nurse and ask him to check up on her.

My legs feel heavy, and I drag myself out of the hospice. The evening breeze is balmy compared to what it's like in Boston. I lean against a pole outside, pulling air into my tight lungs. I have no idea what the hell happened inside Blooming Flowers. I think I said all the right things, told Alice what she needed to hear so she won't worry, but I'm still struggling to process all this, put the pieces in the right order.

There's no dying lover. More to the point, *Alice is still alive.*

Why didn't Faith tell me?

If she'd told me when she first came to my office, I would've given her whatever she needed for her mother.

I run shaky palms over my hot face. Now it's clear why she didn't want a honeymoon. She doesn't want to be away from L.A. in case anything happens to Alice.

But Faith didn't tell me that either. What would she have done if Alice died? Had a secret funeral without me?

I pull out my phone, ready to confront her, then see a text from Elizabeth about Ryder's Thanksgiving party next week.

And just like that, the direction of my anger shifts. If she'd just sent the damned check...

I call her. It takes no more than a couple of seconds before she picks up. She always picks up for family. "Hello, Blake. How are you? Did you get my mes—"

"Two years ago I asked you to help pay for someone's medical care through your charity," I snarl.

"Excuse me?"

"I even sent you a check for it, remember?"

There's a short pause. "Yes."

"Why didn't you do it?"

"I did. Or rather, I had my staff take care of it."

"Your staff fucked up."

"No, they didn't. The check was sent. I followed up on it. To make sure they got it ASAP, we used an overnight courier."

"Then why are they telling me they never got anything?"

A slight pause. "I don't know, but I did everything you asked me to, Blake. There's nothing I can do if people refuse the help. I can't force them to take money." Elizabeth huffs out a breath. "What's this about?"

"I spoke with one of them—the sick one—and she told me there was no offer of help. No check. That's why—" I dig the heel of my palm into my temple. "That's why Faith married... *Fuck.*" I drop my hand and straighten my spine. "I know the couriers you use get signatures upon delivery. I want to know who signed for it."

"I'm not sure that's possible."

"*I need to know.*"

"What's going on, Blake? When you said Faith, you mean your wife?"

"Yes. She was the one who needed help. When it didn't come, she married someone else. I want to know *who the fuck* signed for the letter so I can get to the bottom of this."

"I don't know if we keep records for deliveries that old, Blake."

"Find it for me, Elizabeth. I'm not kidding. I'm going to pull all financial commitments I've made to your foundation if that's what it'll take."

"No need to be so drastic," she says. "I'll dig it up for you, but what does this change?"

What doesn't it change? "A lot." Because it means Faith didn't leave me for money. She thought she had no choice, and I know how she adores her mother.

And it also means I fucked up monumentally by not going after her because I wanted to spare my pride. My teeth are clamped so tight, my jaw aches. I should've taken the biggest club I could find and beaten the shit out of Jack for daring to take her from me.

Love conquers nothing. Hope is for the weak. Pride is all you have left at the end of the day.

My motto in the last two years. It's so fucking pathetic. I let loose a hollow laugh. Love may conquer nothing. And hope may be for the weak. But now I don't even have pride left.

25

Faith

BACK IN TOWN. JOIN ME FOR A NIGHTCAP?

The second I see the text, I say goodbye to Mimi and Andy. I've been crashing at their place; staying at the penthouse while Blake's housekeeper Lenore hovers around makes my skin crawl.

"It's so late. Maybe you can tell him you're spending the night at a friend's," Mimi says.

"I'd love to, but I should go now that Blake's back."

"That woman's still there though," Andy says, ever the pragmatist.

"Yes, but it'll bother me less. I hope." Besides, even if Lenore's presence is unwelcome, there's the warm rapport that Blake and I established before he went to Boston. I don't want to do anything to mess that up.

Sure. Coming soon, I text back.

The drive isn't bad. Traffic's bearable, given how late it is. Still it takes almost an hour. In L.A., getting pretty much anywhere seems to take almost an hour.

The penthouse is dimly lit. I walk inside and spot him in the living room, a bottle of scotch open. It's about two-thirds empty, and his glass is half full.

I smile ruefully. He's probably exhausted from the trip. He hasn't even changed out of his clothes.

"I got here as fast as I could. How was your trip?" I say as I take a seat next to him.

"Went as expected." His voice is marble-like. "Cut it short though." He pours two fingers and pushes the glass my way.

"Are you trying to get me drunk? You don't have to do that to take advantage of me," I tease, hoping to cheer him up a bit. Something probably went wrong in Boston from the dark mood he's in.

His jaw tightens, and he stares at me as though he doesn't recognize me anymore. No, not like that. He's... My inside shrivels as I detect a glimmer of anger and disgust in his gaze.

Finally, he says, "I would never do that because I'll owe you five hundred."

The inflectionless words hit me like a slap in the face. The scotch sloshes in the glass and wets my hand. How can he talk like this after what we had on Sunday?

"Where have you been since I left?"

The question stuns me, then I finally understand the cause of his mood. "Did your spy run to you with my whereabouts to collect her bonus?" I sound so damn bitter, but it's impossible to control the tone of my voice. I was hoping I was wrong about Lenore, but my experience proved correct again. She's just like Jack's maids who watched me and reported to him about exactly how I spent my days—what time I got up, what I wore, what I ate and when, when I left the house and where I went, who came visiting and what mail came for me and what time I went to bed...

"Answer the question."

"I went to see a friend, then stayed with her."

"Does your friend know about Alice, too?"

I blink. My breath stutters. "What...are you talking about?" I say, numb.

"*Don't deny it.*" The tendons in his neck stand starkly. "I *saw* her."

Tremors rack me, and suddenly my belly's full of battery acid. "She doesn't concern you."

"You're wrong." His gaze is cutting. "Did you think sex would convince me to give you more money if one hundred and fifty thousand wasn't enough?"

"Who's turning who into a whore now?"

"People value things they can't put a price on."

"You already had the price," I shoot back. "Five hundred, remember?"

He lunges for me, his hands gripping my arms brutally. "Then why did you give it away for free?"

"It's my way of deciding to move past our history. I can cling to it until I let it turn me into a bitter old bitch or I can let it go. I chose the latter because that's the bigger and better thing to do. If you can't see that, it's on you."

"How the hell am I supposed to move past anything when I don't know what our history *is*, exactly?"

"We met, we fucked, it didn't work out, I married someone else, then became a widow and married you for money."

"You married me for your mother."

I say nothing. A storm of emotions is surging inside me—I recognize rage and resentment. There are others, too complex for me to digest at the moment.

Blake's face is like granite, his eyes so piercing they seem to lance through me. "If you'd just told me the truth when you came to my office, I would've given you whatever you needed."

"Like two years ago?"

"Yes, like two years ago."

"You were a heartless bastard back then." My eyes burn, but thankfully they remain dry. "You held me while I cried about Mom, but didn't lift a finger."

"I sent you money through Elizabeth's foundation."

"There was no money!"

"We'll see about that. I'm having her figure out who took it!"

"Do that if that'll make you happy. If you want a pound of flesh, you can have that, too. I'll even throw in some blood for good measure." Suddenly all the emotions inside me drain away, and I'm left with an acrid coldness seeping through my veins. I shiver. "But never my tears."

He looks at me like I'm a monster. Maybe I am. I can't even feel the tight grip around my arms anymore.

He lets go, then says in a calmer voice, "I'm entitled to the full truth."

"I'm entitled to my privacy."

"I'm going to dig into your past."

"Is that a threat?"

"No. A promise."

"You're welcome to do whatever you want, but you won't find much." He'll probably waste money the way I did when I hired Leslie Kent to look for Jordan Smith. And Leslie came highly recommended.

"You know it's always better if the information comes from you rather than someone else," he says, his eyes narrowed.

"Is that a warning? Because I don't care." I pick up the drink with my shaky hand and down the liquor. It stings my nose and burns my throat. I replace the glass with a thud. "Enjoy your nightcap."

I go to my room and close the door, then lean against it, my head thrown back. I can't decide what hurts more—my pride, or the realization that my desire to move beyond our past was for nothing. A few moments later I hear Blake leave, and I'm alone in a place that's too big and too not mine.

26

Faith

"Wow. That's bad," Mimi says over a latte at a Starbucks near her agent's office. She just got done with a meeting there. Since she wasn't trying to impress anybody, she's in a plain white T-shirt and jeans with a pair of huge sunglasses. I'm dressed similarly except my shirt is pink and glittery, my hair unbound.

"I know, but so what?" I stir the ice in my coffee with the green straw. "I have nothing to hide."

"But Jordan Smith." Mimi wrinkles her nose. "If your husband hears about him and all the bullshit..."

"If he can even find that son of a bitch." I stab the straw so hard it almost folds. "My PI couldn't find him, and I'm sure Blake's people won't either."

Mimi watches me, her gaze soft and sympathetic. "You can stay at my place until things are sorted out."

"No, I can't." Andy won't like it, and I don't blame him. Besides, I don't want to give Blake any reason to back out on our deal. A small part of me prays he won't, but you know what I say about praying? It's what you do during the few seconds your plane's going down in flames.

"But you said your housekeeper is spying on you."

"She has to be." I suck down my iced coffee, letting the caramel flavor wash away the bitter taste in my mouth. "Even if she doesn't send him a daily report, I bet you both kidneys she tells him everything he wants to know about me." I shrug. "It's okay. I told her not to come back until the Monday after Thanksgiving."

"But if she answers to Blake, she might show up again tomorrow."

"Then we'll know for sure who she really works for, won't we?" Sighing, I throw my head back, then stretch my neck left and right. The tension at the base of my skull throbs, giving me a mild migraine. "I just need to figure out a way to talk to Mom so she doesn't get any ideas about Blake and me. I'm not giving her false hopes."

"Would it hurt though? It might lessen her worry."

"But it's lying, and I don't want to do that to her. She deserves the truth, so when she recovers..." I stop. I can't say the rest because I can't accept she's going to be gone soon, but I can't lie out loud either.

Mimi just holds my hand, and we have a moment. "I hate leaving you like this," she finally says, "but I have to go pick up a couple of things from the store before I start my shift today."

I nod. "It's okay. I have to get going anyway."

We leave Starbucks together. A tight hug, then I go right and she goes left. The streets are crowded with busy pedestrians and cars, but I couldn't feel more alone. Only a few weeks ago, I had a home to go to—the studio. It might have been a shitty little place with burglaries and locks that never worked quite right, but at least I was emotionally safe. Blake's penthouse is like some kind of gorgeous prison where the walls close in on me. I can't seem to breathe in there, and having Lenore watching, just like Jack's servants used to, is suffocating.

At the intersection, I stop. A gleaming golden Bentley SUV pulls up in front of me, all the windows tinted black. The back door opens, and a tall wiry Asian man in his late thirties steps out. His face is triangular, like a praying mantis's, and the haircut he sports is conservative and corporate. His suit is a shade lighter than true black, and his shirt matches the color perfectly. He doesn't wear a tie, and his shoes are spotless, freshly polished without a single scuff.

"Ms. Mortimer?" he says, his words slightly clipped.

"Yes?" I tilt my head. The stranger's at least six feet. "Do I know you?"

He gives me a faint smile. "My name is Eugene Cha. Mr. Benedict Mortimer would like to speak with you."

At the mention of my grandfather's name, I stiffen. "We have nothing to say."

"He disagrees."

"Too bad."

"I wish you hadn't said that."

Suddenly he grabs my arm and pushes me into the car. He jumps in and shuts the door. "Go," he instructs the chauffeur.

The car moves smoothly away.

I push my hair out of my face. "This is kidnapping!"

"We aren't taking you anywhere," comes Benedict's deep voice.

"Grandpa?"

I swivel my head in his direction and stare at him. He's dressed in a pale blue shirt, a beige jacket and khakis. His brown loafers are worn, and his eyebrows seem to have grown bushier since New York.

His gaze softens a bit. "Faith. My child." He extends a hand.

Abruptly I realize I called him "grandpa" without thinking. Maybe if my memories of him had stopped the day my father died, I also would've held his hand like a loving granddaughter.

A sharp pang pierces my heart, and I hate myself for that. I glare at him. "I already told you we're through." I dig into my purse and fish out my phone. My thumb taps the screen, unlocking the device. "I'm calling nine-one-one!"

"I'm afraid that won't do." That horrible Asian man

—Eugene Cha—takes the phone out of my hand while simultaneously lowering the window. "I'll toss it onto the road unless you listen to what Mr. Mortimer has to say and give him a fair and calm hearing."

"Are you kidding?" I nearly screech. "You kidnapped me and are now threatening to destroy my phone! You know how much that costs? I still owe payments on that."

"I'm certain money isn't the main concern. Imagine all the data you'll lose."

I gasp. "I'm going to sue you!"

"All Mr. Mortimer would like is five minutes of your time."

"Just listen to yourself. *Mr. Mortimer. Mr. Mortimer*," I mock.

"Mr. Cha, I think that's enough." But Benedict doesn't instruct him to return my phone. Instead my grandfather turns to me. "Faith, just five minutes."

I cross my arms. "Fine. I'll be timing."

A faint smile crosses his face. "I've been trying to talk to you about the matter of your legacy."

I start laughing. "Legacy?"

"Yes. You're an heiress."

I laugh harder, and tears begin streaming down my cheeks. I rest one hand over my belly, drying my face with the other. "God, it's hilarious you want to talk about that when you have nothing I want. Don't you know how rich Blake is?"

"That's a separate issue," Benedict says stiffly.

"No, it's not." The mirth vanishes, abrupt anger

replacing it. "Two years ago, I would've crawled on my hands and knees and licked your boots for a fraction of what you're offering."

"I'm sorry. Jack Villar was an unfit husband." Benedict's voice is full of regret.

That only pisses me off more. "Like you ever cared about that kind of crap? You wanted my mom dead."

He pales. "Faith, I never—"

"You want to force a meeting? Fine. I'll give you one you'll never forget. Jack might've been an unfit husband, but you're an unfit grandfather and father-in-law. An unfit *relative*. An unfit member of what any decent person would want to call a family. You called Mom a mongrel because she's half Asian."

"That was taken out of context."

"Was it?"

"Faith..."

"You know, I could've accepted that explanation. After all, I remember you being nice to me when I was small."

His expression softens, and he looks almost hopeful. And I hate that because I feel awful—worse than awful.

"Why do you think I reached out to you before marrying Jack? But how did you treat me?" I continue without giving him a chance to answer, "You had your people turn me away. I wasn't worth even a second of your time. So cut the 'caring granddad' act. I don't buy it."

He pales, a muscle in his jaw flexing. Maybe he's

finally realized I'm never going to fall at his feet. "Haven't you ever wondered why he approached you—married you—knowing he'd be responsible for a terminally ill mother-in-law?"

I swallow a sudden lump in my throat. I did, but I stopped thinking about that because whatever answer I came up with wasn't good. The more I obsessed about it, the worse it became.

"He knew you were my granddaughter. He wanted to use you to worm his way into my bank account."

"How do you know?"

"He contacted me almost every week after you were engaged, then invited me to the wedding. It was rather too transparent. It's no secret among the people in our circles that the Villars have serious money problems, and they're being investigated for embezzlement at their charity."

My mouth parts. "That can't be."

"Oh, yes it can. We just pretended like we didn't know to spare their pride."

"I *worked* at the charity. It helped the poor..."

"It's easier to steal from the poor and helpless. What are they going to do? They have neither money nor influence." His eyes grow sharp. "You said you worked there, so you may be affected."

"How?"

"They can try to throw you under the bus if that's what it takes to save their hide."

I laugh. "That's pretty original, but no. My work there wasn't anything important."

"Regardless, I'm leaving my legal team at your disposal."

"No, thank you. Are we done?"

Benedict heaves a sigh. "Yes." He gestures.

Cha murmurs something, and the car stops. He climbs out first, then keeps the door open for me. As I step out without a backward glance at Benedict, Cha enters something into my phone.

"What are you doing?" I demand.

"I'm entering Mr. Mortimer's private number, plus the contact information for a partner at the law firm." He taps a few more times.

"I don't need that junk on my phone!"

He closes the door. "You might."

I stick my hand out. "Give me that back."

He does, his face stoic.

"Happy you got to bully a woman in broad daylight in a big city?" I glare at him. "Betcha you got a kick out of it, too, especially since you think you can get away with it."

"Don't be stubborn. Your grandfather loves you. You'll regret it for the rest of your life if you let him go like this."

"How can you work for a guy like him? He considers you beneath him just because you aren't white."

His expression doesn't change. "Mr. Mortimer's always been very fair to me. I don't see why I should abandon him over some hearsay."

My face heats. "Hearsay? How much are you getting paid to say this bullshit?"

"It's not bullshit, and there's no extra pay for my advice." He dips his head once. "Good day, Ms. Mortimer."

As he turns to open the door, I can't help but shoot back, "It's Mrs. Pryce-Reed!"

He inclines the mantis head. "My apologies, Mrs. Pryce-Reed."

He slips inside the car, and the gleaming Bentley pulls out into traffic. My hand tightens around my phone. Even though I demanded he call me Mrs. Pryce-Reed, I'm not sure how long I'm going to be Blake's wife. And the uncertainty is killing me.

27

Blake

I STARE AT NOTHING AND TAP MY RIGHT INDEX finger on the desk. I'm at work because I can't bring myself to go home, even though there's nothing to do in the office.

"Are you all right?"

I scowl as Dane walks through the door. He's neatly dressed in a suit—as he almost always is. I'm sure he puts them on not only to appear cold but austere. "I'm fine."

"No, you're not. I asked you three times, and you just noticed." He shuts the door and takes a seat, placing an ankle over a knee and spreading his elbows on the armrests. "A woman problem."

I say nothing.

"What's the matter? Your wife not behaving like she should?"

"It's her past."

"What about it?"

"It's driving me insane. Somebody's lying to me, but I can't figure out who."

"Hire someone to dig into it."

I've been thinking about that. But that means I have to violate her privacy.

On the other hand, isn't it my life, too?

"I don't know how urgent it is—"

"Very," I say.

"Then hire Elizabeth's guy. She might put you in touch if you give her a mountain of money for her foundation."

"You've done it before?"

"Nope. She turned me down, so I had to use Benjamin."

"Why Elizabeth's guy?"

"Because he used to be Shirley's guy. Elizabeth inherited him when Grandma died."

Both of my eyebrows rise. It was no secret Dane was Shirley's favorite. What did Elizabeth do to get the man? "What's so great about this guy?"

"Fast. Discreet. Willing to go the distance for his employers. Former KGB from what I understand, although I've never had that information confirmed."

"I see." My mind whirls. Whoever the mystery man is, he sounds perfect.

Dane's lips twist. "I was going to ask you to go to lunch with me, but I don't think you're hungry."

"No. Not really." My breakfast hasn't even digested.

"I'll have it with Sophia then."

I snort. "When did I become your first choice?"

"You didn't. I thought maybe you needed someone to straighten you out. You and I will have a drink after work instead."

"What about Sophia?" My cousin never lets his girlfriend spend the evening alone.

"Girls' night out." Dane gets up and leaves.

As soon as he's gone, I call Elizabeth.

"Blake, I don't have the info yet," she says. "I'm still having my people look, but this is one of the busiest times of the year for us. You know that, right?"

"So don't have them do it."

She pauses. "You don't need the information anymore?"

"No. Not that. I need to know more."

"I don't understand."

"I need to know everything there is to know about Faith in the last two years. Since she became engaged to Jack Villar."

"I'm not sure why you're calling me. That's what Benjamin Clark's for."

"Because I want to use your guy."

The silence is so absolute on the other side I can make out people talking in the background. "My guy?" she says finally.

"Dane told me he's fast and effective."

"So is Benjamin."

"You owe me, Elizabeth. If your foundation fucked this up..." I draw in a rough breath. I have to tell her or she'll never agree. "Faith was my first."

She chokes. "That's such a lie! Your first was Meghan Bowden when you were fifteen."

It's my turn to choke because she's right about my virginity. "I don't mean sex. I mean"—I swallow—"love."

"Oh."

"Yeah. *Oh*."

She takes her sweet time. My mouth starts to dry when she finally says, "Okay but you can't tell anybody. He's not some rent-a-PI."

"Fine."

"Also I have another condition."

"What?"

"Promise me you won't do anything rash until you have all the facts. Otherwise you could hurt Faith to the point that you'll lose her forever. If she really was your first love and still matters to you, you'll do that. Else I'm not going to bother."

Angry as I am, that makes sense. "I won't. I promise."

"Okay. He'll either call or text."

"Thanks."

"I hope you find whatever you're looking for, whatever will make you happy, Blake."

~

FAITH

LENORE IS GONE, AS REQUESTED. I'M SOMEWHAT relieved, although the place is still too big and quiet for my taste.

I tap my phone—it's after ten. Blake hasn't come back from work yet. Is he going to spend the night elsewhere? If so, where? With whom?

I close the e-reader app and stare at my contact list. Should I call him? But what will I say? I don't have the right to ask where he is, who he's with or whether he's going to sleep with somebody else. I lost all that when I amended the prenup.

Foolish, foolish pride.

Resting my elbows on my knees, I clasp my hands together and press my forehead against the knuckles. I wanted to show him—and myself—that I didn't care about or need anything from him except money. All that I felt for him two years ago should've been dead and buried, never to reemerge from the grave.

Suddenly I hear the door open. I jerk my head up and stand. A man I've never seen before carries Blake inside. My husband is plastered, totally wasted.

"My God," I gasp, running a hand over his face.

"Stop with the playacting. I'm not easily impressed."

It's a bone-chilling voice, and everything frozen in the world is contained within the man's ice-blue eyes. "Who are you?"

"Dane Pryce. And you would be Faith. Poorly named."

"Excuse me?"

"Where's his room?"

I indicate the way, and Dane carries Blake and dumps him on the bed. Once that's done, he straightens, but I'm not ready to let him leave after that insult. "Finish what you were saying."

The arctic spotlight of his eyes is trained on me again. "I was finished."

"The bit about me being poorly named. Do we know each other?"

"I know you, which is more than enough."

I flush. He must've heard unflattering stories about me from Blake. "What happened to him?"

"He drank too much. Don't worry. It's not too bad, compared to the time when he found out you'd left him for money." He shifts. His mouth smiles, but his eyes stay cold. "All you had to do was wait one more month."

"I didn't have an extra month."

"You do to have billions at your disposal. He would've been too stupid to get you to sign an ironclad prenup. All that money would've been yours."

"You don't know anything. It wasn't like that."

He snorts. "Is this how whores live with themselves? 'It wasn't like that.'"

Outrage burns, but it's a waste of time to confront him. The man's a glacier. Antarctica in midwinter would be warmer. "You know nothing about me."

"I know plenty. You're lucky I didn't decide to break you for what you did to him back then."

"He could've come for me," I say bitterly.

"He wanted to, but I dissuaded him. You simply do not run after a woman who only sees you as a blank check."

"Guess he took your advice, because contrary to what you think his love wasn't deep or true enough."

"You don't get to judge Blake." Dane's voice is a sickle, slicing through everything in its path. "You didn't confront him when you found out who he was, did you?"

My eyes flare. So he heard that too. "I didn't think he cared. And I was done begging for crumbs."

"Yet you ended up with crumbs in the end. Have a great night, Faith." He gives me a wintry look. "Hurt Blake again, and I will personally destroy everything you hold dear."

He stalks out, shutting the door behind him. I stand shaking. *How dare he?*

I run an unsteady hand along my cheek, then march toward Blake's room. I need something to keep me occupied so I don't let the ugly encounter with that horrible man mess with my head.

I undress Blake, starting with his shoes. He is unbelievably heavy, his solid body a total deadweight. When I'm finally done, I pull a sheet over him.

"Y'know whass really sad?" he says.

"No. Do you want something to drink?"

"Scotch."

"Sorry. Only water's on offer."

"Cruel woman." He drags an arm over his eyes. "Shoulda jus' gone wi' the flow. Sex, a lil pillow talk... then *poof*—divorce."

"Yeah, you should've." I push some hair off his forehead, unable to help myself. "Why didn't you?"

"Jus' couldn'." He drops the arm and turns his head, his eyes bleary and sad.

My heart squeezes, and melancholy spreads through me. It's like his sadness has a special frequency that I resonate with.

The next few days crawl. Blake and I don't talk about what happened after Dane dropped him off, and he stays away, spending all his time in the office. Lenore, surprisingly, follows my instructions and doesn't come back.

I try to maintain my routine—mainly visiting Mom. She's deteriorating rapidly. It is so scary that I don't tell her the truth about Blake, lest it stress her out. She can believe whatever she wants.

But the rest of my days are painfully empty. I see Mimi when I can, but she's busy with work and her career. I have no purpose, no job, nothing. My life has come down to one thing: watching my mother die and agonizing over it.

Fed up, I boot my laptop. The folder labeled CHARITY on the desktop stares back at me. The work

I did there was sort of routine and basic, but it was a job and it made me feel like I was making a difference.

I can do it again. I just need to get an education, because that's what everyone wants to see on a résumé.

Pulling up Google, I look up community college enrollment information. It's about time I do something proactive.

28

Blake

IT'S THE WEDNESDAY AFTERNOON BEFORE Thanksgiving, and I'm in the office. Nobody's here but me.

The strained silence and awkwardness at home is killing me, and I'd rather avoid that. Faith left early this morning, too—presumably to see her friends although I bet she went to Blooming Flowers to see Alice. The app on my phone tells me she visits every day.

If I'm going to be in the office, I should at least get some work done, but I can't focus. It's been days since I told Elizabeth's guy what I needed. Surely he should have something for me by now. Or has Dane overestimated the man's ability?

No. My cousin's more likely to cut somebody down than to build them up.

A text arrives, and I glance at it. *Check your email.*

I rush to my laptop and sync. A new message pops up with the subject, WHAT YOU ASKED FOR.

I swallow, my mouth suddenly dry. I double-click. There's nothing in the main message, just a PDF attachment. I open it.

Whoever Elizabeth's guy is, the man is scarily thorough. It has two sections. The first one is about the check delivery. It was given to a man whose signature reads *James Brown*. There's a picture of the actual signature. Another signature sits next to it—Jack Villar's. I study both carefully and suck in a breath. The way the J's, A's and R's loop and slash is exactly the same, and it's obvious Jack himself intercepted it. And that explains how he found out about Faith's predicament and swooped in to play Knight in Shining Armor.

Anger courses through me. That fucking weasel. When I ran into him a few times in Vegas, I assumed he was foolishly trying to rebuild his family fortune through gambling. After all, he wasn't a bad poker player. But this... I never suspected. He must've done his homework, and much better than I would have given him credit for.

The second section contains information about Faith's marriage—her daily routines, any deviations from them, where she went, what she did, who she saw. There are names and dates and places. It's so detailed I wonder if Elizabeth's man has been following her for the last two years, writing all this down while he watched her through binoculars from a nondescript sedan.

Two months into her marriage, she miscarried. Jack's baby. I feel for her loss, but am also intensely envious Jack had his child growing inside her. That was my dream at one point.

A short hand-written note catches my attention. *Jack's sterile. So whose baby?*

What the hell? Did she have an affair? Simone practically said as much.

There's more. She met several times with this Jordan Smith, and there's a copy of a sworn affidavit from the man saying he had an affair with Faith while she was married to Jack.

I text Elizabeth's investigator. *I need to talk to you. I have a couple of follow-up questions.*

Approximately three minutes later, my phone rings. Unknown number. "Hello?"

"Blake Pryce-Reed." The man's voice is gravelly and accented. Russian. But otherwise his English is excellent. "Ask your questions."

"Did Faith have an affair with Jordan Smith?"

"Most likely not, but difficult to say for certain."

"Your report says there's a sworn affidavit."

"Yes, but Jordan Smith isn't his real name—Neal Simms is—and he's in a particular kind of business."

"Like what?"

"He seduces married women whose husbands wish to divorce without paying alimony. If he can get them to sleep with him, he makes sure there are photos that can be used against the women. He's quite popular among a certain set. Regardless, in Faith Mortimer's case, the photos were staged to look like they were intimate, but they weren't overly incriminating. If I must guess, she never liked him enough to do more than have coffee with him from time to time...although with lonely wives, you never know."

"Jesus. Jack was trying to divorce Faith?"

"He wanted to get closer to Benedict Mortimer through marriage, so no."

The back of my head hits the cushioned headrest on my seat. So. *That* was his motive... I used to wonder if he loved her more than me somehow and convinced her he'd be the one to take care of her better than I could.

"I suspect his family didn't want to give her anything," the man says. "It's no secret they're drowning."

I grunt. Now that I've pulled the plug, they *will* drown.

"Anything else?" he says.

"Whose baby is it?"

"Jordan Smith told me there was a lover before she married Jack Villar, but he didn't name names."

I suck in a breath.

The man continues as though he can sense I need to hear more, but his voice has the flat stoicism of a person reciting a chemistry textbook. "The miscarriage was spontaneous. No medical reason given. She can have other children if she wishes. Sometimes, as they say, shit happens."

Jesus. I run a hand down my face. Sometimes shit does happen, but it isn't just "shit" if it's happening to *you*.

"Let me tell you something else. Don't bother Elizabeth with stuff like this again. My loyalty is to her. I won't have anybody coerce her into farming me out like some cheap online freelancer." He hangs up.

I barely register his comment. My mind is focused on the miscarriage. *A lover before she married Jack Villar.*

I take risks, but I don't bet on things I know I won't win. That's how I made my fortune after all. But the baby being mine...

I'd wager my own beating heart.

Why didn't she come to me when she found out? Surely she would've known before she married Jack that she was pregnant with my child.

I stagger to my feet and pick up my phone. My fingers move on autopilot, and I hear the ring.

"Blake?" comes Faith's voice.

"Where are you?" I rasp.

She hesitates. "I'm with Mom."

"I'm going there right now."

"That's not a good idea."

"I don't give a shit."

"What's wrong?"

"Everything," I snarl.

"I'll see you at the penthouse then."

"Fine. Get over there *right now*." The privacy of our home is better for what I need to say. I don't trust myself to be civil or quiet. The emotions storming inside me...

They expand like a hurricane gaining volume and power. My chest feels too small. I don't remember getting behind the wheel of my Aston Martin. My heart beats like I've had a bucket of pure caffeine, and my hands shake, palms sweaty.

Calm the fuck down or you're going to get yourself killed.

Wouldn't that be a fucking pointless end, à la some messed up literary novel about the futility of life, how nothing matters, nothing means anything?

A helpless laughter chokes me, and I put a fist against my mouth. The whole revelation from Elizabeth's man is no laughing matter, but I can't stop because it's either that or break down, and I'm not ready for the latter just yet. I need to sort out what the hell I'm feeling and how I plan on dealing with Faith.

With the past she blithely said she's moved beyond.

29

Blake

BY THE TIME I MAKE IT TO THE PENTHOUSE, Faith's already there. Her dark hair is pulled back, and she's been pacing. The moment she sees me, she stops and rubs her palms down her jeans. There are slightly damp spots on her shirt, and I know she's been sweating.

The sight of her distress only inflames my fucked-up whirlwind of emotions. She must know why I wanted to meet. I stare at her, not even certain where I should start. My temples throb.

"So. What did you want to talk about?" she asks, her voice low and hoarse.

"Jordan Smith said you were pregnant and lost the baby."

Her jaw trembles, and she clenches it while

breathing hard through the nose. After a moment, she says, "How did you find him?"

"Why? Want to reconnect with your lover?" The question slips out. I'm being unfair—I know that—but I'm too angry, too much in pain to care.

"He's nobody to me."

"Not according to what he said."

"Yeah, well... He's the type who'd say anything for a buck."

"And you wouldn't?"

"Blake, what do you want me to say?"

"I want you to tell me why you didn't come to me when you found out!"

"For what? I was engaged to Jack, and he'd paid for Mom's initial treatment already."

I fling an arm in the air. "So you were going to pass *my* child off as his?"

"No. I couldn't do that to him. I told him, and he said it was okay. He'd raise the baby as his own."

"*My baby!*" I pound my chest. "That was my baby, not his! He couldn't father one himself, so he was going to steal mine!"

"He wasn't stealing anything. Back then you didn't want me. The check you claim you sent—"

"I *did* send the damn check. Your fucking dead husband stole it!"

"What?"

"He signed for it using a fake name. That must have been how he knew your mother needed medical treatment and decided to come riding in to save the day."

She blinks once, but other than that small motion, she's absolutely still, her face pale.

"I never had a chance, did I? You needed whatever excuse to be with a man who didn't love you. Jack only wanted to use you to get to your grandfather." I clench my hands, try to control my breathing so I don't sound like a crazed bull in a ring. "All along you thought you were using him for money, but he was using you...for money! Isn't that fucking ironic?"

"He..." She doesn't continue. She merely stares at me as though I'm some sort of escaped lunatic.

Maybe I am. I've never felt intense emotion like this, and I'm not capable of coping with it. It sears through me like a wave of lava, turning my insides into ashes layer by layer.

"You should've come to me," I say bitterly. "You should've come to me if only to slap me and spit in my face."

And a small part of me wishes she'd do that now. Maybe then we could break this unbearable tension and ice.

But she doesn't. And I can't stay anymore.

I spin around and stalk out.

Back in my car, I realize I have nowhere to go. Lucas is staying at the multilevel penthouse, and Dane's out of the question. I'm not fit to be company for anyone.

I drive until I find a hotel. It looks expensive

enough. I toss my fob to the valet and walk up to the front desk and get a room. A suite because that's what they have left, and I don't give a shit.

Then I shut myself in the room and order five bottles of whiskey...to start.

~

BLAKE

WHEN I'M FINALLY SOBER ENOUGH TO PERCEIVE what's going on around me with any sort of clarity— clarity being a loose term—I'm in my bedroom at the loft penthouse. How the hell did I get here?

I spot more than a few bottles of scotch, whiskey and vodka. Looks like I went through my liquor cabinet with the thoroughness of an alcoholic on a binge.

Cringing, I notice my wrinkled shirt and jeans. They're ripe as well; I must have been wearing them for days...although I have no idea when I changed into them from my suit.

"Finally, you're awake," Lucas says as he walks into my room with a bottle of water. He's dressed in a tux. Why, I have no idea.

"How did I end up here?" I rasp through a parched throat. Thankfully he offers me the water and I chug half the bottle. He hands me four aspirins, and I down them as well. "Did you bring me from the hotel?"

He gives me a look. "You don't remember?"

"No." Did something really bad happen? I should probably have Cecilia call my lawyer to sue whoever screwed me over while I was out of it.

"You don't remember showing up at Ryder's Thanksgiving party drunk? Giving me some kind of... er...relationship advice the next day? I even asked if you'd found out you were terminally ill."

I try, but... "No."

He shakes his head. "Man."

My skull is pounding. The aspirin better kick in fast. "Did I do anything stupid?"

Lucas rocks his weight onto the balls of his feet. "Define 'stupid.'"

"Ah, geez."

He sighs. "You didn't do anything too bad, considering. You must've been worse off than I thought. I'm surprised you were that functional."

"The Pryce metabolism." My mother's side of the family drinks alcohol like it's the fountain of youth. "Why are you dressed like that?"

"I just got married."

"When?"

"Today."

"How come I wasn't invited?" I ask, then wince. What an idiotic question. Who the hell would invite a passed-out drunk to a wedding? "Never mind. Who's the bride?"

Lucas beams. His smile is so bright, my eyes ache. "Ava."

"So you went back to her."

"Actually, she came to me."

"Must be nice." Bet she didn't go to him for money.

"We decided to fight for each other. That's all."

My petty jealousy evaporates. What the hell is wrong with me? Lucas deserves to be happy. "Hope it works out."

"It will."

I finish the water. "So why are you here instead of on your honeymoon?" Ava Huss—or Reed, as she's probably called now—doesn't have a dying relative she has to be close to.

"An email from *our father*."

"What email?"

"Didn't you get it? Check your phone. It was sent to everyone."

Everyone as in all five of us with the rotten luck to be born to that cock-sucking bastard. I look around and locate my phone on my nightstand, plugged into a charger. At least I did that right.

As I unlock it, I notice the date. Monday. *Jesus.* Then I see a notification for a few missed calls, including one from Faith on Saturday. She also sent me a text, but I can't deal with her at the moment. Every inch of my insides feels like it's been scraped with a rake, especially my heart. Maybe she had enough time to come to terms, but I need more time to digest, get sober.

The email from Julian is curt and to the point.

Subject: Meeting

Come to my house at 10:00 a.m. on Tuesday. If any of you fail to show, I'm burning every painting your grandfather ever created.

–J

I read it, then look at Lucas. "Is this legit?"

He nods. "Yeah. What do you think it's about?"

"Don't know and don't care. I'm going, if only to tell him to go fuck himself with a cactus."

Lucas chokes.

I stand, then stop as the floor underneath my feet shifts...or at least it feels that way. I've got to stop drinking so much. I'm going to need all cylinders firing if I want to deal with our despicable father. "I'm flying out tonight. You want to come with?"

He eyes me. "Sure..."

"Don't worry. I'm not going to drink anymore. You won't have to babysit me."

"Good. Go shower up and we can get going."

BLAKE

I ALMOST FEEL HUMAN AS WE CLIMB INTO THE SKY.

A gallon of water and sports drink helped. Only then do I allow myself to have some coffee. The cabin attendant is more than happy to accommodate me.

The flight brings Faith to mind—how much she hates flying but did it anyway to fulfill the terms of our contract. She went the distance for her mother. I've seen her love and devotion, and I'm envious. And I hate feeling that way because it makes me a petty bastard. Who the fuck gets jealous of the relationship between a dying woman and her daughter? Yet here I am.

My phone rings mid-flight. Faith again. I ignore it.

"Who's that?" Lucas says.

"My wife."

He chokes on his wine, then starts coughing. "You got married?"

"Yes. A few weeks ago."

"You tell anyone?"

"Elizabeth knew."

"Isn't there anything she doesn't know?"

"It's nobody's fault you're a hermit." As soon as I say it, I shake my head. "Sorry. Didn't mean that."

"Yes, you did...but you're right. I've been an idiot. That's going to change though."

"Good," I say slowly. "*You*'ve changed." The last time I saw Lucas, he was sullen, resentful and depressed.

"I'm happy."

"I'm glad. You deserve it."

"So do you." He tilts his head at my phone. "Call her back. Could be important."

"Not yet."

"Are you trying to make her sweat?"

I snort. Like she's capable of that.

"Just what did she do to put you through a wringer like this?"

"She..." I take a deep breath, then tell Lucas in the most succinct way possible, starting with two years ago.

He finally nods. "So she's the reason you were so out of sorts with Ava."

"Yes." Although "out of sorts" doesn't do justice to my behavior...not that I remember precisely what I told her. I was basically a nasty fuck to everyone during that time. But what I'm feeling now is worse. It's a kaleidoscope of anger, bitterness, grief and resentment. But underneath all those ugly emotions is the current of love I still feel for Faith—something that might've been reduced to a trickle at some point, but never quite stopped.

"I know you're still upset, but you've got to figure out who you're most angry with and let it go."

I cock an eyebrow. "Who do you think?"

Lucas doesn't fall for it. "Are you angry at yourself because you weren't there for her? Or are you angry at her because she didn't tell you?"

"What if I told you I'm angry at her late husband?"

"Bullshit. If you were, you wouldn't be ignoring her calls. Look, if you don't decide and don't let it go, this is going to eat at you until you end up losing everything that matters. It did with me, and I couldn't accept the love and happiness that was mine for the taking."

I look away, muttering under my breath. It's easy to talk about moving on and letting it go, but *doing* it is...

I'm afraid it's beyond me at the moment, because I don't have an answer to his question. I don't know who I'm most furious with. All I know is there's an ocean of rage inside that's threatening to engulf me.

30

Blake

Darkening the doorstep of my father's obnoxiously ostentatious mansion in McLean, Virginia, is the last thing I want to do, but I'm not going to let my siblings down. I'm actually one hundred percent sober and sharp after two cups of coffee and zero alcohol since getting on the plane in California.

Jarvis, the butler, opens the door, his back comically stiff, like somebody's stuck a couple of oars up his ass. Ryder finds him amusing, but I find him ridiculous with his insistence on "no last name" and that he will one day make it big in Hollywood. Apparently the idiot failed basic geography because Virginia isn't anywhere near California.

"If you would follow me, Mawsters Blake and

Lucas," Jarvis intones in a faux British accent—a brand-new pretension since our last visit.

I almost gag. Lucas just wrinkles his nose.

We walk up the winding staircase. The interior is a fucking mess—an expensive mess, but still a mess. One thing money can't buy is taste.

Father's study is as flatulently pretentious as the rest of the house. Bookcases are filled end to end with leather-bound classics and poetry collections. Dad hasn't read any of them—he doesn't read fiction—and I'd bet my bottom dollar that neither has Wife Number Six. Any word with more than five letters is beyond her, unless it happens to be a pricey designer brand. Then all of a sudden she's multilingual.

Ryder's sprawled in a seat, texting. Probably writing something sappy to his pregnant wife Paige. Even in a ripped shirt and jeans, he looks disgustingly well put-together. He's the guy who ruined the hand-some curve in Hollywood.

Elliot, Lucas's twin, is sitting on a couch nursing a scotch. Elizabeth's seated next to him, talking in a soft voice. She's dressed conservatively in a muted pink dress and nude pumps, her hair twisted into one of those fancy things women like to do.

"Finally, you're here. Thought you'd never come," Elliot says.

"Of course we're here. I'm not letting you guys down," Lucas says.

I study him. It's amazing how different he's become. Less than six months ago, he said he wasn't going to marry—because he couldn't—and he didn't care if he was letting us down or not.

"Are you feeling better?" Elizabeth asks me.

"Yes. Much."

"Good." She pauses, then opens her mouth to—

Just that moment, the door opens and Father walks in, sans Number Six. Did he get rid of her already?

Julian Reed is petty, but he's also purposeful. His stride is long and his arms pump with vigor. The interior lights glint on his golden hair, and he stops right at his desk and spins around.

"You think you've won?" he says in a deathly quiet voice.

I tilt my head. I've never heard him speak like this before.

"What did we win?" Ryder asks.

"The portraits."

My gaze slides to Elizabeth. Did she get married? My brothers look surprised as well. But there's no way a marriage as high profile as hers would go unnoticed. Unlike some of us, she's always in the spotlight for her charity work and advocacy.

"Are you trying to weasel your way out of the deal?" Elliot demands.

"No," Father grinds out. "I'm giving you your damned portraits early. But mark my words. Blackmail only works once. Try it again, and I'll burn down every piece of your grandfather's art just to make *my* point."

A small frown creases the spot between Elizabeth's eyebrows, then vanishes quickly. Her gaze is cool and thoughtful as she regards our father, and something about her demeanor jars me.

If someone's blackmailing our father, it would have to be one of us. But I don't know who could've found something bad enough that he would cave. If there were anything, I would've found it a couple of years ago when I decided to dig into his background.

But Elizabeth's Russian... He seems capable of finding anything he sets his mind to. Dane said he used to work for Shirley, and she only hired people who could get her what she wanted, by whatever means necessary. And what did the Russian say about Jordan Smith—real name, Neal Simms? He's the guy husbands hire to divorce their wives without paying alimony... Did Dad use him to get rid of his exes, leaving them penniless, and the Russian found that out while researching Faith's past?

"Jarvis will show you where the portraits are. You will take them before leaving this house in the next hour, or I'm tossing them all into the fireplace," Julian snarls the last word.

"Fine," I say.

"You may now thank me," he says between clenched teeth.

"Why the hell would we do that? You are only doing this because you have no choice, not because you actually want to be nice." I shrug. "I hope you understand I want to check my portrait before leaving, to make sure."

He turns beet red. "You son of a bitch."

"Guess that makes you a bitch." I smile thinly. "*Dad.*"

Elizabeth chokes.

Dad's hands clench, knuckles white. His entire arm vibrates with anger.

Jarvis walks in. "If everyone is ready to view the portraits..."

"Let's go," Elizabeth says hurriedly, jumping to her feet and leaving first.

I follow quickly, keeping up with her short, fast strides. "Was it you?" I whisper under my breath as we walk down the long, carpeted corridor.

"Was what me?" she asks.

"The blackmail."

She gives me a sidelong look and laughs. "Don't be ridiculous, Blake. I would never. It's not my style, you know that. My method would be to make him donate so much money to my causes that he has nothing left to lavish on himself."

"But—"

"Look, we're about to get what we want. Let's not quibble over how we're getting it."

"Sure. Still, it's convenient how you didn't have to marry."

She raises her eyebrows. "Did you want me to?"

"Hell no. You're better off feeding orphans than chasing after some guy."

She smiles. "Agreed."

Jarvis opens double doors at the end of the hall. It's dark inside, and he flips switches. Light floods the room. There are numerous framed canvases on the walls, but only five are covered with curtains. What a surprise.

"It's a temperature- and humidity-controlled environment," Jarvis says. "I suggested to the new Mrs. Reed that she should install such features for storing your grandfather's works. Fortunately, she agreed."

"Nicely done, Jarvis," Ryder says.

The man has difficulty maintaining a properly stoic demeanor. "My pleasure, sir. It is my job as butler to advise, ensure everything is properly taken care of."

"I want to see them," I say. Grandfather painted them when we turned eighteen, highlighting our potential and all that we were at that time. I want to see if they're as grand as I remember.

"Certainly." He starts to push the curtains out of the way, one work at a time.

The first one he unveils is Elliot. There's sharp intelligence in his dark gaze, a wicked little curl to his mouth that says he knows something you don't. He could've looked like a smug punk, but there is a general warm glow to him that softens the effect to one of warmth and mischief.

"Damn," Elliot whispers.

The second one uncovered is Ryder. He literally glows, every feature unnaturally perfect. One of his hands is open, palm tilted forward. On it are small dates and hard candies. His smile is inviting as though to say, "Come share with me." But then that's him—

always generous, even when psychotic women want a piece of him.

"Perfect," Ryder murmurs.

The third is Lucas. He has no shield, no armor and no hardness in his expression, just pure sweetness. There's such candid vulnerability to his entire demeanor—from the wide dark eyes to the almost shy smile—that it hurts to see the portrait. But that is not a weakness, I realize, because it makes you want to open up to him and fight for his cause by his side.

Lucas sighs softly.

The fourth one revealed is Elizabeth. I blink. Her smile is so soft, like an angel's, her cheeks lightly flushed, but her eyes... They're as sad as a trapped bird's that wants to soar free. If the piece had ended with that, she would've looked merely tragic, but there's more—the firm, steely line of her jaw. It's so subtle, but it alters her bearing from a weak victim to something much more complex.

My gaze finds hers, and she blinks rapidly, then smiles. Somehow she looks wistful.

"The last of the series," Jarvis announces, jerking my attention back.

My mouth dries, and I feel my heart beating in my chest. He finally pulls the curtain off mine.

I look so different in the portrait. Younger, of course, and maybe a little more innocent than I am now. Empathy glimmers in my eyes, but my mouth is set in a flat, unsmiling line as though I don't want anybody to know what I'm really thinking and feeling.

The line of my chin is stubborn, unforgivingly so. And I finally understand what Grandpa saw in me.

I never wanted to wear my heart on my sleeve, let people know how I felt about anything deep inside. Maybe I was afraid people would reject me, even laugh, finding me weak and pathetic. After all, making yourself too vulnerable is a terrible lapse in judgment.

Except... It didn't really work out the way I hoped.

I never told Faith I loved her back in Vegas. Even though I railed that she should've waited a month—that she should've contacted me when she found out she was pregnant—why should she have done that? What reason did I give her?

With that clarity, I finally have the answer to Lucas's question. Although I can't be sure I could've done anything to prevent her miscarriage, I should've been there to support and care for her. The disappointment, anger and bitterness are about me—my failures —not her.

"Pack that up," I order Jarvis, then turn away. I need to call Faith. Tell her I'm sorry. Tell her I screwed up.

But when I call, she doesn't pick up. I try again, but again I'm punted to her voicemail. I start to hit the green button one more time, then I remember her text. Perhaps I should start with that, so she knows the conversation won't be an ugly one.

I see her text.

My mom passed away.

Spots swim in my vision, and I expel a rough breath. I stagger, almost falling to my knees.

She tried to reach me on Saturday afternoon at 2:34 p.m. Today is Tuesday. She tried to call me again today on the plane. For four days she's been without me. My cold thought when I found out about Alice rings in my head—whether Faith would have a secret funeral for her mother without me by her side.

But Faith ended up having one anyway. Not because she kept me out of the loop, but because I wasn't there for her. I was busy drowning myself in alcohol.

I call her again, but she doesn't answer. My fingers shaky, I start texting.

I just saw your message. I'm sorry.

Faith, can you forgive me?

Can you call me when you get this? Please?

I had to go to Virginia, but I'm flying home right now. I'll see you in six hours or less.

I get Cecilia on the phone and I'm in the air as soon as she can arrange it. I bite my knuckles. For every second Faith doesn't answer, I feel like a drop of blood is drying in my veins.

I'm on a plane now. I'll be there soon, I text.

Nothing. Not that I blame her.

What a fucking moron I am. I deserve to be beaten. Or worse. Far, far worse.

31

Faith

I sit on the cold living room floor, a pretty spring-green urn in my lap. The shade was Mom's favorite, and I wanted it for her.

I'm struggling to accept that she's gone. The only consolation is that I got to say goodbye before she drew her last breath.

"So sorry...about you and Benedict," she whispered as I crouched by her bedside.

"No, Mom. Don't waste your energy on that man."

"My fault..." A tear slipped from a corner of her hazy eyes. "Love you."

I gripped her hand in mine. "I love you too. And we can still beat this. Just one more time..."

But we didn't.

Blake's penthouse is dark, with the curtains drawn.

I'm only here because he isn't. I can't face the world—or anybody—right now. I'm a raw mess.

My mother's gone. I can barely feel anything. My eyes are so swollen, it's amazing that I can still see.

My phone beeps again, but I ignore it since it's probably Benedict. Again. The only person I want to hear from is Blake, even though he walked out on me when he found out about our baby. But it's Benedict who keeps calling. I don't know how he found out, but I do *not* want to talk to that man...hear his upbeat voice... see his smug expression. He must be thrilled now that the "mongrel" is gone.

If he thinks he can waltz in and fill the vast emptiness Mom's death has left in my life, he's wrong. I'd rather drink bleach.

The penthouse seems so cold. Or maybe it's me. Blake hasn't tried to get in touch, not even once. I don't believe he didn't see my text on Saturday. I even called earlier today, hoping for... I don't even know what I was hoping for. But when he didn't pick up, I knew...and a part of me shriveled.

It's crazy that his desertion hurts this much. It isn't like we're a real couple. We did it for calculated mutual benefit, nothing more. There's no reason for us to stay married. Or at least, I don't have one. He still has time. We can quietly get divorced and he can find some other woman to marry before the deadline. I'll find a way to pay him back the money he gave me. That should be a satisfactory outcome for him.

The doorbell to the penthouse rings. I sigh, but I

don't make a move to answer it. The housekeeper has the keys, although I told her not to come back in no uncertain terms. I can't deal with a stranger hovering over me.

Blake, of course, would just walk right in.

It rings again. Then suddenly I hear pounding. "I know you're in there, Mrs. Pryce-Reed!"

I flinch. That voice is familiar. I put down the urn and go to the door for a peek. It's Eugene Cha in an austere black suit and a black dress shirt, no tie. I don't see Benedict with him.

"Go away," I say.

"Open the door *please.*"

"So you can manhandle me? No, thank you."

"I won't. I promise."

"Your promise means nothing to me."

"Don't be stubborn, Mrs. Pryce-Reed. I'm here only to talk to you."

"Then talk."

"Do you want everyone around to be privy to your business? This concerns your mother."

"Neither you nor your boss are fit to speak about her. Tell him to leave me alone."

"I'm afraid I can't do that. You have no one."

I grit my teeth. "I have plenty of people who care about me. I don't need Benedict."

"Very well. You leave me no choice but to do this the uncomfortable way."

What is he going to do now? I take another peek.

He sits on the floor and opens a briefcase I didn't

notice. "Date—May tenth, nineteen ninety-six. Subject —Your family. Dear Benedict, you cannot withhold money like this. Your son's working like a dog to support us, and I cannot believe you're disowning him for marrying me. I'm not going to lie and say I didn't marry for money. You're right; I like money, and I would've never married a poor man. But you aren't just hurting me but your own flesh and blood as well. Think about that. Don't try to blackmail me with this email. You'll regret it, and I'll deny everything. Charles loves me.

"Date—October twenty-fifth, nineteen ninety-eight. Subject—Funeral. Don't bother to come, you bastard. Your son's been cremated. We had no money. But you know what? Even if you had given me money for his funeral, I would've cremated him as soon as possible so you couldn't say goodbye. You know we miraculously recovered the body from the wreckage? And it actually looked recognizable. But I don't care. I hope you regret every penny you've hoarded because that's the only joy you'll get out of life. Faith is mine, and I allowed you near her only for Charles's sake. Now you'll never spend another second with her again. I'll make sure she won't remember you.

"Date—December twenty-seventh, nineteen ninety-nine. Subject—Christmas. Stop sending gifts to Faith. She'll never receive them, and she'll never be grateful for them. She knows why her dad died— because of you. You were too cheap to do the right thing and give us money like I asked. That's why he had to work so hard, and that's why he died. If you think you can bribe your way into her life, forget it. I'm all she has, and she loves *me*. I'm going to make sure she knows what a horrible man you are, starting with how you're a racist pig who hates me because I'm 'yellow'. I'm sure telling her you called me a mongrel is going to go over well." Cha stops for a second. "Just so you know, I've never, ever seen Mr. Mortimer use derogatory racial epithets in my twenty-six years of employment."

Bastard. "Like I'd believe that bullshit! You can't be more than thirty-five."

"Thank you, but I'm actually forty-seven." He continues reading. "Date—December twenty-ninth, nineteen ninety-nine. Subject—Re: Christmas. Don't you dare ask me why I'm doing this. I am absolutely entitled to. She sometimes asks me about you, which breaks my heart because I still haven't been able to make her see how hateful you are. I love my daughter. I'm not going to lose her to you, and I'm sure you don't want a penny of your money going to me. If you give her anything, she'll give it to me, so think about that and choke on it."

I can't stand to listen to any more of this. *How dare he!*

I yank the door open. "You bastard! Stop it!"

"Why?" He looks at me, his expression stoic. "It's all true. I have printouts of all the emails she sent your grandfather."

"I don't believe you."

"You think I'm making this up?"

"Why not? You'll do anything to please Benedict."

"I would never compromise my ethics. For him, or anyone else." Cha's black gaze is steady and open, but I know he's lying. He has to be.

"Mom was a great woman. A fantastic mother. The best any girl could have. She was always there for me, always kind and ready with advice! *Always!*"

"You're a very foolish young woman. You confuse her being a friend to you with her being a mother. She didn't take care of you. You took care of her."

I laugh. "Did I? She paid the bills. Bought the groceries."

The smile he gives me is full of pity. "Did she? Tell me, did you ever see her work?"

I stop. I don't remember her holding a job. But... "What does it matter? She never failed to provide for me. We always had enough to live on."

"Because of your grandfather."

The veins in my forehead are throbbing. Cha is lying, I know, but I can't find the words to dispute what he's saying because he's too clever, too good of a manipulator. The printouts he has... They have to be fake. Every single one of them.

Mom. Loved. Me.

"Your grandfather paid the premium on your father's life insurance policy when your parents couldn't afford it anymore after you were born. Your mother lived off that without having to work...as was her grand ambition in life. Then you started working in retail when you were old enough. Alice was very good at maintaining a loving maternal façade, and you never wanted to face the truth because you were afraid of losing the only parent you had left."

I clench my hands, stiffening my arms straight. Every atom in my body seems to vibrate. "*Stop lying!*"

"I have proof of the payments," he informs me calmly.

"Which you fabricated!" But even as I say that, I know that isn't true. Mom's final words... She was sorry about me and Benedict...blamed herself. But...I can't believe she lied to me about what kind of a man my grandfather was all this time. It's too awful. "Why are you doing this? Why do you try to defame a dead woman?"

"Because you've done enough to hurt Mr. Mortimer."

"He hurt me first. He wouldn't help Mom."

"He didn't want to help a woman who drove a wedge between him and his granddaughter. He didn't think she was truly ill. It seemed to be just another ploy to see if she could get some money out of him." Cha pauses and sighs softly. "I'm not sure if you're aware, but your mother was out of money by the time she was diagnosed with the tumor. It wasn't entirely...unfeasible for her to fake an illness to get him to open his wallet."

I put a fist over my mouth. What little lunch I had earlier churns in my belly.

He reaches into his inside pocket and pulls out a handkerchief. "Here."

I stare at the plain white cotton, then blink. I didn't know I was crying. "Did Benedict send you?"

"No. And if he finds out I'm here, he'll probably terminate me." Cha starts wiping away at my cheeks, his touch surprisingly gentle.

Awkwardly, I take the handkerchief and dab at my eyes. "Then why are you doing this?"

"Because she's dead," he says bluntly. "Your parents are gone. You only have a grandfather left, and he only has his granddaughter. It's been that way for a long time for him, since your father died. I want to do whatever I can to correct your misconceptions." He takes a breath. "You must understand, Mr. Mortimer abhors people coming after him for money. Given his circumstances, it's understandable."

I shake my head, but I feel awful, like he's taken a hammer and tenderized my already bruised heart.

"You have nothing here," Cha says. "Go to Dallas, be with your grandfather. He loves you. Don't deprive yourself and him of whatever few months you have left. He's an old man, Mrs. Pryce-Reed. He won't live that long. And you are certainly familiar with mortality."

"I want to talk to him," I say. "Now."

Wordlessly, he takes out his phone and dials. Then he hands it to me.

"Mr. Cha?" Benedict's voice is cordial. "I thought you had the day off."

"Benedict," I croak.

He's so quiet, I can hear him breathe. "Faith?"

"Yes."

"Good lord. Are you all right? How are you holding up? Do you need anything?"

I can't stop the tears from flowing again. Everything he's said so far is about my well-being, his voice taut with worry.

"Whatever you need, just tell me. I'll make it right."

"Mr. Cha came to see me."

A pregnant pause. "He shouldn't have."

"But he did. Why didn't you tell me?" I sniff. "You could have when you cornered me."

He sighs. "She was your mother and the only parent you had left. No child should be disillusioned like that."

"Even if it makes you a villain? Even if I might've hated you until the day I died?"

"Even then. Grandparents aren't the same." His voice cools. "Mr. Cha had no right."

"No, but he had an obligation to be truthful."

"Faith... Are you angry?"

"I don't know." And that's the real answer. I honestly have no idea how I'm feeling at the moment.

"If you want..." He clears his throat. "If you don't mind, I'd love to have you in Dallas. Or I'll visit you in L.A. I don't want you to be alone."

"You know."

"Yes. I've been keeping tabs on you. I know Blake went to Virginia."

I exhale long and hard. I just feel...drained. All the

resentment and anger I had for my grandfather was for naught. It's difficult for me to accept Mom wasn't the perfect angel I thought she was, but Cha was right about her never having worked. I never questioned where the money was coming from or how she could afford anything because, well...it just never seemed that important. Now I'm starting to realize that my incurious attitude was more self-protective than anything else.

I realize something: I want to get to know the man who protected me at such great cost to himself. I've seen my classmates stuck in custody battles. They were always ugly, with adults flinging horrible accusations at each other and dragging the kids into the fight. Neither side cared about the children, so long as they won.

"I'd...like to spend some time together," I say. "Is it okay if I come see you?" As much as I hate flying, this place isn't mine, and I don't feel comfortable staying in L.A. anymore.

"Of course," he chokes out. "Can I talk to Mr. Cha?"

"Yes." I hand the phone to the stoic man.

"Mr. Mortimer?" He listens intently, then nods a few times. "Most certainly, sir." He puts the phone away. "We're to leave whenever you'd like. Do you need help packing?"

"If you don't mind, sure."

I lead him to my room and take out a suitcase, plus a huge duffel bag from the closet. While he lays my clothes into the suitcase, I pack the duffle bag with my toiletries, underwear and other personal items. I take the pearls from my father, but leave the diamonds from Blake in the jewelry box.

"I'm done. We'll send someone for the rest," Cha says.

"Okay." As I turn, I notice the sparkle on my finger —the rings Blake gave me.

I study them. They look so elegant, so beautiful. I thought them perfect, and my heart ached that he picked out such exquisite bridal jewelry. The whole farce might've been easier if he'd been some ogre with hideous taste in everything.

Slowly, I pull them off, one by one, and lay them on the vanity top. They gleam like a beautiful dream beyond my reach. Everything about this marriage has been beyond my reach from the very beginning.

"Are you ready, Mrs. Pryce-Reed?"

"Yes. And you can call me Faith. Or if that's too informal, Ms. Mortimer."

"Very well, Ms. Mortimer."

I turn and let Cha lead me away. I don't look back.

BLAKE

A HELICOPTER IS WAITING FOR ME WHEN I LAND. The pilot takes me to the rooftop of my penthouse, bypassing the insane traffic below. But the flight still seems to take forever. Why don't we have Star Trek teleporter tech that can shift people from one place to another instantly? We're living in the twenty-first century for fuck's sake!

I jump off before the landing skids hit the ground.

"Faith!" I call out as I enter the penthouse. My voice seems to echo in the vast space. "Faith!"

She isn't in the living room...or dining room...or kitchen or on the veranda. Maybe she's in her room, trying to cope with losing her mother. God, she adored Alice. She must be devastated. *I should've been there.*

I'm going to make it up to her. I don't know what it'll take or what I have to do, but I'll make up for this even if I have to crawl over broken glass.

I knock on her door, then push it open. It's like a tomb inside, the curtains drawn over every window. I flick the lights on. Something glints on the vanity.

Agonizing pain explodes in my chest. I fall to my knees, unable to draw a breath, my vision blurring with unshed tears.

This can't be happening.

32

Faith

The second we're ensconced in the cream-colored limo in Dallas, Cha hands me a bottle of Coke. "Here. The sugar will make you feel better."

"How did you know?"

"I used to hate flying, too."

I give him a wan smile. "You noticed?"

"Yes."

Our flight was commercial, but very comfortable in first class. The cabin crew treated us as though we were gods. I actually think it was Cha and his connection to my grandfather. He's probably a majority stakeholder or some such. I survived the trip by telling myself I owe Benedict this much.

But he didn't come to the airport, and I can't help

but wonder why. Maybe he's in a meeting or something like that. He's got to be a busy man.

"You know my grandfather isn't going to kill you, right?" I say, wanting to fill the silence in the bright interior.

"Murder is difficult to cover up, Ms. Mortimer, even for a billionaire." A corner of his mouth lifts. It's the first time I've seen him with a non-stoic expression. "But getting fired... That's a possibility. I've already asked a few headhunters about openings."

It's hard to tell if he's serious or not. "Well. I won't let him fire you. I'm sure he'll do me that favor."

Cha smiles. "He'll give you the world on a platinum platter if that's what you desire."

"Maybe." I swallow. I'm nervous about meeting my grandfather. Our past encounters weren't pleasant.

"New beginnings aren't always easy, but you'll be fine," Cha remarks. He grows serious. "You should know that I do not only work for Mr. Mortimer. I also work for you."

"What?"

"All of Mr. Mortimer's interests are my concern, and you're number one on his list."

I swallow. "Thank you. If that's the case, can I ask a favor?"

"Certainly."

"I need a lawyer."

"What sort?"

"A divorce attorney."

"I understand. It'll be arranged."

"Thank you."

Our limo stops a few minutes later in front of a grand mansion, the kind I've only seen in movies. Jack lived in a penthouse like Blake, but obviously Benedict doesn't want one for his main residence.

The property sprawls on a lush multi-acre lot with immaculate landscaping. The main house is three stories tall, with soaring, white columns and a huge fountain in front. Water jets from the rectangular pond, fracturing the bright Texas sunlight and creating multiple mini-rainbows.

Cha gets out first and helps me climb out. Somehow the brilliant sunshine and warmth on my skin thaw the ice that's formed inside me since Mom's death.

Suddenly the door to the house opens, and there's Benedict. He's in a crisp white button-down shirt and dark brown slacks. He walks down the steps, then engulfs me in a tight hug.

"I thought you might not come after all."

Love, pain and regret all rush through me, leaving me shaky. I nearly sag in his embrace. "I wondered if you were upset or something when I didn't see you at the airport."

"I wanted to meet you there...but I was worried you might run the second you saw me and hop on a return flight to L.A."

I swallow. "I'm sorry."

"No, no. You're here. That's all that matters."

As he tightens his arms around me, I blink away tears. "I'm so glad I'm not alone."

"You won't be. Come on. Let's go inside. I had the housekeeper prepare a rogues' gallery of snacks. If you're anything like your father, your favorite's probably double chocolate chip cookies, but your grandmother was partial to oatmeal raisin..."

33

Blake

I CHECK EVERYWHERE. BLOOMING FLOWERS IS NO help. The people there only know that after Alice died, Faith had her cremated, then donated all of Alice's things except for some photos. *Jesus.* I feel bile rising in the back of my throat. There should've been a funeral. There might've been one if I'd been around.

The crematory also has no information.

I call Faith over and over again, send more texts, but nothing gets an answer.

Two days later, a huge crate arrives from Virginia, containing the portrait. I should hang it somewhere, but I don't have the energy or time to worry about that.

Where is Faith?

I scroll down my contact list, but I don't know who

to reach out to. I know very little about her. Does she have any friends in L.A.? She said she did, but she could've been lying in order to spend some time alone. She probably hasn't gone to Benedict, assuming that he even came to L.A. to be with her.

Worry consumes me, but I grit my teeth. I can't let myself believe the worst. I call Benjamin Clark, and have him look into where Faith's gone. "Discreetly," I add.

"Of course," he says in a clipped voice.

I shouldn't have bothered though. Friday after lunch, I get a delivery to my office, which Cecilia signs for. It's from a law firm in Dallas. I have no business interests there...but that's where Benedict lives.

Suddenly my stomach curdles. This can't be anything good.

I rip it open. Papers spill out, plus a cashier's check for seventy-five thousand dollars.

Sweet Christ.

My heart in my throat, I scan the documents. Certain words jump out at me.

...quietly...

...efficiently...

...maintain the appearance of an amicable front for the sake of everyone's reputation...

Faith wants a divorce. She won't take anything from me.

I clench my hand around the papers, crumpling them in my fist. This... This is bullshit. Shouldn't we at least try to work something out? She should give me a chance to make it up to her.

Do you really deserve a chance?

Breathing hard, I surge to my feet and brace my hands on the edge of my desk. My neck bends, head dipping forward. There has to be—*has to be*—a way to fix this. If I lose her now, I'm going to lose her forever.

"Are you all right?"

I flinch when I hear Dane's voice. "What?" I say, straightening.

He's leaning in from the hallway. "We have a meeting at two."

The small clock on my desk says it's five after. "Sorry. I'll have it rescheduled." I give quick instructions to Cecilia over the intercom. I'm in no condition to attend anything.

"What's going on?" Dane comes in and shuts the door behind him.

"Faith wants a divorce."

"I take it you don't."

"No. I can't let her go like this. I fucked everything up." And I tell Dane the story... Her miscarriage. Her mother's death. How I wasn't there for her.

How I failed her.

"Guilt can make you do peculiar things," Dane says.

"It's not guilt." I swallow. "I love her."

Dane's cold eyes warm a fraction of a degree in sympathy. "You know my history with Sophia."

"Yes." He destroyed her lifelong dream in a careless moment.

"When she found out, she wouldn't believe anything I said."

I wince.

"But it wasn't just the obvious. She was afraid, too. To accept my love...to believe it would be true and steady for life...it takes an enormous amount of trust."

"How can I make her trust me when she won't even see me?"

"Easy. Lay everything on the table. No more hiding. No more bullshit."

I swallow. "Everything?"

"Yes. She has to see all the cards you're holding and decide if it's worth it. Women's hearts are fragile and easily hurt. So their shells are harder to crack, especially if they've been hurt before. But bare your soul to her only if she's the one for you, not because you feel bad that you weren't there for her. Guilt will eventually fade, and you'll end up resenting the poor choices you've made."

I look down at the papers. Faith is the only one for me. She was the first woman to steal my heart, and she's never given it back. It belongs to her—it beats only for her.

Laying everything on the table for her to examine and see if I'm worthy of a lifetime with her sends a wave of terror through me. But a lifetime without her? I might as well jump off a skyscraper.

"Cecilia," I say through the intercom. "Cancel all my appointments for the foreseeable future."

"Sir?"

"And get my plane ready to take off for Dallas."

"Yes, sir."

As I exit the office, Dane gives me a firm clap on the shoulder. "Good luck."

34

Faith

THE WEATHER'S BEEN SURPRISINGLY WARM IN Dallas. There's no breeze, and the sun is bright and pleasant on my skin. I lie on a hammock in the garden, my eyes closed. Benedict leaves me alone to enjoy the sun. I think he knows I need some solitude, to give myself time to sort everything out after both losing my mother and learning that she wasn't who I thought she was.

I feel guilt at having been so cold and hateful to him all this time. I wish Mom had come clean when I was old enough to handle it. Or maybe Cha was right... I saw the signs but didn't want to really sit down and figure out what they meant because I didn't want to lose the image of my sweet, loving mother.

Benedict's mansion is full of maids and other staff to take care of our needs and maintain the vast property. I thought I hated having people around, but I realize I just hated having people who I suspected were spying on me. I adore his maids, who are sweet and welcoming. His oldest housekeeper fusses over me like I'm five.

I don't check the news much, but Cha let me know when he came by earlier today that Simone's been arrested. His announcement leaves me speechless. So she really did embezzle money from the family charity. I don't understand how she could steal from the poor to give it to herself, but maybe Benedict is right: it's easier to take from the weak. "Benedict said she might throw me under the bus," I told Cha.

"She can try, but it won't do her any good. Mr. Mortimer's not going to let some scheming bottom-feeder like Simone Villar drag you down. I promise."

He sounded so confident and calm, I had no choice but to accept it as true and consider my unpleasant chapter with the Villars finished.

"Miss? You have a guest," a maid says, interrupting my lazy reverie.

"A guest?" I blink, opening my eyes. My breath catches when I spot Blake behind her.

"Hi, Faith."

I swing my legs over to stand. Of course, the hammock has to sway wildly, making me lose my balance. Blake reaches over and steadies me.

He's dressed impeccably in a pale sage dress shirt and black slacks. The collar's undone, and his hair's slightly messy, as though the nonexistent wind blew through it a time or two. I, on the other hand, am dressed in an old white T-shirt and frayed jeans, my feet bare.

Suddenly uncomfortable, I look away. "Why are you here?"

"Your lawyer contacted me."

"You didn't have to come here to talk about that. You could've had your lawyer deal with it."

"Actually...I couldn't." He sits in a rattan chair by the hammock. "Why are you breaking our deal?"

I look away. "My mom died."

"I got your text on Tuesday. I'm sorry."

"She didn't have a funeral."

His throat works. "I'm so sorry."

"It's okay. I don't know if she wanted anything extravagant. I think she was worried about money at the end."

"Jesus, she shouldn't have. I would've never let anything happen to you."

I merely shake my head. This is not the kind of conversation I want to have right now. I know why he wasn't there for me, and I don't blame him for wanting space and time to himself. But I also don't want him feeling guilty or bad about my mom's death and making promises he'd never make otherwise.

"How did you end up in Dallas?" he finally asks.

"After she died, I learned that all the horrible things I believed about Benedict were untrue." Which is just so damn sad. I've spent my entire life hating a man who did nothing wrong.

Blake is quiet for a moment. "Well. I'm glad you have him."

"So am I. I don't know what I would've done otherwise."

He winces. "I'm sorry. I should've been with you."

"Stop apologizing. Where were you?"

"Virginia."

"So Benedict was right," I murmur. "What were you doing there?"

"My father called us all there."

"For what?"

He hesitates, then finally says, "He gave us the portraits."

"The ones your grandfather made?"

He nods.

"I thought you had to stay married for a year."

"Yeah, but I think he was coerced somehow."

I nod. "I'm glad, Blake."

"Why? You should want the worst for me."

"But I don't. Your getting the painting means we don't have to stay married now. We're free to go our separate ways and pursue whatever we want. Right?" I trace the bold lines of his nose and cheeks with my eyes, committing them to memory. "You can find the woman you really want and be happy now that you don't need me anymore."

"Faith...that's not true. I do need you."

"I don't understand."

"I love you."

I close my eyes. "Oh, no. No. Don't say things like that out of pity...or guilt. You don't really love me."

"Yes, I do. What did you think the engagement ring was? You think I got it off eBay or somewhere?" When I don't answer, he continues, "I bought it two years ago to propose to you. I kept it all this time. Maybe I harbored a foolish hope that one day you'd come back to me."

"You were angry with me about Mom and the baby." The last word could be a grenade.

"I was angry at *myself*...for not realizing what you were going through sooner. Because I should've known better. I should've been there for you."

Abruptly I stand. I can't bear this anymore. "Blake, I'm going to college. Benedict said I could, and I want to."

"Then go, but it's not going to stop me from loving you."

I continue as though he hasn't spoken. "I don't want to be some ignorant woman with nothing to her name."

"You're Benedict's sole heir."

"That's his money, from his accomplishments. Not mine." I clasp my sweaty hands together. "I am *not* allowing something as confusing as love to muddy my thinking until I'm certain I'm okay."

"That's fine," Blake says.

I narrow my eyes. He's giving in too easily.

"But I'm not giving you up. I'll wait until you're sure."

35

Faith

"I HEARD BLAKE CAME BY YESTERDAY," BENEDICT says conversationally over a breakfast of waffles and two sunny-side up eggs.

I cut into my French toast with a fork. "Yes. He did."

"Is he going to fight the divorce?"

"I don't know."

"Your terms were fair."

"I thought so too." Then I pause as something else occurs to me. "Do you think he wants your money?"

Benedict snorts. "Blake Pryce-Reed? He spits on other people's money. He started his VC firm with his cousin when he decided he'd rather die than take a penny of his father's fortune. Julian Reed is a piece of work."

"You know him?"

"Oh, yes. It's a good thing Blake isn't close to his father. Julian's one of the few people I simply cannot abide. Believes his money makes him better than everybody else."

"Don't you?" I tease.

He grins. "My money affords me a lot of opportunities and luxuries, but it doesn't put me above others. I'm just a man, like any other. Perhaps when money can confer divinity, we can talk. Until then, best to be humble and good."

We chat about my plans for college. Benedict prefers I choose someplace in Dallas. I agree, which makes him beam. Cha's right that Benedict and I don't have that many days left, and I don't want to be apart if I don't have to.

Cha arrives soon afterward. I say, "You know it's Sunday, right?"

"Yes."

I look at Benedict, who shrugs. "He enjoys working."

"Are you married?" I ask Cha.

"Yes. With two children. But my wife prefers I go out and do something useful rather than laze around in the house."

I bite back a smile at his deadpan delivery.

Benedict gets up from his seat. "Right. Let's go to the office to review a few things."

Just then a maid interrupts. "Miss?"

"Yes?"

"You have a delivery."

"What is it?"

She disappears around the entryway, and Blake walks in, holding a huge bouquet of tropical flowers. Their sweet scent fills the breakfast room. But it's him I notice—the somber, determined look and the small smile. My heart flutters. He used to bring me flowers when we were in Vegas. Since our marriage, he started buying me silk and diamonds, but it's the flowers that bring warmth to my heart.

"Blake... What are you doing here?" I ask almost dumbly.

"Not giving up." He kisses me on the forehead and hands me the flowers. Then he dips his head lower and whispers in my ear, "I love you."

My throat closes. Before I can say anything, he walks out.

"Well," Benedict says.

Cha merely cocks an eyebrow, while I feel my cheeks heat.

And the routine doesn't stop. Every morning after breakfast, Blake shows up with a different bouquet, tells me he isn't giving me up, kisses me on the forehead, whispers, "I love you"...and leaves.

Ten days into this, I put a hand on his sleeve before he can straighten after "I love you" and say, "Why are you doing this? Don't you have to work?"

"I already told you, Faith, I'm not giving you up. I said I'd wait. So I'm waiting."

"What if I decide I want the divorce after all?"

His gaze flickers with pain. "If that's what you really want, then we'll divorce, but I'm not stopping." As though he can't help himself, he presses another kiss on my forehead and leaves.

"Hmm." Cha nods. "I believe he is courting you, Ms. Mortimer."

"As he well should," Benedict says. "The boy also needs to ask me for my blessing."

"Uh, we *are* already married," I point out.

"Better late than never."

I sigh. Neither of these men is helping.

Still, Blake can't stay in Dallas forever. I'm sure he'll return to Los Angeles tomorrow to spend Christmas with his family. Every morning visit is drawing me a little closer to him. It reminds me I have someone else in my corner...if only I'll let him in.

But I'm too scared. What if we don't want the same things? I pluck a plumeria from Blake's latest bouquet and bury my nose in it. It smells amazing. Blake has work in L.A. and Boston. He likes his penthouses, the convenience of being close to the city center. He was upset about the miscarriage, but that doesn't necessarily mean he has any desire for a family. He may want a married life in a bustling, cosmopolitan city without pets or children. His Aston Martin is too small for a family, and I can't imagine him driving a mommy mobile. And then there's the travel. He seems to enjoy flying to exotic locations in his fancy jet. I've seen photos of him at all sorts of beautiful spots in the world. I can't give him that. Flying that much would drive me insane, but I'm too petty with jealousy to let him go to a tropical beach by himself, surrounded by beautiful women in tiny bikinis.

A lot of people desire that sort of life. But I'm too much on the staid side for that kind of thing.

If I tell him what I really want, he may run like hell the other way. Or worse, he'll sacrifice everything he wants to make me satisfied because he's driven by guilt and he wants to make amends. And one day he's going to realize what he's given up and grow unhappy.

I love him too much for either scenario.

When I call Mimi for her wisdom, she says, "You should give him a chance, hear what he has to say. Maybe he'll surprise you."

"How do you know?"

"Because the man loves you. I can't believe you think he's doing it out of guilt! If he's feeling guilty, he would've agreed to a divorce and just given you a bunch of money. He doesn't have to stay in Dallas and come by your grandfather's place every morning just to give you flowers!"

"But you don't understand."

I can almost hear her draw herself up. "Explain to me what I don't understand."

"Look at him. He's rich, handsome and accomplished. He built Digital Angel with his cousin without using any family money, and he's highly respected. He has everything anybody can want."

"Except you."

"But I'm so...ordinary."

"Okay, here's the deal. Friends lie, but best friends tell the truth. So I'm going to tell you the truth, girl. The whole truth and nothing *but* the truth. Unvarnished."

Oh shit. "Um...okay."

"You are so *not* ordinary. You're one of the most extraordinary people I know. You are loyal, dedicated and loving. You didn't cheat on Jack—who by the way was a fucking dick—not because of the prenup, but because you aren't that kind of person. You supported your mother throughout her illness, never once complaining about wasting the best years of your life. If anyone but you had been reconciled with someone like Benedict, she would've been on a crazy shopping spree, but you're cool about it. You're trying to figure out what steps you're going to take next, how you're going to make something of yourself because you don't want to live off Benedict's money and name. That's pretty fucking admirable in my book, and I'd seriously wonder about Blake's mental health if he *didn't* find you worthy of love. So. Stop with the crappy self-talk. *I mean it!*"

"Yes, ma'am," I answer meekly.

But still I hesitate and think endlessly.

On Christmas Eve, I put on chunky silver heels and a festive red dress with a flirty skirt that flares around my calves. The cook has sprinkled extra powdered sugar on my French toast and placed a marshmallow snowman on my plate. I smile at the cute table decorations, trying not to think about Blake, who won't be coming today. Perversely enough, I miss him already.

"Why so morose?" Benedict asks as he loads enough sugar for three breakfasts onto his buttermilk oatmeal.

"Me?" I force an even brighter smile. "I'm fine."

"I can read you, my dear. Now what's wrong?"

"Nothing. Just...holiday blues."

He's thoughtful. "You miss your mother."

"That, too."

He sighs. "I really wish things had gone differently. Despite our differences, I believe she loved you."

I nod. "Thank you." I take a big bite of the French toast. After a sip of coffee, I say, "So. Anything special planned for Christmas?"

"Yes. I'm going to stay in, enjoy my hot chocolate and the rum cake a colleague sent. You?"

"Maybe I'll stay home and share the rum cake with you."

"You could invite some friends. I wouldn't mind."

"I know, but the only ones I'd want to invite are going to their folks' place. And I'm pretty sure they're going to get engaged soon." Andy and Mimi are too in love not to.

The maid comes inside. "Miss, the flowers are here for you."

I blink as Blake walks in. He's perfectly groomed, his jaw freshly shaved, his hair neatly cropped since yesterday. A black blazer lies elegantly over a cream-colored shirt and black slacks. My jaw trembles for a moment, and I pull my lips in so I don't babble like an idiot. Seeing him when I wasn't expecting it makes it extra special...like I've been given a gift.

"Hi. I didn't think you were coming," I murmur.

"Of course I came. I told you I wasn't giving up." He kisses me on the forehead. "I love you."

My throat closes, and it's all I can do to tilt my head, my eyes closed. Right now I *feel* loved.

When he straightens, I grip his forearm. I don't want him to go. Mimi's right. I have to talk to him, sort out the kind of life we can have together.

He thinks he's the one who's not giving up. Well I'm not giving up either. Not like this. Not this time. Contrary to what I told my lawyer, I don't want to divorce Blake. I want a forever.

Blake gives me another kiss, then turns to Benedict. "Mind if I steal Faith for a few hours? I have something to show her."

"Must be something pretty good if it's going to take a few hours," Benedict says archly.

"I believe it is."

"Well then, ask the lady. She's an adult."

I jump to my feet. "We're leaving now."

A lopsided grin tugs at Blake's face, and he extends his arm, which I take. It's formal, and courtly, and I feel like a teenager in love for the first time.

Well. It *is* the first time...for me anyway. He's my first and he'll be my last. I recognize that now.

The car outside is an Aston Martin. It looks exactly like the one he has in L.A. I peer at it.

"Yes, it's the same car," he says as he opens the passenger side door.

I climb inside and look at him. "When did you have it brought over?"

"When I realized I was staying. I needed decent wheels." He shuts the door and gets in the driver's seat.

"So. Where are we going?" I ask, my mouth dry as he starts the engine.

He takes my hand and kisses the knuckles, his warm lips lingering. "It's a place I like to think of as Blake's Last Stand."

36

Faith

AFTER THAT, BLAKE DOESN'T TALK, AND I REMAIN silent on the drive. I'm too nervous to speak.

I sense Blake doesn't want us to continue as we have been. After all, just seeing each other briefly in the morning is getting old. And the local florists have made enough of a profit off him already.

I keep rehearing what I need to say. I could start with "I love you"...but it might be better to save that for the end. Maybe confide my fears to him? Or are they too much of a downer? Maybe I should begin by telling him my dreams.

"We're here," he says suddenly.

Only then do I notice that the car's stopped, idling in front of a gated estate. The clock on the dashboard says we've been driving for no more than fifteen minutes. "Oh."

"What were you thinking about?"

"Um. Nothing important." Then I realize what I just said and shake my head. I'm not being truthful. "Some stuff I wanted to tell you."

His brow creases. "Can it wait until I've said my piece first?"

"Sure."

He blows out a breath. "Okay."

He punches a code into the security pad, and the double gate opens. He drives slowly down the long, winding road. The garden is impeccably maintained, with an expansive lawn and a few big trees I don't recognize. I spot a pool in the back, and a sizable garage.

"I know it's a bit too big," he says. "But I couldn't find anything smaller that was close and available."

"Are you buying this?"

He nods, his gaze sliding to me, assessing my response. "Already bought it."

"Wow..."

"Come on." He parks the Aston Martin in front of the main house and helps me out.

I don't let go of his hand. His grip tightens, he pulls me up the steps, and we walk inside the huge mansion. The foyer is made of marble and stone, contemporary chandeliers hanging prettily from the vaulted ceiling. A staircase corkscrews up from the living room like something out of Tara in *Gone with the Wind*.

But it isn't the luxury inside that makes my breath catch. It's a statue of a golden retriever puppy by the entryway.

"A puppy?" I rasp, my throat tight and hoarse.

"One. I think one's good...unless you want more."

"I think one's good too."

Then he leads me up the winding stairs to the second level. All the rooms are empty—but sizable—with sitting areas and huge walk-in closets. Then there's a huge suite with two bedrooms and a shared sitting area. Statues of two children—one girl and one boy—sit on the floor, their heads together conspiratorially. Their facial features are just like mine.

I swivel my head in Blake's direction. "I don't understand." I'm afraid to understand, because things this good can't happen to me...right?

He turns around and takes both my hands in his. "It's my deal involving our future."

Suddenly I can't speak. Tears blur my vision.

Blake dries my cheeks with his thumbs, cradling my face. "I envision this as our home, so you'll be close to your grandfather. I know the house doesn't have a white picket fence. There wasn't time to swap out the iron fence, but it can be arranged. The house will come with a puppy—a live one, of course—and, eventually, two beautiful children who are just like you. I'm having Cecilia look into how quickly we can get a decent SUV. But if Bentley or Rolls-Royce can't come through in time, hell, we'll just get a Sienna."

Hysterical laughter bubbles inside my chest. I can't

picture Blake behind the wheel of a minivan manufactured for your everyday suburban parents with kids, but I also know he's going to do it because he said he would.

"Laughter is not the response I was hoping for," Blake says teasingly, then sobers quickly. "Everything about the package deal I just told you is negotiable, except one point—it comes with me. You don't have to accept right now. Look around first and see if there's anything you want to change...or add. The offer is on the table indefinitely until you're ready."

I swallow, then nod. My heart seems overfull, and I'm bursting with all the love I feel for this man. "How did you know?"

"Alice told me. I didn't even know what I wanted in my future, but when I heard, I knew your dream was what I wanted too. I want a life with the woman I love, children with the woman I love. I know I screwed up... monumentally. I have zero experience with this kind of stuff. You're the first woman I fell in love with, and you're going to be the last."

"For a guy with zero experience with this kind of stuff, you're pretty good." I give him a tremulous smile through tears. "I was always afraid I wasn't good enough—to get a job, to be okay, to be loved. I was always afraid I'd be alone. Now I know that's not true. I have people who love me, accept me the way I am. And you're one of them." I wrap my shaking hands around his wrists, feel the pulse leap and throb against my bare skin. "I have zero experience with this kind of stuff, too, you know. You're the first man I fell in love with, and you're going to be the last man I'll ever love."

"Faith..."

"And my answer is yes, as long as the package is you and me."

His throat working, Blake drops to one knee. "Faith Mortimer, will you marry me?"

I laugh. "We're already married."

He shakes his head. "It's not the same. I'm asking you to marry me because I love you and I want to build a life with you."

I understand. "Yes."

He slides the marquise diamond ring back on my hand, then pulls me down for a lingering kiss.

I kiss him back, my fingers digging into his hair. And we don't leave the empty house for hours.

37

Faith

—Fifteen months later

I walk into Blake's office in Dallas precisely at lunchtime. It's guarded as usual by his assistant Cecilia. She nods her golden head, her gray eyes warm. "He's ready."

"Great! Thanks."

I float inside. Or at least I feel like I'm floating on the fluffiest and whitest cloud in the world.

Blake smiles from his desk. "You're glowing."

"Hard not to." I bite my lower lip, but I can't help it. I still end up grinning the biggest grin. "I'm so happy I feel like I'm going to burst!"

He puts his arms around me, pulling me closer. "You know your smile turns me on, don't you?"

"I thought it was my soap," I tease.

"That too. And your skin. Your hair. Your eyes. Your nose." He punctuates each with a kiss.

I rest my hands on his wide, strong shoulders. "Mmm. If you keep going, we'll miss our lunch with Benedict."

He pulls back. "You invited him?"

"Uh-huh. I'm going to make a big announcement. If you want, we can get your brothers and sister on a Skype call or something so they can hear it live too." His siblings are currently all over the country.

He arches an eyebrow.

I debate. I was going to wait until everyone, including Cha, who's become a surrogate parent of sorts, was there to hear it. But Blake is my husband, and this impacts him more than the others. "Okay, you can hear it before anybody else."

"I'm all ears."

"I'm pregnant."

He blinks, then sweeps me into his arms and spins around, letting out a loud whoop.

I laugh. "My goodness, stop. There's more to the announcement!"

"All right." He stops spinning around, but he doesn't let me down. "What's the second part?"

"We're having twins."

"Twins...! Holy hell, that's... Wow. That's amazing. Boys or girls?"

"Too early to tell. We could end up with one of each, you know."

Urgency turns his gaze flinty. "We have to finish the nursery, stat." We sort of started on getting one ready, but having twins changes things. "And get the SUV!"

"There's always a minivan." I giggle. "I believe a Sienna was your top choice..."

"I know, but I'm trying to preserve my reputation."

I laugh.

"Ah, screw it!" he says with a wide grin. "Who cares about a car when I have you?"

"My precise sentiment." I kiss him. "Who cares when we have each other?"

Arms wrapped around each other, we leave to share the good news with our loved ones.

Thank you for reading *A Final Deal*. I hope you liked it!

Would you like to know when my next book is available? Join my mailing list at
http://www.nadialee.net/newsletter.

If you enjoyed *A Final Deal*, I'd appreciate it if you would help others enjoy this book, too.

Recommend it. Please help other readers find this book by recommending it to friends, reader's groups and discussion boards.

Review it. Please tell other readers why you liked this book by reviewing it. If you do write a review, please contact me at nadia@nadialee.net so I can thank you with a personal email.

I love to hear from readers! Feel free to write me at nadia@nadialee.net or follow me on Twitter @nadialee, or like my Facebook page at http://www.facebook.com/nadialeewrites or join my reader group at http://www.facebook.-com/groups/595788263841144. Say hello and let me know which one of my characters is your favorite or what you want to see next or anything else you want to talk about! I personally read all my emails, Tweets and Facebook comments.

SEE WHAT'S NEXT FROM NADIA LEE

A super sweet and sexy romance featuring a virgin and a hot lawyer. *big grin*

That Man Next Door

I'm a twenty-two year-old virgin who's had five one night stands. How that's possible? Easy. I've never gone all the way. I just chicken out and bail. Thank God, I've always selected men I'll never run across again...

...until that sexy-as-sin Matt from last weekend moves in next door...

...then shows up as a new in-house counsel at Sweet Darlings Inc. where I work.

Oh...crap.

But it was dark in the hotel room. If I put on a boring office outfit and Clark Kent glasses, he won't recognize me...

Right?

Want to know when That Man Next Door *is available? Sign up for my mailing list at http://www.nadialee.net/newsletter!*

TITLES BY NADIA LEE

Billionaires' Brides of Convenience

A Hollywood Deal

A Hollywood Bride

An Improper Deal

An Improper Bride

An Improper Ever After

An Unlikely Deal

An Unlikely Bride

A Final Deal

The Pryce Family

The Billionaire's Counterfeit Girlfriend

The Billionaire's Inconvenient Obsession

The Billionaire's Secret Wife

The Billionaire's Forgotten Fiancée

The Billionaire's Forbidden Desire

The Billionaire's Holiday Bride

Seduced by the Billionaire

Taken by Her Unforgiving Billionaire Boss

Pursued by Her Billionaire Hook-Up

Pregnant with Her Billionaire Ex's Baby

Romanced by Her Illicit Millionaire Crush

Wanted by Her Scandalous Billionaire

Loving Her Best Friend's Billionaire Brother

ABOUT NADIA LEE

New York Times and *USA Today* bestselling author Nadia Lee writes sexy contemporary romance. Born with a love for excellent food, travel and adventure, she has lived in four different countries, kissed stingrays, been bitten by a shark, ridden an elephant and petted tigers.

Currently, she shares a condo overlooking a small river and sakura trees in Japan with her husband and son. When she's not writing, she can be found reading books by her favorite authors or planning another trip.

To learn more about Nadia and her projects, please visit http://www.nadialee.net. To receive updates about upcoming works from Nadia, please visit http://www.nadialee.net/newsletter to subscribe to her new release alert.

Stalk Me!

nadialee.net/newsletter
facebook.com/nadialeewrites

CPSIA information can be obtained
at www.ICGtesting.com
Printed in the USA
LVOW11s2318080418
572690LV00007B/657/P